TWO MEXICAN KIDS, BARACK, AND THE WALL

(In the Land of the Fee)

Néstor Lacorén

ARCHWAY
PUBLISHING

This book is a work of fiction. Names, characters, places, and incidents are the
product of the author's imagination and or used fictitiously. Any resemblance
to actual events, locales, or persons, living or dead, is coincidental.

Archway Publishing books may be ordered
through booksellers or by contacting:

Archway Publishing
1663 Liberty Drive
Bloomington, IN 47403
www.archwaypublishing.com
1 (888) 242-5904

ISBN: 978-1-4808-3177-3 (sc)
ISBN: 978-1-4808-3178-0 (e)

Library of Congress Control Number: 2016907924

Print information available on the last page.

Archway Publishing rev. date: 08/08/2016

CONTENTS

To Helene, the love of my life.

For the children: Melanie, Ava, Kayla and Lucas

ACKNOWLEDGMENTS

Writing this book was a huge and solitary effort and it took me a lot of time, energy and ability to finish it. There were two people that helped and inspired me the most, Helene the love of my life and Lucas, my grandson. Both of them helped in different ways. Helene is the very best, not only is she intelligent and patient, but she is blessed with more common sense than most people I know. She kept me centered and focused. Lucas on the other hand, my friend and "accomplice", without knowing it helped my inspiration during the few days we worked together. Next come "the girls"; Ava, Melanie and Kayla, because they have made my life richer, and to receive their hugs is an inspiration and the greatest gift of all.

Thank you to Shelly Frape from England, via La Linea de La Concepcion in Cadiz Spain, my copy editor. She caught all the errors and "horrors" in the book. She is fantastic. If you find one single error do not blame her, blame me.

And finally, muchas gracias to Claudio Nasso a great artist from Buenos Aires, Argentina, nowadays "nicotine free", for designing a wonderful cover.

CHAPTER 1
The Delivery

My name is Juan Sintierra and I'm the happiest kid alive. I was born in Sinaloa a few miles south of the Elota River, the only place in the world where the mountain range at a distance looks like a big, greenish Mexican *poncho*. The weather in my pueblo is very warm. If you sit down in any corner of my town and gaze long enough, you can see the reflection of the sunlight dancing a hot *quebradita* with the yellow dust. From time to time, a strong wind blowing from the north, carrying the sand and the debris to the foothill slopes, explodes like a *mariachi fiesta* enveloping the whole valley. Daily during the summer the wind and the sand, by the grace of God, get together and put on this special show just for me, little Juan Sintierra. Four times a week, while waiting for my *primo* Miguel to help him out with his deliveries and having nothing else to do, I sit on the sand by the riverbank until dark and I think about my *amigo* Barack who lives faraway in the north. Since I can remember, I replay in my head, the picture of the beaten path among the mountains that eventually will take me to him. Barack is the *presidente*, the big boss, the *mero-mero* of the North, the first black president in the history of Gringo-Land. I still remember when a long time ago my *abuela* told me: "Brown is beautiful." Ever since, I kept imagining that the world was either brown and beautiful, or white and ugly. That we the dark ones, because of our hostility toward the whites, were always the problem, when in reality, if the browns and the whites worked together in peace, they could be part of the big solution for the world. Now, *hoy*, I finally learned that the real problem facing humanity is the colorless people, those folks that are so hard to see, that they are almost invisible. And when these *pinches* invisible *chingones* sense that the people in every walk of life are trying to get together, they will do their best to keep them apart by breeding hatred and fear among them. The colorless folks are those *que tiran la piedra y esconden la mano*, the same *pinches cabrones* who stoned and nailed Jesus to the cross. Anyway, who cares? All I want is not to be bothered and have a chance to visit my friend Barack. I'm sure we can be like brothers and *buenos amigos*. I hope someday soon we'll get together, shake hands and sit by the fire in his beautiful white house - that pretty white house built by hand by his ancestors - and have a long and smooth talk about the *mexicanos'* and *gringos'* similarities. We are going to be nice to each other, and nobody is going to hunt, hurt, kill or steal from nobody no more. Looking at the river, right there and then, I felt an uncertainty in the air, but at the same time a feeling of change, and the gain of new and unfamiliar things coming my way. "Maybe black is beautiful too, *abuela*," I whispered, thinking about my friend Barack's smiling black face.

Late as usual, Miguel came down the road very fast in his four by four yellow *troca* from the direction of the Culiacán-Mazatlán highway. Interrupting my thoughts, he nearly ran me over.

"Juancho!" he screamed. "Juancho *por Dios*, don't think so much."

I didn't move. He got out of the pickup truck, leaned over and picked me up.

"Juancho. You are going to go crazy in the head. You are going to get sick from so much thinking."

Miguel was big, smart and quick, an extremely weird Mexican. He would always be the smartest person I'd ever known. He shook my shoulder, his long brownish face smiling at me the way a father smiles at his young son. My *primo* was my hero, my best friend and he was strong like a horse. Like a Mexican horse! Of course!

"Thinking is good," I said. "You too should think sometimes *primo*."

He smiled.

"I'm not sure that thinking is that good, Juancho," he said hopelessly.

He plunged his entire big hand under the white canvas covering the back of the pickup truck and uncovered the cargo.

"Look what we have to deliver tonight," he said.

"Looks like too much flour to me *primo*," I answered nervously.

"I know it's too much but we'll deliver the whole thing, very quick, *en un dos por tres*," said Miguel softly.

"Ain't sure that the way things are right now, it's a good time to do it."

"Jesus Christ, Juancho! We can just as well ride off and hide forever, or do our job and kill those *putos* bastards, and take over the whole fricking distribution business once and for all," said Miguel looking down at the ground in despair.

Suddenly his right hand went into his pocket.

"Do you have your revolver with you Juancho?" he asked.

"I ain't got nothing," I said.

"Juancho, we are not playing games here. We are not going to Father Bernardino's church for Sunday mass you know. I don't have to remind you that all the *puñeteros carteles*, the DEA and the *federales* are working together, and they are looking for us. If we see them, *una de dos*, we shoot to kill, or we run as fast as we can."

"You told me that, two or three times already," I said angrily.

"I just want to make sure you don't forget it."

Miguel walked to the driver's side of the *troca* and got in. He laid back and crossed his hands behind his head. I sat down on the passenger seat, imitating every move he made, turning my head to see what he was doing. Smiling he looked at me as if I smelled bad or something.

"Juancho, I can get along with you so easily and so nice, but if you do not stop acting like a girl and making fun of me right now, I'll kick your little sorry *culo*!"

For a moment we lay quiet in our seats, the motor running and after a while Miguel said:

"Juancho, you know, you and me, we are gonna do very bad things tonight."

"I really hope we don't have to," I whispered.

Suddenly pressing the gas pedal, he accelerated and made a U-turn in the direction of the highway at very high speed. He took off his baseball cap and threw it out the window.

"Miguel!" I said sharply. "For God's sake, you have been drinking again! Are you going to go *loco* and trigger happy, like the last time?"

"You should drink some tequila too, Juancho, for sure it will clear your head. Go ahead take a good big swig. It's good for your little brain."

Holding the steering wheel with both knees, he grabbed a half empty tequila bottle from under the seat. He smiled happily, shaking the bottle close to my face.

"You drink some, Juanchito."

"I ain't sure it's good tequila," I said, trying not to make him feel rejected, "Looks kind of cheap to me."

Miguel stared morosely at the road. The rims of his eyes were red and wet.

"Our first stop is at the governor's mansion. After all he's your *cuñado*. I'm sure your brother in law is going to be more than happy to see you!" He smiled.

"He is not my *cuñado*, you crazy *puto*," I yelled.

"I forgot," Miguel said softly.

"Try hard not to forget that anymore, you *pinche primo* or next time I'll kill you!"

He smacked my head and said:

"Wow! What a *macho* man! I'm so scared of you!"

Miguel wore a black silk shirt, his favorite *camisa negra*, brown cowboy boots and blue jeans. With his brownish long face, his restless eyes and sharp strong features, he looked like a smaller Mexican version of John Wayne. Every part of his body was defined, big strong hands, slender arms and a well-shaped nose.

"The hell with what you say, Juanchito. You just remember to cover my back at all times."

He grinned and handed me a 38 silver revolver. It was fully loaded, to my relief.

The full moon reflected the giant cactus shadows on the open road. As we got closer to the *hacienda* we saw a small army of about twenty dark figures guarding the path, their machine guns pointed directly at our truck. Miguel reduced the speed, my throat was dry and my pulse gradually accelerated, as we got closer to the main house.

"Remember the first time you killed a man, Juancho?"

The question took me by surprise, and before I could answer it, I saw a glow ahead of us and then a huge building leaped up in the dark. A tall tower next to it lit the pathway all the way to the wooden doors of the house. My sister standing by the entrance was holding a baby in her arms, her eyes wide open, and she looked terrified.

"*Tranquilo*, Juanchito, this is it. Let them see your hands, your little *manitas*, and don't go *loco* over your sister. Just be cool."

After saying that, Miguel paused and placed both of his hands on the steering wheel, and we came to a full stop. When we got out, I felt a cold sweat running down my back and I started to pray. I felt sick. I paused, puffing noisily, the blood pounding in my ears. At that moment I became something less than a kid. I was a grown man.

Five huge *gueros* carrying M-16's slung over their shoulders walked heavily, dragging their feet in a single file down the path to greet us. I noticed that, even in the open, they stayed one behind the other. All of them were dressed in black with long leather coats, black Stetsons, and black cowboy boots. Distracted by this show of brute force and firepower, nervously and without thinking, I stepped beside them. Puzzled they looked at me.

"Juancho! *Por la Virgen de Guadalupe!* You crazy bastard; get out of there! Help me unload," said Miguel, coming to my rescue.

"Ok, I'll be right there, *pinche cabrón!*" I yelled back, while walking fast to the back of the pickup truck.

"Let's do this."

Miguel stretched out his hands and slowly pulled the canvas to show the merchandise. Somebody snapped his fingers sharply and, at the sound, everyone turned around. Smiling pleasantly, the governor himself approached the *troca*.

"Who let the dogs out tonight?" he joked.

Miguel's eyes narrowed, he laughed. I knew that laugh. I also knew the smell of death. I started shaking. Miguel stared the old man hard in the eyes and said:

"The dogs are here now, let them be. It will be a sacrilege not to feed them."

It was amazing how soberly and cool Miguel acted, and handled the whole situation that night. He was in control the whole two hours it took us to unload, close the deal, kill all of them - but one - collect the cash and leave. Too bad for us we didn't take into account the immensity of the act we had committed, and all the future consequences.

CHAPTER 2
The Governor

The whole community knows I'm weird and old, but no matter how weird I look, I'm still the governor, and the big boss. Sometimes I even forget to come to the office. I'm the absolute weirdest *machotote* in the whole *pinche* Mexican Republic. Yes, and *es verdad,* most of the time they have to send down a good looking *chamaquita* to my house to wake me up, take a shower together, have breakfast and then go to the executive office and take over my duties as governor. That's right, sometimes I go to work in my pajamas. Everybody in the office likes me because I'm a good boss and I don't ask too much of the people. I mean, how can you expect the citizens to work hard if you show up in the office wearing your pajamas and in flip-flops? I know it's weird but the majority of the people in this country are very poor, actually living in one-room shacks or old trailers. You cannot ask too much of them. They drink a lot to feel closer to the earth. To tell you the truth they are a bunch of losers, always waiting for a savior. When they see a bunch of UFO's crossing the sky, they believe they are cronies of the devil. My people pay too much attention to a lot of nonsense. They are just too slow and too distracted to know what's going on in the real world. Some of them don't like me, and most of them hate me. Either way, who cares? I have all the power and all the money - in that order. I have a big house, long and rectangular, with huge square windows and a solid door surrounded by a very

tall wall. Because I'm the governor by state law, I have the national
army, the police, the *federales* and even the DEA to watch over
me, but I know better so I have my own private army to protect
me from all of them. The inside of my house looks like a palace,
with expensive paintings hanging all over the walls. There are
also shelves loaded with different articles, diamonds, silver, gold,
precious stones, ivory, crystals, you name it, huddled all the way
up to the ceiling. Some of them are presents from very important
people, and most of them I took from very rich people myself. In
every room in the house, there are oak and ivory trunks full of
money, millions and millions of dollars in cash. Nowadays, with
the terrorist menace all over the world, plus the financial crisis,
I never know when I will have to travel unexpectedly overseas.
Just in case, I have five jet planes and four helicopters standing
by in my private little airport. I also have ten armored cars. I
never use the official vehicles the government provides me with,
because somehow, in the past, they tended to explode every time
the former governor and his family were inside! Weird, right? Most
of my friends, including my first wife and my older son, tell me that
I'm paranoid. That those explosions were something unusual that
happened in the past. That I should overcome my fear, and at least
once or twice a week drive all over the city in an official car with
the governor's seal on it, to show to the people that their governor
is moving around town doing his job. Anyway, I don't know why,
but somehow I don't trust any of them. Every time I asked my
wife or my son to ride along with me in an official vehicle, they
refused claiming they were busy or not feeling well. They hurt me
with their words when they tell me: "We would love to go along
with you! You know how much we love you papa!" I know, they lie,
and it hurts like a broken bone. I don't want you to think that I'm
rude or anything, but sometimes I wonder if maybe I should force
them to take the ride themselves, so they'll get blown up to pieces!
Pinches traidores!

Of course I was commended to be governor by my great *presidente*, Zorro Porro Neto. Right after he stole the general elections and elected himself president, he invited me over to his house and told me, face to face, that he needed a yes man. It was no accident that he called me to make such an important offer.

"This is the first time I chose somebody like you for this job. I hope you don't disappoint me."

After he said that, he sat in his chair, and talked and talked for hours. Sitting in front of him, looking at the big black moustache across his upper lip moving up and down, I was ashamed, not being able to understand a word he was saying.

"Can I offer you a drink?" he finally asked.

"You bet," I said.

I was nervous. Why was he being so friendly? Was he framing me up? Maybe he was planning a sneak attack on my reputation? Zorro Porro just sat in peaceful silence for a long time staring at me straight in the face. I didn't know what to do or say, so I just sat there quietly as he did. The silence got so heavy and real that it felt like a *troca* was parked on my chest.

"Do you know why I selected you to be the governor?" he finally asked.

I knew it was a tricky question. I knew I needed to answer it correctly or I would fail.

"Because I'm corrupted and stupid?"

"Yes you are very stupid, big time stupid and you are a crooked politician, and that's good enough for me."

I was starting to get upset.

"I didn't mean to offend you," he said. "I was aiming for your ego, just being honest. I didn't intend to upset you."

I was getting more and more freaked out, and I still didn't know what he wanted.

"What about that drink, *jefe*?" I asked.

He looked up at his wall-to-wall bar. It was a huge bar. Well decorated with mirrors, tall crystal glasses, hundreds of expensive bottles, candlesticks, chandeliers, you name it. Looking at that bar, I could feel the eyes of the *Virgen of Guadalupe* and the holy saints looking down upon us. I got up and walked towards the bar.

"Pour me a Ley 925," he said.

It sounded like an order to me.

"A *Pasión Azteca?*" I asked, just to show off.

"Yes," he glanced coldly.

I felt humiliated under that look. Uneasy, I shifted on my feet. The only two things that kept me from smacking him across the face were the superb glass of tequila I was holding in my right hand, that I didn't want to spill and go to waste, and knowing deep in my soul that I was a despicable ass kisser and a coward.

It was strange how we got drunk that night. It was three hours before we started singing *"Cielito Lindo"*, and four hours before we sang an obscene song, and it was very late when we started talking about women. By that time, our minds turned to fighting. We were almost too drunk and too sleepy to fight. That evening was a highpoint in my life. Next day the news of my nomination for a second term was all over the media. My smiling face was on every newspaper and every TV news channel.

"My mother is going to be so proud. Now I can go on stealing forever," I thought.

The following week the whole town started to arrange all the details for the big celebration. They washed the sidewalks, the streets and even the town walls. My staff inspected my nostrils, my ears and my hands. They also selected my outfit, my trousers, my tie and my blazer. They even brought me my father's hat. They persuaded me not to carry my jewel-studded forty-five caliber pistol in my belt during the ceremony. The item of shoes gave the most trouble, since I had only cowboy boots to wear. After spending more than two hours with my hairdresser, my make-up artist and my tailor, I was finally ready. Once again, I walked in front of my family and my friends in order for them to inspect me.

They looked at me critically. They stared hard and gave me their opinion.

"Pick up your feet, papa," my son said.

"Don't drag your heels," said my niece.

"Hold in your belly," ordered my sister.

"Stop picking at your hat," my aunt instructed.

"Turn around and smile," my wife demanded.

"Stand still," said my uncle.

"Whatever you do, don't you ever fart in public, *pendejo!*" my grandfather yelled at me.

"If you don't look sharp, those people who see you today for the first time will think you are not in the habit of wearing good clothes," my mother said.

"When you go to mass today, if your constituency notices that your tie doesn't match, they won't like it," said my older brother helplessly.

Suddenly, Blanca came to my mind. At that moment, I felt like two different people inside one body. Like a magician slicing myself in half, with all these people living in the North Pole, and Blanca and myself in Cancun, by the sea, dancing nude on my yacht. She is so pretty and her dark green eyes so beautiful. She is the prettiest girl I have ever seen. She is movie star pretty. For the first time in my life, I think I'm in love. The feeling is so special and so profound, that today on this happy occasion I would like to apologize to everybody I hurt. I know deep in my heart that I can't apologize to everyone I injured or killed in the past, but there is something that I know for sure; I can apologize to little Blanquita. I harmed many little brown Mexican kids when I was younger. It was a different time, a bad time, very bad. It was wrong. However, I was young, stupid, and full of hate. Just like all the *pinches gueros* like me all over Mexico with all the power, all the money, all the guns, no brains and the will to kill. *Lana o plomo* -money or lead - it was our motto. What I just said, I'm sure it seems to you like a contradiction. But when you hold so much power, like I do, you can lie and cheat, and contradict yourself and others with total impunity. To have all that power makes me special. Better than everybody! I even have my own *pinche* web site, where I can give the Mexican people in my state advice on the best way to drink tequila, know how to hold it, and when to throw up!

As I walked down the street, I felt naked and unprotected without my forty-five. It was as if one of my senses was gone. I was scared to be disarmed. Anyone might attack me. I walked bravely on, through the streets, into the plaza and out to the Church of *La Cruz*. My bodyguards, my best men: *Puñeta, Foker, Dronko and Burro*, were watching me closely. I order them to wait for me outside. The doors of the church were wide open. I got inside before the service began. I dipped Holy Water out of the marble font, made the sign of the cross before the Virgen of Guadalupe, and I sat down. The church was rather dark, but the altar was a fiery *fiesta* lit with a thousand candles. The odor of incense perfumed the air. Looking at the altar, I tried to repent, but the sentiment was too remote from my heart, too unapproachable. My eyes sought something warmer, something that would not frighten me. There she was: Blanca! Standing next to the figure of Saint Jude holding a golden candlestick and in it, a tall red candle was burning. I could not stop looking at the red candlestick and at her face. It was beautiful. I could not believe that she came to see me, and that she smiled a little now and then. The recurring smile of somebody, who thinks of pleasant things. With her presence, there was a new beauty in the church.

"Everybody rise," Father Bernardino said.

Quickly, all the *pinches chingones* in the church got up and blocked my view. I couldn't see Blanca anymore.

"Curita pendejo, hijo de la chingada!" I whispered.

I knew *Padre* Bernardino very well. He was not a PRI lover. All his sermons were full of caustic comments against my political party. I was sure that the *pinche* priest was going to take the opportunity and use the occasion to blame me and my *presidente* for the corruption, the poverty, the drug trade, the police brutality and all the bad things going on in the country. He'll make the people angry by breeding in them hatred and fear, telling them to revolt. He was our worst enemy and I knew that eventually, *por las buenas o por las malas,* I would have to stop him. I knew very well what went on in the church's basement, and his dealings with Miguel and Juan. This priest was in league with the devil, and that always leads to death. Religion is not for revolutionaries.

Padre Bernardino climbed onto the podium. I couldn't stop looking for Blanca. At last, the service began.

"Welcome everybody to the house of God and *que Dios los bendiga a todos.* Today I am very happy to tell you that there is a new splendor in our church, one of the children of our parish has given a golden candlestick to the glory of *San Judas.* However, I also have to tell you that I'm very angry with the people in our government. I am ashamed of them and I'm stricken with grief. I know very well what these corrupted politicians do behind closed doors. They do not care about the people and their families. Worst of all, they do not care about our women and our children. Our children are the future of The Republic and not taking care of them is a sacrilege! The men in power would be more than glad if I accepted their bribes and stopped telling the truth *a los cuatro vientos.* They attacked my friends, broke into their houses and threatened to kill them. You, the people, do not have to be afraid. I am not afraid of them. Together we can change this town to the way it was before. God is on our side...."

All of a sudden, a rushing sound came from the main entrance, the priest stopped talking, with his eyes fixed down toward the commotion. All my bodyguards came running and swarmed over my body to protect me. The people ran for cover, most of them rushed for the door. I heard five shots. I saw Father Bernardino falling backwards and collapsing face up on the altar, a lot of blood pouring out of his forehead. He was dead before hitting the floor. A furious roar like a howling broke out. With my ears still buzzing from the crack of the shots, trying not to panic, I strolled outside the church. A long moment passed before the police and the ambulance arrived. Once I got out of the church, I noticed that everybody was upset. They looked at me in a violent threatening way.

"Father Bernardino was a good man. I'm sure God our Lord needs him in paradise. That's why he took him upstairs," I said solemnly.

The people lowered their eyes. At least they were silent. At that moment, it felt good to know that I still had a remote soul and nerves of steel.

"Now, we have to catch the killers and bring them to justice. As your new governor, I swear to you, I will. I'll wipe out these *cabrones!*"

The people sighed in dismay. I had had more than enough for one morning and I still had to attend the party celebrating my nomination. My cell phone rang.

"Hello," I said.

"Tell all the press to hold the news about the ambush for at least twenty four hours. We need a scapegoat, even better, a dead one."

I knew that voice very well.

"Okay *Señor presidente*, as you wish," I said.

"You talk too much, *pendejo*, you give too much free information, you must learn to shut up, you stupid idiot!" he shouted.

The line went silent. I noticed some revulsion in his voice.

"C'mon governor, get in before these *sucios chingones* start going crazy again," Lagarto my driver said, opening the car door. When I got in the car, the crowd went wild.

"*Viejo criminal*, crook, son of a bitch, *hijo de la chingada*," they yelled at me.

They began to run after the car, throwing rocks, bottles, candles and *avocados*, smashing the windshield and all the side windows. The shattered glass hit my face and blood splattered all over my white shirt.

"This will not come to a good end. Lucky for them I don't have my forty-five with me," I said angrily, wiping the blood off my face with my handkerchief.

The situation was getting real bad. We escaped at high speed down the narrow streets. I saw the Indians jumping for cover to avoid being hit by the fast moving car. I don't know why, inside that speeding car, *de pronto*, out of the blue, at that exact moment, I remembered when I was eight years old and I was running away from my grandfather. I could still see the old man holding a gun, shooting at my feet, yelling:

"Jump you little fairy, learn to be a man."

I wanted to kill the old prick. I remembered my parents, and my dead sister. How depressed I was when she died. I thought about crawling into a hole and disappearing forever. I remember my mother coming to my rescue.

"She went away so you and your older brother could learn about life and death. Death is strong and mean," she said. "Never forget that. So you might as well gut it out."

My mother is my best friend, I know she cares about me, she always would tell me the truth. If I were gone, I know that nobody would miss me but my mother. However, she would never admit that she would miss me. She is a self-made woman, too tough for that kind of emotion. Aside from my mother and Blanca, I know nobody else will miss me. I was a nothing, zilch, *un cero a la izquierda*, a round big zero, a nobody, especially for my father, who, luckily for me, I saw very few times as a kid while growing up. He was a heavy drinker and a hard puncher, and because of that, every time after I met with him and we had a nice chat, about me and my future, next day I would be walking around with two black eyes, a bruised face and a split lip. However, what hurt me the most was that my mother ignored me. She didn't believe in physical punishment.

"Your father was born mad and he needs to hit you. You are his favorite punching bag and you seem to enjoy that. Therefore, in a way, you two are exchanging favors. Go and wash your face."

I wasn't too sure, but somehow it seemed to me that boxing was not the sport of my choice and that she was very upset about the whole situation. Growing up, I guess I took after my father. Since I was very young my favorite sport has always been, shooting, kicking and punching people, and to beat the shit out of any *pendejo* available, no matter what age, color, nationality or social status. I really haven't changed much since then.

"We are here," Lagarto, my driver, said. "Don't get out yet, *patron*, I'll keep you covered."

I gazed at the facade of the house, the sunlight patterns blinded me for a while, and I saw my mother standing by the front door smiling, waiting for me, holding her right breast with both hands like when I was a baby when she used to nurse me and feed me with her warm and sweet milk. Maybe I was hallucinating, but that day thanks to the apparition of my mother holding her right tit, I finally felt protected.

The phone call came directly to my private line. The call was from *Los Pinos.*

"We have an emergency meeting tonight at *Los Pinos*," the voice said.

"What about my *fiesta*, my inauguration, all the dignitaries, the VIPs? I asked.

"Who cares? You *pinche* idiot! Cancel everything you stupid jerk!"

I knew that voice and I knew it was an order! I told my mother to take care of everything. She was the only person I trusted one hundred per cent. We knew that people would be coming in large numbers, friends and enemies alike; they all waved the white flag that day and would let me celebrate in peace. Too bad, there wasn't going to be any celebration because Father Bernardino decided to get killed, on my special day. He was dead *para siempre*, for good, but he kept haunting me from the grave.

"*Curita cabron!* Just for that, I'm not going to your funeral, *pinche* Bernardino," I whispered angrily.

Lagarto my bodyguard knocked on the door.

"The plane is ready, *patron!*"

When I arrived at *Los Pinos*, I realized that I didn't have enough time to prepare myself for the meeting. I felt helpless and stupid. I was mad at God. I was mad at Father Bernardino. I was mad at Jesus. I was mad at my *presidente*. I was mad at my Mexico *lindo y querido*, and I was mad at my Mexican brothers. I felt like all of them were mocking me. I thought about killing myself, my boss and killing God. I was so depressed that I don't know how I found the strength to get off the plane and go to that joyless meeting with Zorro Porro Neto. He didn't say hello.

"Wait outside," he said.

"Kiss my ass," I thought and I smiled.

He was wearing a red shirt and black pants. By his attitude, I could sense that he was totally freaked out by the reaction of the Bishop and the people in general, about the assassination of Father Bernardino. I waited outside for almost one hour. As I waited, I counted more or less five hundred pine trees.

"No wonder they call this place *Los Pinos*," I thought.

Finally he called me inside and started screaming, walking around the room like a madman.

"What's wrong with you?" he asked.

"He's dead!" I shouted happily. "He's dead!"

"I know, I know," he said. "Yes, *pinche* Bernardino is dead but you had him killed like a dog. Now I don't have the confidence and the trust of the people anymore," he yelled.

He opened the desk drawer grabbed a gun and aimed to my head.

"I wish I could kill you myself!"

He put the gun down and went on a tirade, on and on:

"How could you order the murder of a priest? Our own *Padre* Bernardino! In full daylight, in his own church. The entire *pueblo* was watching! And to top it off, killing him like a dog, on the altar next to The Virgen of Guadalupe and Jesus, as a witness looking from the cross!" I started to cry. I touched my face and it was dry. There were no tears coming out.

"I can't remember how to cry anymore, boss." I said, and I couldn't stop shaking.

"You are a sick and crazy bastard! Pour me a Ley 925, and have one yourself. Let's have a toast *pinche* psychopath!"

We raised our glasses.

"To Bernardino, wherever he is, in heaven or hell, and whatever he's doing up there!"

After saying that, we smashed our glasses in the fireplace.

"Now you have to lay low for a while," he said to me.

"I'll do that, *jefe*, no more trouble," I said.

"Hide in the *hacienda* with your new girlfriend, enjoy her company."

"How do you know that, boss?"

"I know everything about you, *pinche pedófilo*."

It was just the two of us, seated facing the fireplace drinking in complete silence. He got up, went behind his desk, and turned off the lights. The glare from the fire now lit the room. From the darkness, for the first time in a long time, he called me by my nickname.

"Are you ok, Tarantula?"

"Yes *jefe*, I feel great," I replied happily.

"We are taking over the whole *pinche* country, just you and me!"

"Sure we will, boss," I said.

"Everybody is going to respect you."

"I thought you were mad at me."

"Not anymore, *cabrón*. Do you have a gun with you?" he asked standing up behind me.

"No boss, no need for that, I just came to see you."

He laughed, I laughed too. Suddenly I realized that he was not laughing with me. He was laughing at me!

"What's so funny?" I asked.

"You are a fucking pedophile, you are one creepy *chingón*. And that's bad for our party."

Now he was laughing louder.

"I'm quite aware I'm a little different, *jefe*, but I wouldn't classify myself as a creep," I answered.

"Don't get me wrong, Tarantula, I think it's great that you are a creep. I mean if you look at all the great criminals in our history and the history of the world, dictators, kings, presidents, generals, you are looking at a bunch of creepy people," he said.

In reality, at that moment, after drinking almost three bottles of tequila, neither of us was that drunk. We were awake and alert.

"Don't start something you can't finish," he said, filling my glass up to the rim. "Drink up, Mr. Governor. Be happy!"

"What the hell," I said.

Then I couldn't hold it anymore and I broke down.

"My life is in ruins anyway, *jefe*. In this country, the morals and the humanities are lost forever. Now we have gone too far, we are the real criminals. You and me, we are not human anymore, we are beasts. We even kill women and children. Our only hope to be saved is to wipe the darkness from our brains, but now it's too late, we are lost forever."

He was standing by my side.

"You are right Mr. Governor, but there is one thing I want you to know. There is somebody here to see you."

I knew he was pulling the trigger. I anticipated the blast of the shot climbing to the top of the five hundred pine trees outside and rolling down again back into my head. I saw myself falling slowly forward to the floor, finally dead. At that moment, a brilliant light pulled me straight upward and I saw Juan Sintierra holding a silver revolver and smiling at me. Blanca seated next to him, holding the candlestick with the red candle in it, and a baby on her lap, was waving good-bye.

"Last night I realized my son was dead when my heart started to cry and I felt his mouth sucking my right nipple. He was struggling. I sensed he wanted to live."

That was my mother's only statement when she became aware of my death.

"I wonder what really happened last night," her voice was trembling, stricken with grief, when she said that. "I'm angry at the president, I know what he did. My son loved all the children especially little girls. He believed in love and friendship. Since he was a little baby, he loved to play with dolls. He never hurt anybody, not even a doll."

After saying that, with her head down, she walked back into the house and locked herself in. She never came out again. Never!

Again, my name is all over the news. My smiling face is on the front cover of every newspaper in Mexico. According to the national news, I'm a national hero. To cover it up, they say that I saved Zorro Porro Neto's life, sacrificing my own. However, the sad truth is that right now I'm all the way up over here. Up, up high in the sky. Now that I'm dead, for the first time in my life with a warm heart, I have a great view of the church, the river and the whole town. This place up here is too cold, too holy and too remote. There is no God here, no *San Pedro* holding the famous key to open heaven's door, no cloud nine either. I don't see the Devil, the angel Gabriel, Father Bernardino or my sister walking around. If I make a real effort, I can see Blanca's green eyes fixed on me. Now she is not smiling anymore. Wait, I'm trying to cry, trying to repent, but I can't. I still can see Juan Sintierra sitting by the riverbank. He is watching the river flow, and he's trying to tell me something. "Brown is beautiful," Juan Sintierra said sternly looking up at the clouds, or was he looking at me?

It's getting cold and dark, very dark up here, pitch black. "Brown is beautiful," I said.

At last, forever and ever, *por siempre y para siempre*, I'm vanishing into the black.

CHAPTER 3
Juan Sintierra

Lucky for me, my father died before I was born, so when I finally came into this world, I had one less problem to deal with, one less person to bargain with while I was growing up. Unlucky for me, the persons I had to cope with were my mother and my sister, and let me tell you, it was not an easy task. It was more than enough. I was born with practically two brains. Okay, so that's not exactly true. I was essentially a very bright baby. My brain was fast, so fast that it worked like a jet engine. My way of thinking was weird, sometimes serious, sometimes poetic, most of the time very funny, so it seems more accurate to say I was born with the power of knowledge. My mother, my sister, my grandmother and my grandfather thought I was a very special little child. I also had, and still do, all sorts of physical abilities. However, let me tell you, there is nothing more dangerous in this world than being a kid with brainpower and showing it. For the adults, still fairly cute if you show your intelligence when you are six, seven and even eight years old, but it's all over when you are nine or ten. Then they don't like it that much anymore. After that period of "babyhood", your intelligence and your wit turn you into being a pain in the ass. You become the danger. In addition, if you are twenty years old, and you are still thinking and showing your intellect, then you become the biggest menace in the world. Everybody in my town called me Brains, or *Cerebro*. When the teacher made me read history books at school, I always wondered why they forced me to read lies written by such retards. Do you know what happens to bright people like me in Mexico? No matter how old you are, you could get beat up or killed. It's safer to shut up and be quiet. That's why I think all the time. I think about my mother, my father, my sister, and my friends. I think because words are too limited and they get me in trouble. I speak and I write in Spanish, Mexican Spanish. I'm sure that only a small percentage of people will understand what I mean. When I think and I don't talk, thanks to my sixth sense I know, or at least in my perception, I assume, that by keeping my mouth shut and being silent, everybody will understand me.

I'm only seven years old and I feel important holding a revolver in my hand. I want everybody to pay attention to me. I know that when I grow up I'm going to be important. I'll be the *mero-mero*, I'll be the *presidente*, maybe a famous one like my friend Barack. So I think about that, and many other things, and I feel that having a gun in my hand, might be my only real chance to make money and escape to the North. I don't want my life to be a series of broken dreams. *Bueno,* now you know that I'm a thinker, and I believe I'm very good at it. But right now, before anything else, I wish I could perform some magic trick and get out of this lousy town once and forever. I'm too poor, *muy pobre,* and there is no way out, and that's not even funny anymore. The worst thing about being poor is that most of the time the whole family misses a meal, or two, or maybe three. Sharing one taco, *uno solo,* after going twenty four hours without eating anything is a blessing from *La Virgen de Guadalupe,* and no matter what's in it, I can assure you it tastes great. Being hungry is no joke; makes people sick, especially old people. My *abuela* was the first victim; she was the first to go. Initially, we thought she had heat exhaustion, on that particular day the temperature was over one hundred and three, and plenty of old people were getting sick. My grandmother was no exception. That afternoon she was lying in bed, her face was red like a hot jalapeno-pepper and she was screaming in pain. I tried to give her some water, but she didn't want any of that.

"Get me some *tequila pendejo,* I'm dying anyway," she screamed.

I went to the kitchen to get her drink and when I got back, she was dead. I patted her on the head. *"Adios abuelita,"* I whispered and I drunk the tequila myself.

Since I was four my grandma would give me a tang of *tequila* or *mescal,* occasionally.

"Just to keep you warm and sharp, Juanchito." She would say.

My *abuela* was not a drunk. Like my mother, she was a moderate social drinker. They didn't want us kids to be drunks.

I was seven years old when my grandmother died and Blanca was sent away to Guadalajara, to live with my uncle for a while. I had mixed feelings about her trip and she having to stay by herself at my uncle's place. But in the end it didn't matter how much I loved her, how much I worried about her or how much I'd miss her, the most important thing for me at that time was how much extra food we were going to have on our table, at breakfast, lunch and dinner, with one less person living in the house. I also had the whole guacamole and the bedroom just for my miserable self. The hard part was to go back to school without my sister; she was my best friend and my protector. My school was so poor and so boring that the whole class had to try to stay awake smacking each other on the head. It was impossible to learn anything under those conditions. In my humble opinion most of the teachers were slow or mentally retarded. To top it off, our dean was Mrs. Malamilk, a decrepit mean old woman with an ugly face. "I'm sorry, *pendejo,* but I have to suspend you for two weeks," was her favorite line. There was no room for arguments. In addition, you were lucky if she didn't kick you in the *cojones,* call the authorities and send you to jail. Every time I confronted her, I wasn't sure what to do or say. I'd just stand quietly facing her, ready to take in the ear-piercing screaming, followed by the interrogation and the insults.

After my grandma's death, I sensed that something started boiling inside me, and I knew I couldn't take the witch too much longer. I started feeling restless, to the point that I started remembering my grandma's teachings and our special dialogues.

"No matter how much they *teach* you in school, it's all nonsense."

"I know, grandma."

"The real teachings are out there on the street."

"You're right, *abuelita*."

"When I started teaching in your school they fired me, because I smacked a student in the head with my *machete*, and when the father came to whine about it, I hit him with the *machete's* blade flat on his back, chasing the two *pinches pendejos*, father and son, all the way out to the street."

"*Juazzzz!* I love it, *abuela!*" I laughed.

"I was taught to be a teacher the old fashion way, to save, enrich and develop the brain of the children. Teach the kids to be free, to be good Mexican citizens."

"All my teachers are a bunch of retards!" I said.

"Teachers like me were trying to enhance our Mexican roots, our culture."

"I know, *abuelita*, I know."

"Most of the teachers nowadays are trying to kill the truth, to go backwards, to create a generation of reckless robots, just to serve the idiots in power for a salary."

"You're right, *abuela*, in my school Mr. Retard and Mrs. Retardee are in charge!"

"You know, Juanchito, I was Blanca's teacher. She was the smartest girl in her class. She was smarter than you."

When my grandma said that, I was happy but jealous at the same time.

"Your sister wanted to be a singer."

"Are you kidding?" I asked.

That statement astonished me. I didn't think it was serious.

"She never mentioned that to me," I said.

"She always thought people would make fun of her."

"Why? I would have thought maybe she could have wanted to make musical videos and movies, and be famous!"

"She was not shy about the idea of being a singer; she was shy about the kind of songs she wanted to sing. She wanted to write songs with a social meaning, like urban revolutionary songs. Like the black people sing in *El Norte*."

I giggled at that comment and I remember my grandma got upset.

"You are not supposed to laugh at your sister, *pinche pendejo*," she said.

"*Disculpa*," I said. "Those songs are just sort of silly and old fashioned, aren't they?"

"That's the difference between your sister and you, *pinche* Juan. You hide your ideas; your sister exposed her ideas to the whole wide world!"

"Why does she do that?" I asked.

"I don't know," my grandma said. "Maybe something shifted in her head, after she came back from your uncle's house."

"Yeah," I said. "She came back with a black eye and walking funny."

I remember clearly talking with my grandma all night. I didn't anticipate at the time that she would be dead in a few months. After we buried her, I decided to quit school. No stupid rules, no more. "From now on I'd live by my rules. I would accept my *primo's* offer and work for him", I said to myself, and I felt responsible for my decision.

"Juanchito," my sister said. "Don't go with Miguel, he's up to no good."

"How horrible is that?" I asked.

"What he does is ugly, violent and cruel. It hurts too many innocent people, and even he doesn't know it yet, he can already consider himself dead."

"I'm going anyway!" I screamed.

Blanca was mad. She looked at me with the angriest look in her eyes. She was furious. My sister and I had big dreams since we were little kids. We dreamed about being something other than poor, but we never got the chance to be anything because nobody paid attention to our dreams. That is why we decided very early in life to do something about it - grow up fast, and start believing we were destined to be rich and famous.

"I love you, Juancho," she said, disrupting my thoughts. "You have no idea what Miguel is doing, and he's going to get you killed."

From the sound of her voice and the way she looked at me, I could swear to you that I understood what was happening inside her head. She knew what I was going to do. She knew I was not scared. She knew I wanted to run away as fast as I could. She also knew as I knew it too, that no matter how fast you run, you cannot run away from your own self. She knew me well. We hugged, and held on to each other for a long time.

"I got to go," I said.

My sister just froze! I felt it in my gut. I was petrified myself. Like in a silent partnership agreement, we did not speak a word and said goodbye. For some reason I did not understand why this was happening. There was something about Blanca's glow on that particular day that hit my heart with the force of a punch. At that moment, I also noticed that, over the years, my sister got very good at staging goodbyes. Thanks to her, I learned that, no matter what, life could be beautiful, sacred and magical. Anyway, after that day, we rarely saw each other that much anymore. Certain that we needed to change our way of life, right there and then, we started walking in the opposite direction.

On Sunday, *El dia de los muertos*, at daybreak, I met with my *primo* Miguel by his girlfriend's house where he was living at the time. He came out carrying a rifle on his shoulder and stood on the porch looking up at the sky for a long while, completely ignoring me. Suddenly he came up to me and cleared his nose, holding his nostrils one at a time with his forefinger and blowing furiously, aiming big greenish snots at me. That was his distinctive way of saying hello and showing affection. Then he said.

"I have to cut your hair, you look like a girl."

"You do that and I'll cut your *cojones* off, *pinche cabron!*" I answered sharply.

He paused for a moment and walked slowly to his *troca.*

"When you grow up, you'll be my driver."

"I'm going to drive you all the way to Gringo-Land. I promise."

We started to laugh. *Juazzzzzzz!* We were still laughing aloud as we rode off to town at full speed. *Juazzzzzzz!* I was laughing at my poverty, at my parents, at my sister, at the whole *pinche pueblo*, blaming them for my bad luck, and for all the other sickness in the world. *Juazzzzzzz!* When we reached the center of town, we noticed it was practically deserted. We only saw a *mariachi* band in the town square playing beautiful music, and three police officers and a mailman walking by the Town Hall on their way to their jobs. At a normal speed, we quietly passed them.

"I want you to say it," Miguel shouted without warning.

"To say what?"

"I want you to repeat after me that you and I together are going to kill a lot of people."

I could not say that. It was not true. I wanted to believe that killing people was just a game, as if I was playing Play Station, but I really could not. I wanted to believe that I was just a kid having an adventure, having fun.

"You have two big *cojones*, Juan. You ought to be the king of Sinaloa," he said.

I wanted to cry, I wanted to tell him that I was not a killer. I felt so weak.

"Gracias Miguel," I said instead.

"*De nada*, Juanchito. Now you say it!"

"I can't!"

And then I cried. Tears rolled down my cheeks.

"I'm sorry," I said.

"From now on you don't have to be sorry for anything, Juanchito. The ones that are going to regret it are the *pinches cabrones* we are going to whack, and don't you ever feel bad about killing them or about crying." *Juazzzzzzzz!* Miguel laughed suddenly. "This town is already conquered, it's ours!" he yelled.

Holding the rifle out the window, he opened fire. I saw the mailman run for cover. The policeman was bleeding, lying face down on the sidewalk. He was not moving. The dudes from the mariachi band, with their mouths wide open and their eyes fixed on the dead cop, stood motionless in complete silence, holding their instruments close to their chests, as if to protect themselves. By the time the police started shooting back at our truck, we had escaped down the avenue at full speed.

"We are hurrying toward our destiny, there is no way back now," I thought.

"You should try and shoot some people, Juan, it's a real good feeling," Miguel said.

"It's a real good feeling? I don't understand?" I asked.

"Yes! It tickles!" he shouted.

"It tickles?"

"You're finger, stupid, when you pull the trigger. It tickles!"

Miguel drove me back home. It was very late.

"I'll pick you up tomorrow evening by the river bank. We have a very important delivery to make," he said.

I was still in shock for what had happened in town, and for not trying to do anything to avoid it or to stop it.

"Listen, I have to tell you something else. But you have to promise me you'll never repeat it."

"Ok," I said.

"Promise me," he insisted.

"Ok, *lo prometo*. I won't repeat it."

"Not to anyone, not even your mother."

"Nobody," I said.

"Ok then,"

He leaned closer to me because he did not want the birds or the trees, or anyone to hear what he was going to tell me.

"You have to leave this house, move out."

"What?"

"Yes, I mean you have to leave soon and forever."

"What do you mean?" I was confused.

"You were next to me when I whacked that cop in town. You are guilty of a crime."

I thought someone else was saying these things. Such a situation would never have occurred to me - killing people.

"I betrayed myself," I thought.

I got off the *troca* and I felt defeated, I was only seven years old. I was crying. I could not believe what was happening.

"You can't give up now! You won't give up!" Miguel screamed, before driving away.

It was a lot of pressure to put on a kid like me. "I don't want to fight, but I have to," I said. I have been fighting since I was born. I fought in school. I fought off all the drunks and drug addicts in town, including my despicable uncle, just trying very hard to be myself and keep my dream alive. When I walked into the house, my mother was awake.

"It's late, why are you looking so sad?" she asked.

Do not ask me why, but I think she knew my plans. We studied each other's eyes, as if we were sending radio signals.

"I want to live by myself," I said.

"You want to go to your uncle's?" she asked.

She was completely in denial. It seemed to me it was almost as if she had been waiting for a long time for me to tell her the bad news. I even knew what she was going to say next.

"I know you are running away because you want to find something. Your sister is going to be very angry at you."

I noticed a big box by the door with a red ribbon and a card.

"Is that a present for you?" I asked.

"No, Juan, it's from the governor, for your sister," she said.

I ran out of the house and sat on the porch for a long time, and thought about my sister and me. I thought about our situation and all what we were doing. We both knew it was wrong. We were heading to our ruin, and we should stop that before it was too late. Somehow, deep inside, we believed in our ability to make it. What the heck am I supposed to do? It felt like *la vida* just kicked me in the ass! My mother came out and sat next to me, holding a glass of *mescal*.

"I want you to stay home," she pleaded.

"No," I said.

From the porch, I could see the whole field in the back of the house filled with my mother's plants. About one hundred meters over the fence, there were many houses packed with people poorer than we were.

"You don't want me to be like them," I said gesturing at the homes.

"You could maybe wait until the semester break, or until next year. Get a fresh start," she said, ignoring my comment.

"Why is Blanca never here?" I asked.

"After school your sister goes to the governor's mansion to learn public relations," she said proudly.

After she said that, I knew I was going to be very angry with her for refusing to see the obvious.

"Public relations, mother? My foot! You know what the whole town says about the governor, don't you?" I asked.

"I know that he has a temper and stuff, but he's been nice to her."

"Mother, do you ever wonder why he's so nice to her?"

She looked at me, raised the glass and took a deep gulp.

"Are you crazy? Do you realize the absurdity of your thought? Your sister is very young, she's just a child!" Like you!

Right at that moment, I was beginning to understand my mother. She was giving up. She could not fight forever. She was trying to keep her hope alive, living in denial.

"We have to do something to help Blanca. If you don't, I will," I said.

I kissed her on the cheek. I knew that just like me, she was bleeding inside. I paused a second and then I walked out. She was crying.

The day after I decided to move out, I reached an agreement with Miguel to make it happen. I did not say goodbye to my mother. I wanted to tell her that she was the best person in my life and that I loved her, but because of my extreme anger, I could not say those things to her face. Therefore, I just gathered my stuff and left. It was very sad. I felt *muy triste*!

The place that Miguel got for me was a small trailer by the riverbank. Inside, there was one bedroom, a bathroom with a shower, and a kitchen. The walls were yellow, with red tiles covering the floor. There were two small square windows, one on each side of the trailer. Hanging on the walls, a cheap portrait of Frida Kahlo and a color picture of our president Zorro Porro Neto, smiling while standing tall by the iron-gate at *Los Pinos*. Near one wall, there was a small round table and two chairs.

"This place brings me good memories. The last guy that lived in this place was a good friend. Too bad he got killed so young," said Miguel, and laughed at his own joke.

"Screw you!" I said angrily.

"Nothing terrible will happen to you, Juanchito, you are blessed! *La Virgen de Guadalupe* is watching over you, *pendejo*," said Miguel. "I have to go now. Have your cell on, I'll call you tomorrow." He left.

At last, I was by myself and I had my own place. I walked into the bedroom. I looked underneath the bed, and inspected the blankets and the mattress. Everything was clean. I put my things on a shelf by the bed. I went to the bathroom. A bar of soap, a razor, one old comb and a bottle of pills were all inside a metal cabinet. The mirror on the cabinet's door was busted. I sat on the toilet and started to cry.

"Where the hell's that new man Juan?" I asked myself.

I heard a noise coming from the front door. I ran out of the bathroom. The front door was wide open. A huge stocky guy stood by the entrance. He wore black jeans, a white silk shirt and a black vest. His thumbs were stuck in his belt, on each side of a round, gold buckle. A heavy gold chain was hanging from his neck. His high-heeled boots with golden plates on the tip were proof that he was not a workingman. Kicking the door shut, he stepped into the room, giggling, looked quickly at me and said:

"*Hola* Juanchito, I'm *El Lupe* and I'm here to make sure you drink your milk, brush your teeth, take a shower and go to bed early."

"I don't need a babysitter," I said.

"*El Charro* told me to be here in case you needed something."

"*El Charro*, who's *el Charro?*" I asked.

"*El Charro* is Miguel, your boss. You are just a little boy and the farther and farther you get involved in this business, you are going to run into more and more surprises."

"What surprises?"

In the North across the border, they love the stuff we are bringing them illegally, but they don't like us, the *ilegales*. Our brothers living in the North are even poorer than you would ever think possible."

"I don't believe that," I said.

"You are only seven years old, and you don't know shit."

He got up, stared me hard in the eyes, and then spat on the floor.

"You are getting me mad," he said.

I did not know the guy. I just met him. I didn't want to get him mad. When we Mexicans get mad, we get mad real fast, and it takes us days to get un-mad. In addition, while we are mad we can cause a lot of damage to other people, like killing them, cutting them in little pieces and feeding them to the dogs. Therefore, I thought it was better for me to keep quiet for a long while, to give him time to calm down. After all, he was at the house to watch over me. He was my personal bodyguard. However, I had to speak eventually and, when I did, I knew that my bodyguard would become my friend.

"Those white people in the North aren't better than us." I said.

He turned around and headed for the door.

"Miguel told me that you are brave, you are a warrior. I'll be around, call me if you need me," he said.

That felt good. It was the best thing he could have said to me. I stood alone in the house and watched *El Lupe* drive away in a shiny black *troca*.

"I deserve to be here," I thought.

I was tired and I went to bed. I couldn't sleep. I fantasized about all the beautiful girls waiting to go to bed with me, and I started to masturbate.

At about ten o'clock in the morning, Miguel woke me up. He was all dressed up.

"Where are we going?" I asked.

"We are going to see *Lobo Bobo,* the big boss. He's our private supplier."

"What's his real name?"

"What?" He laughed. "In our business there are precise rules, Juancho. You must memorize the rules, and live your life by those rules. If you ask fewer questions, you'll live longer."

"Okay," I said.

I went along with Miguel that morning, completely confused. I was only seven years old trying to be a man, but I was completely terrified. I had heard about these mafia type people, their private wars and their criminal organizations. I imagined that these guys could kill us easily. Just like flies. I realized how much my life depended on Miguel's sense of safety and his experience dealing with these killers.

"Pay attention, Juan. I want you to take a good look around here. I want you to remember this place, can you? The hacienda from where *Lobo* operates is about twenty miles to the north. We just have to follow the river."

"Sure," I said. "Of course I can remember this."

"Listen Juan, in case we get in trouble, I want you to come right back to the trailer and hide."

"Hide inside the trailer?" I asked.

"Yes hide inside the trailer till I come for you. Can you remember that?"

"Sure I can, Miguel. Let's hope nothing bad happens today."

"I'm not so sure about that," he said.

"*Lobo Bobo* was expecting you tonight," the guard at the gate said, pointing at us with his gun. "You can go around the house by the stable," he said, indicating a narrow path at the back of the hacienda.

Miguel led the way. I walked close to him all the way to the main house. Finally, when we got to the front door it was wide open. I saw a middle-aged guy wearing a brown leather jacket and a young woman standing next to him. She was dressed in red and smiling at us. *Lobo Bobo* rubbed his hands, leaned over and inspected our faces closely. Immediately Miguel shook his hand and kissed the woman on the cheek. *Lobo Bobo* seemed happy and satisfied.

"Come in boys," he said. "I thought you guys were coming tonight. We are ready to eat breakfast. Where the hell is my money?"

"Can I have some coffee?" Miguel asked and sat down.

"Sure *charro.*"

"*Charro*? Me?"

"Yeah! You are a typical *Mexicano chingón*, and a crook, and just for that, you get me pretty mad sometimes, but I don't give a damn, as long as you deliver for me."

Miguel looked down at his feet, before answering.

"The last time, your people made a big mistake with the cargo and we had to drive one hundred miles around the mountains to avoid the *federales*."

Lobo Bobo squinted his two eyes.

"Well next time I have to send out my elite team. Anyway, it will not do any good to talk about that now. What's your name, boy?" he asked me.

I hesitated to answer. He put his laptop on the table and opened it. Miguel stared angrily at me. I nodded to show him that I understood what was happening.

"So, what's your name, little boy?" he insisted.

"Juan Sintierra."

Lobo typed my name quickly.

"You got your school ID with you?"

I reached into my pocket, produced my fake ID, and handed it to him.

"I'll be back."

He got up and went into the next room. I noticed that he walked with short, slow steps, like a very old man. After a while, he came back out.

"Your name's been entered in my book. Now we are family. Where did you work before?"

"Up around Elota," I said.

"Just like Miguel?" *Lobo Bobo* asked.

Miguel nodded. *Lobo Bobo* pointed a playful finger at me.

"You are seven years old, huh? You have some balls kid!" he said, and smiled.

"Yeah, and he's a hell of a good *sicario*, fast as a rabbit!" said Miguel.

"Then why don't you let him answer? What are you trying to sell me?"

"What I'm saying is that Juan is bright and fast. I'm sure he can do a delivery all by himself!"

"I wonder what stake you got in this kid? What plans do you have for him? I had never seen a *cabron* like you take so much trouble to ride with a little boy. I just would like to know what your real interest is. Your business is my business, and you know that very well, Miguel," he said.

"He's my cousin. I told his mother I would take care of him. He's ok, and he can do anything you tell him," Miguel said.

Lobo Bobo turned his head, looking straight at us.

"All right kids. I'm warning you, don't try to put nothing over, because you won't get away with anything. I have seen wise guys, *pinches chingones* just like you before, and I took care of them real fast! When you go out there, you are my team, my family. Never forget that! If you forget that even for one minute, you are as good as dead."

Abruptly he got up and went to the front door, but before he opened it, he turned around and looked at us for a long moment.

"Where's my money *cabrones?*" he asked.

"I'll bring it to you later," Miguel said.

"No *lana* no merchandise, Miguelito." *Lobo* sounded upset.

"I'll bring it to you today, I promise *Lobo*," Miguel persisted.

"Okay then, Juanchito stays with me till you bring the money *puto!*" he said and glanced coldly at me. He stared hard at Miguel.

"No money, no Juanchito, you *pinche charro!*"

I had no idea what was happening. *Lobo* wasn't laughing at all, he was mad now. At that moment, I felt stupid and immature. I didn't know what to do or say. I was confused. We had followed the rules, we had behaved exactly the way we were supposed to behave, but this *pinche Lobo* had ignored the rules. Miguel didn't know what to say, he just stood there his face red like a stop sign. Three bodyguards appeared standing next to *Lobo Bobo*, like a pack of wild dogs.

"Take the kid inside," he told them. "You *charro,* go and get the money."

A look of shock came over Miguel's face. He opened his mouth and cried out.

"I'll be back in three hours," he sounded insulted.

The bodyguards pushed me into a backroom.

"Let's see how tough you really are, *pendejito,*" said one of the guys punching me hard in the stomach.

Considering the situation, I realized how much of my self-worth, my sense of safety, was based on Miguel's guts and goodwill. It was good to know he would never let me down.

We Mexicans are like an ancient tribe. Any chance we get, we like to sit around a table, a bar or a campfire, have a tequila or two, or better yet, four or five, and recount sagas of brave deeds. Telling and retelling heroic tales from Cuathemoc to Pancho Villa, not discounting one or two anecdotes of our boxing champions, and three or four of our baseball and soccer players. Each of us spends years and sometimes a lifetime trying to stay united as one people, one nation, under one flag. The fact is that, being so close to *El Norte*, we never can reach an agreement on which people or what flag we are talking about .However, don't think for a moment that this situation discourages us in anyway. Somehow, in some mysterious fashion, believe it or not, that dilemma is the pulse and the heartbeat that drives our country forward. Possibly, our problem is that we haven't grown up yet and we are still playing games, or maybe our illusions lie in another direction. We thought we could find some kind of a formula to get away and be completely isolated from the gringos, but at the same time, we're still trying to figure out how to get through the border, by car, by train, by plane or by simply walking and climbing up the wall, and we keep doing it, forever and ever, warming up one another with our common dream, to be standing on the other side, in *El Norte*, Gringo-Land, Dream Land, the dollar sign, just to climb the wall and live there, is always in our head.

"I thought you might want to know that Miguel is on his way with the money," *Lobo* said.

There is a smell to danger. A stench floats in the air. Just as dogs can detect the odor of fear in a person, so could a seven-year-old kid like me sense when a man is going to kill another man. By the tone of his voice, it seemed to me that all *Lobo Bobo* wanted was his money, and make peace with Miguel. He walked over to the bar and poured himself a big glass of tequila.

"It's a bad habit to drink when dealing drugs," I thought.

When Miguel arrived, I was in the living room seated next to *Lobo*. The bodyguards were smoking in the patio outside. I looked up and smiled as I saw him approach. He was carrying a backpack.

"It's nice to see you, Juanchito," Miguel said, blinking an eye at me.

Miguel had this young and innocent look on him.

"Can I see my money?" *Lobo Bobo* asked.

"It's all here," said Miguel holding the backpack with his left hand, and placing it on the coffee table.

Right there at that moment I smelled danger, the disgusting odor was so powerful that it filled the whole room. In a split of a second, Miguel leaped on top of *Lobo Bobo*, holding a gun to his head, clutched him by the neck and pushed away stepping back towards the front door. The bodyguards came into the house pointing their guns toward Miguel and *Lobo*, not knowing what to do.

"Run, Juan, run! Wait for me in the *troca*," Miguel yelled, while spraying the bodyguards with *plomo*.

The impact of the bullets lifted the bodyguards up one by one, and I saw them slamming down on their backs dead, with their eyes wide open. A smoking gun bounced on the floor and landed next to my feet. I picked it up. It was still hot. Breaking free from Miguel's hold *Lobo Bobo* was trying to get away. I aimed at the head and shot him in the mouth. He rolled around, falling to the ground like a clumsy child. He probably never saw the bullet that killed him, and never really felt Miguel's trademark, the ten bullets flaming down into his chest. Each time a bullet hit *Lobo*, his whole body and his hands would jerk and jump up, as if he was trying to grab the backpack. I'll never forget that sight.

When Miguel came out, I was waiting for him by the *troca*. He looked weakened and in shock, unable to talk. He was the one doing the thinking now. As in a dream state, we loaded the merchandise.

"*Lobo Bobo* doesn't need anything anymore," Miguel said.

We got into the truck. We could hear each other panting. We were not thinking straight, fighting the shock and the agonizing stomach spasms. We were fighting the horror, waiting for our strength to come back and be able to drive away toward the highway. We cut back south by the river, as planned, to avoid being followed, to return to the trailer, store up the merchandise and hide for a while.

"Till things cool down a little," Miguel said, "we hide in the trailer."

We had provisions for more than three weeks. El Lupe was not around anymore. When I asked Miguel about him, he told me he was on vacation.

"No news about *El Lupe*, and no news at all about *Lobo Bobo* and his *putos* bodyguards, is good news. Nobody cares if they got whacked."

"I do care, *cabron!*" I said.

I was ashamed. I might have impressed Miguel, but I still hated myself. I knew that my grandmother, wherever she was, would never approve my actions. I felt stupid and naïve. Of course, after killing *Lobo Bobo* everybody in the business started paying more attention to us. Miguel became the most popular dude in the business, but nothing much changed. In my mind, I was still an outsider in a foreign land. Miguel treated me pretty much the same. He didn't really say much to me about what happened, and I didn't really say much to him. I wanted to ask Miguel for his advice about crossing to the other side, but I couldn't. I felt like a zombie. In fact, if you think of everybody with a body, soul and brain as a human, I was the opposite of a human. It was the loneliest time of my life. I remember when my *abuelo* used to think I was smart, and my brain was useful. It would be impossible for him to understand how I got in trouble, drug-dealing trouble. It had nothing to do with me. *Nada.* Yet they were driving me into it.

"Thanks for sticking up for me back there, and helping me to kill *Lobo*," Miguel said.

"I was so scared, you saved my life!"

"I promised you I was coming back. We are one, Juan. We have to stay together or we got no chance. Neither one of us. *Ninguno de los dos.*"

He cut me off before I had a chance to answer.

"Don't talk. Save it, kid! Before I forget, no phone calls, no text messages or e-mails from this location," he said.

By the next evening, my fears had evaporated. Slowly the emotions regarding *Lobo's* killing began to die down. A full moon, the one that makes everybody crawl out of the woodwork, was all the way up in the sky. In an emotional state, Miguel started talking.

"We have to quit depending on computers and start trusting our instincts again. The only way we can keep the business flowing in peace is to sit down with the heads of the cartels, the DEA and the *federales*, and negotiate face to face. No cell phones, no e-mails, no texting, no twits, just people talking to people, shaking hands and looking each other in the eye, exchanging ideas and finding solutions. Our business is the most serious business in the world. It's goddamned hard work being successful. It takes courage, balls and personality if you want to make it big time without getting jailed or killed."

I stepped away from the window. After that speech, for a moment, I felt important. Then I realized that Miguel maybe had been drinking too much *tequila* or smoking too much *yerba* that evening. There are all kinds of addicts. I guess they all have pain. Still they all look for ways to make the pain go away. Miguel drinks his pain, and then throws up, and after flushing it away, falls sound asleep. As expected, that's what he did on that particular night. "My grandpa wouldn't define that as pain, he'd call it vomit!" I thought.

I couldn't sleep. Therefore, I got up and I went back to the window. I had the sudden urge to hug my sister. Not following Miguel's orders, I decided to make it simple and send a text to Blanca.

> *Hermanita, it's been a long while since the last time we talked. I wanted to know how are you doing? How is mama? I'm ok working for Miguel and having lots of crazy momentos! I wish I could make enough money, so you and I together can have a good life in El Norte, in Gringo-Land with my friend Barack on the other side of the wall. I hope to see you soon.*
>
> *Luv you, Juan*

After sending the text I felt lonely, sad, isolated and terrified. No matter what, my sister and I were always connected. We are the freakiest brother and sister in the whole Mexican Republic. But we loved each other. Her answer came back real fast:

> *Juanchito, It's a beautiful night. The full moon is magical. I'm still mad at you, but I miss you so much. I'm glad you are ok. I don't like you working with Miguel. He's going to get you killed. Mama is very sad because you are not here anymore, but I think she understands. Between school and my work at the governor's mansion, I'm very busy. I'm not at home most of the time. Today I drove a car for the first time. I like my job a lot. Yesterday I went to a nice restaurant, right in the lobby of this great hotel. On the menu, they had tacos. I ordered two tacos for twenty dollars each! Insane! I didn't think they would be any good, especially not as good as mama's. They served the tacos on this beautiful silver plate and so I ate them. Let me tell you*

Juan, they tasted great! They were almost as good as mama's! I just kept imagining that you were next to me all the time. Too bad, it was just a dream! I love my life! I love Mexico! I love you!

Tu hermana, Blanca

I stared at the text for a while. I was angry with her. I knew what was going on in that mansion even though she wouldn't tell me. "I have to whack that *pinche* governor," I thought.

CHAPTER 4
Miguel Meromero

It was Saturday morning. I was standing by the trailer's door waiting for Juan to get up. I stood outside holding my cell phone. My right hand was trembling.

"Hurry up Juan, *El Lupe* is waiting for us!" I yelled.

It was a big day for me after three long years of dealing with hard-core criminals and gambling daily with death. With a simple phone call, the big Capo of the cartels gave me the ok to take over the distribution in the whole state. It was a very dangerous and nerve-wrecking job, but I loved it more than any other job in the whole world. I know very well that the capos of the cartels are wild, insane characters, and have a parade of self-centered megalomaniacs and ungrateful idiots working for them. They all are a wild pack of brainless, vicious and destructive sons of bitches! However, as far as I'm concerned, if they are a gang of idiots with no brains, all the better.

"It's a big day today, Miguel! Let's do it, boy!" I said to myself.

When we got to *El Lupe's* place, he was waiting outside. Seeing him at a distance, reminded me when three years ago, I picked Juan up for the first time at his mother's house and helped him move to the hideaway trailer by the river. Of course, this time was a very different time, and I was picking *El Lupe* up for an entirely different reason.

My name is Miguel Meromero. I'm sixteen years old. I was born in El Hujal, Zihuatanejo, State of Guerrero, into a family of healers and raised in rural Mexico by my *curandera* mother. According to my father, I came out from my mother's womb with a forty-five in one hand and a machete in the other. Since the very beginning, I knew how to fight and really hurt people. I was rowdy and ready to punch anybody at any moment. Very early in life, I also learned how to concentrate and reach my Zen mode, trying to make this whole fighting thing a spiritual experience. That combination, violence and Zen, one contradicting the other, helped me to improve the condition and the quality of my life. Later in my profession, when I became a killer, in the process of killing somebody I could stop, forgive the victim and let him live, or just carry on, whack the guy and just as easily forgive myself. The wisest advice in the world - learn to reach your Zen mode. If someone pisses you off, you won't have to punch him in the stomach or kill him. Let it slide, smile, be cool and save that bad energy for the next kill. You never know, in my profession to save bad energy is key, and it always comes in very handy.

I'll never forget the first time I met Juan. He was five years old and I was eleven. There was a family get-together, a welcome party for me after I came back from my uncle's house in Monterrey. We were playing in my aunt's living room and he said:

"You better keep your hands off my toys, *primo*. I'm only playing with you because you are family, but if you piss me off I'll punch you in the nuts."

Everybody in the family that were present laughed at his remark. I sensed that he was dead serious. I was glad!

"Don't laugh at me," he yelled at them.

"They are not laughing at you," I said. "They are laughing at what you said."

"That's the whole problem with this family! Nobody takes me seriously!"

"Come on, Juan, it's kind of hard to take you seriously when you are quarrelling about toys and threatening to punch me in the nuts."

"It's serious enough for me," Juan said.

"Why don't you stop talking nonsense and tell me what you really want to do with your life," I asked.

"I want to be the king of Sinaloa."

"Wow! That's cool!" I said. "You want to be a king? Why?"

"I want to change things around here. I want to be recognized."

I kept silent. I could not make fun of a five-year-old boy. Besides his dream was my dream too.

"Mexicans boys don't suppose to dream at all, especially the brown young boys from small towns. They don't suppose to dream big either. In Mexico they expect us, the browns to be happy with our own limitations, but looking at you tonight, I feel that we are wired, that we are connected and there is no way that you and me are going to sit still. No way, like a Mexican eagle, we both are going to fly high. I think its super cool that you want to be the king of Sinaloa and be recognized, but you won't make it halfway if you go around punching guys bigger than you in the nuts," I said.

Juan turned slowly with his eyes wide open. He watched me carefully, smiling.

"I can tell the future. Together we'll be like an army of two, Miguel. You'll see," he said.

Maybe I don't know much about life, but I know a little bit about people. That night I thought that Juan was the perfect *socio*, the ideal partner to start my enterprise. It was only a matter of time, only a few years for him to be ready. In a few years the little apple-cheeked kid would turn into a cold-blooded killer. And a good one too!

When Juan was only five, I was already working for *Lobo Bobo*. At the time he was the most powerful and respected boss in Mexico. His name was all over the papers. He was a big star on U-tube, where this monster posted his videos, showing gruesome images of the brutal massacres his people committed all over Mexico. Politicians, top models, and the most famous divas in the country fought each other for the privilege of asking for favors or going to bed with him. He was not a handsome guy. He was short, in his fifties, with gray hair, a big red nose, small bluish eyes, and a little paunch. He reminded me of a miniature Santa Claus, with a bad temper. Every day he would wake up around noon, relax by the large swimming pool at the back of his hacienda and call a meeting with his whole staff. There were twenty-five guys and there were always six of them heavily armed to the teeth surrounding him. *Lobo Bobo* never learned their names. "I'm impressed with you *Charro*, you are the only one listening", he would tell me at the end of every meeting. That nickname he gave me sounded pretty good coming from him, since he trusted no one, not even me. The nickname *Charro* was a huge compliment. *Lobo Bobo* was smart. I wished he would become governor or president. Of course, having so much power, *Lobo Bobo* most probably would kill many people or, on the other hand, maybe he would become a superhero fighting for truth, justice and the brown Mexican way.

"The people here in Mexico call me a criminal because they don't know that I'm the only protection they have against predators, starvation, and slavery. The people from the North are constantly threatening the strength of our people. If we are no good at defending our identity, making food, shelter or babies, then we'll be conquered," he told me once.

"Don't get sentimental," I said.

"I'm not getting sentimental, *pinche Charro*, I don't think I could live through that humiliation," he said.

Deep in his soul, he was a romantic, a romantic and a beast. Before smashing a person's head with a baseball bat, he would say a prayer, covering the victim's head with a heavy-duty plastic bag and a red poncho, to avoid seeing the head explode. Of course, at the same time it would keep the blood and the brains from splashing on his clothes or all over the walls. "I love people and I respect my enemies, and when I'm sending some *cabrón* on a one way ticket to the other side, I would never do anything disdainful to disrespect him." After killing a guy or ten or whatever, *Lobo Bobo* would organize a party and celebrate, and dance all night long, "To honor the dead," he would say. He loved to dance, that was his way of showing that he was happy to be alive.

We, his loyal militia danced too, all night long, like in a trance. In a way, we were all so happy to be alive together like brothers, knowing very well and deep in our young hearts that it could be our last dance. In our business, death is nearby every day.

He invited loads of young girls, hot and horny for sex, drugs and money. *Lobo* danced every single dance, taking turns with all of them. I pretended to be happy. I pretended I belonged, hiding my true feelings. Of course, you cannot lie forever. Lies have short shelf lives. Lies go bad. Eventually lies rot and stink, and consequently they are discovered. When *Lobo Bobo* called me for a private meeting in his hacienda, I thought something was wrong. Smiling, he waved me in.

"How are things?" he asked. "I heard there's a new kid working for you, that he's only seven years old."

Juazzzz! Lobo laughed. I almost fainted. Lobo stretched his arms and laughed again. *Juazzzz! Lobo* was a psycho; brilliant maybe, even a genius, but a certifiable lunatic.

"Why didn't you tell me?" he insisted.

"He's family, he's my *primo*. I didn't have a chance to tell you," I said.

Lobo studied my face, as if he was searching for something.

"He's too young. Are you sure we can trust him?" he said.

"He's one hundred percent reliable. He's good and I need him."

"You are the first one who's leveled with me."

As it turned out, *Lobo Bobo* couldn't see the future. For the first time in his life he was mistaken. At that moment, he didn't realize he would never survive his second mistake.

The days and the weeks dragged on, and so did the months and the years. The summer was so hot that it almost melted the stones. The yellow dust, pushed by a very warm wind stuck in our hair, our nostrils and our eyes. The dust piled up on the doorways, covered the roof and the walls of all the houses in town. It was hot as hell. The people divided in two bands, hated each other. There were those who helped the cartels, and the traitors who helped the police and the army. Both groups' silent; waiting for revenge. Many of them believed they were fighting for a better town and the ideal way of life. Soon they found out that the control the government took was insecure. People that were neighbors for a long time looked at each other coldly and never spoke again. There was a smell of death in the air, hovering and waiting. Many folks were murdered in reprisal and it made no difference. Now and then young people killed each other just for kicks. The army and the police raided the neighborhoods killing some of both their friends and their enemies. It did no good. The hatred grew. Now the authorities were alone among silent enemies. No one could let his guard down, even for a moment. Delivering merchandise became too complicated. Every day somebody would disappear and the family received the corpse. Accidents happened to governors and mayors alike. Most of them got killed in their cars and in their homes, killed by a bomb or a lonely gunman. The hatred was deep in the eyes of the people, beneath the surface. Everybody was armed. Now it was the police and the army, that were losing ground, their men had to go out on patrol in groups of twenty or more. Most of them detested our town and the people, and gradually fear began to grow in their ranks, a fear that would never be over. They were afraid that one day; they would be ambushed and killed. Their nerves wore thin and they shot at everything that moved. The fear crept into the police and made them vicious. Sometimes they would shoot an old man in the back, for holding only a stick, or a little girl holding a flashlight. Everybody in town was a menace to them. Juan and I just went on with our work. The riverbanks were rotten with bodies. We were very lucky that we knew how to avoid the squads.

"These people will not spare us. They will kill us like dogs," I said to Juan.

"No way, they have to catch us first. They are a bunch of fools. They can't plan and execute the way we can."

There was a little street not far from our trailer where all the prostitutes congregated to work their tricks. My friend Perlita was the leader of the pack. Sometimes she would give me a free blowjob, and keep me informed about the coming and goings of the police and the army. She would talk to me while on her knees and holding my *pinga* as a microphone to shun suspicion. Perlita and the girls would stand by the corner, on the sidewalk or leaning against the walls, waiting for their clients. Their business, like ours, never stopped. They would deal with the police, the soldiers and with the town's people the same old way, without hesitation. "We are a democracy here, either on top of us or between our legs, everybody is equal," they joked. One Sunday night, when the army patrol came down to their street, after drinking tequila all night at the local bodega, abruptly their thin street-democracy was over. They took all of them away in an army truck and we never saw those poor girls again. The street is very quiet now. Twice a week, high in the air, two police helicopters circle the sky, watching the area. They drop a few feet and then gain altitude again, turn and fly back in the direction from which they came from.

"I don't think those murderers will achieve anything from the air," I said.

"Let those cowards, *hijos de la chingada*, keep the sky. Down here on the ground we are in control, we are king. If they dare to come down here, I'll cut their *cojones* off myself!" said Juan.

In a little town like ours the news spreads quickly. It's communicated by whispers on the street, in doorways, in the park, by quick glances or a telephone call. For that reason I wanted to tell Juan about his uncle, and Blanca and me, before he could find out by himself, get upset, feel betrayed and try to kill me. Maybe I'm exaggerating, but telling him the whole truth about our dysfunctional family, was not an easy task.

When I met Blanca I fell in love with her at first sight, with my body and soul. It was the happiest time of my life. It was destiny. The first time I kissed her, she started crying, telling me about how lonely she was and how everybody wanted her to be perfect, because she was the only woman in the family. How scared she was all the time, but nobody would let her be scared because she was strong, pretty and smart. I was older. That made me wonder how was it that in my dumb head, such an innocent girl could be so sexy, and become my perfect match. I suddenly understood that love and lust could make you go crazy. Now I also understand why, when my father met this girl much younger than my mother, he moved out in a hurry and married her one week later. I'm not so mad at him anymore for leaving us and moving to Monterrey with his new young wife. From day one, Blanca and I became very close, but we couldn't show it to the world. For everybody in town, we were just best friends. We held hands occasionally, and kissed once or twice, making sure nobody was looking. I didn't know what I meant to her. I thought she wanted to go a little crazy, or she was only using me as an experiment, or she was bored or trying to tell me something, some awful secret. Maybe something terrible, that she been hiding inside her for a long time.

"Miguel," she said one day after a long walk by the river. "I hate this *pueblo*. It's too small and too poor. Everything about this town is small. The people here are mostly stupid. They have small ideas, small dreams. Most of them, all they want, is to have a *troca*, go around delivering drugs and shooting people, and keep doing that forever."

"What do you want to do?" I asked.

"I want to leave this place as soon as possible, get away from it really fast; before it's too late for me."

After saying that she started crying, she was very dramatic.

"Where you want to go?" I said.

"Let's go anywhere, but the North. I want to go to a civilized place, where people are well educated, polite and sophisticated. Where people's life is precious, and more important than money and material things, where I can go to school and learn something significant to help build a more rational world for my kids. I want my children to be educated, I don't want them to be indoctrinated," she said.

"Blanca, people are the same all over the world. People care more about money; than anything else, they never have enough. Wherever you go, it's the same bullshit."

I figured she was sad and depressed, and ready to give up on the world.

"There are millions of people on the planet, but this feeling and this love between you and me is unique. Just think about it." I said.

The next time we met by the riverside. Unexpectedly she started talking about how she felt about me, and her particular idea, about love and dreams. All the anguish and the pain she had to endure to be with me. How she ached from the wanting and the passion she felt for me. I just stood there listening, not saying a word, not really knowing what she wanted, but knowing very well what I wanted. She was sobbing. Looking at her, I was overcome by an unbearable feeling of desire. "It's all right," I said, and my gentleness made her cry even harder. I put my arms around her waist and held her cozily. After that, neither of us ever knew how we got into the trailer, and who made the first move. What started as a gentle, understanding and romantic walk by the river; became a sensual, animal wanting desire. We were kissing hungrily, and I was holding her tightly. I felt her body pressing against mine. "I need you Miguel," she said. I took her clothes off. Nude, with her eyes closed, she looked like a sleeping angel. Then I was naked in the dark, lying on the floor beside her, not knowing what to do. There was urgency in both of us. Still with her eyes closed, she climbed on top of me and moaned once, holding me fiercely. I began to make love to her, gently, filling her, completing her, making her body whole. It was an ecstasy, an unbearable rapture, two childish animals coupling, and Blanca screaming: "Love me Miguel, *ámame!*"

At that instant, I was part of her. We were one. We embraced in the dark for hours, and talked and laughed, and it felt like we belonged together always. We laid on the floor and I held her in my arms protectively, and started singing. I don't know why, at that particular moment, I remembered Perlita.

"This is what love is?" I thought.

Blanca turned and gazed at me. She looked beautiful. I never loved anyone so much. As in a flash of blue light, I saw Perlita's face smiling at me and whispering my name. I closed my eyes trying very hard to erase that image. I just kept singing.

"I want to marry you," I said.

"Sure," Blanca said, "Father Bernardino can officiate our wedding in his church. I can picture myself wearing a white wedding dress and walking down the aisle. I'll be the most beautiful bride in the history of the whole *pueblo.* The only problem would be that we are too young and we are cousins. Not the most natural thing in the world!"

We hugged tightly and started laughing. Juazzzzzz! Laughing aloud, so loud and so hard we couldn't stop! Juazzzzzz!

It was not until hours later that I realized what I had done. I didn't even remember how it all started between us in the first place. I felt I had degraded her. I experienced guilt and I was sick to my stomach. I wanted to run away, not see her anymore, flee, evaporate, and disappear. However, I couldn't. She had touched a chord so deep in me that no one else had ever struck before. She told me so many things about herself. About our uncle in Monterrey, a well-known pedophile throughout the whole state and how he abused her every time they sent her to his house on vacation. I believed her because the *pinche puto* also tried the same shit with me once, but I kicked him so hard in the balls that he never bothered me again. She told me the endless suffering he caused her starting when she was very young. She wanted to pay back all the people who had hurt her and made her short life miserable. She wanted vengeance.

"I promise you, Blanca, from now on, you are going to have your revenge," I said.

I understood her completely, because, in a way, it was the whole family's fault for letting this sickening *pedofilo, hijo de la chingada*, get this far. They suspected he was abusing all the children in the family, but never did anything to stop it. I tried not to let Blanca see the shock on my face. I knew I had to be extremely careful how I handled the situation. But whatever it took, I couldn't let that *pinche* psycho get near Blanca ever again.

"Next time I see him, I'll shoot his balls off, let him bleed and suffer for a while; then I'll whack him for good."

Our town sits on the slope of a hill, with the river below it and with a forest of tall, dark trees as its background. The lower part of town is populated by the poorest people in the world, together with the most dangerous criminals in the state. However, up on the hill where the governor's mansion is, the streets are sparkling clean with bright lights on every corner, and huge luxury houses with beautiful gardens full of flowers and enormous green yards. The people in this part of town are the very rich. They control the politics, the businesses and all the money. They are white, good looking, very sophisticated and have all the power. All of them without exception are more treacherous and threatening than all the dangerous criminals put together!

"They have no brains and no balls, but yet they manage to keep everybody under their thumb," my grandfather used to tell me. "Miguel, if you put yourself to it, you can take over this town anytime you want. You have something they do not have, youth and balls. And I'm not joking."

At that time I didn't understand my grandpa's definition of the power elite, I didn't mind that they had all the power. I have no desire to take over the stupid pueblo. I had enough problems just growing up. I wanted to make money and, like everybody else, without remorse leave town and go to the North. That was the agreement I had made to myself.

When *Lobo* took Juan hostage, I went directly to Perlita's mother's house to pick up the money I had stocked in a backpack and buried in her back yard. As I got off my *troca*, I noticed she was waiting for me outside the house and looked very nervous.

"Miguel, I tried to call you. I'm sure this will come as a shock to you, but *El Lupe* was here one hour ago and took all the money," she said.

I took a long breath. All my money was gone, and now Juan's life was in danger. *Lobo Bobo* will kill him for sure.

"Ah, it's nothing," I said to her, trying to hide my anger.

I couldn't waste any time. I would take care of *El Lupe* later. I grabbed the empty backpack, walked into the house and I proceeded to fill it up with magazines and newspapers.

"Are you ok?" she asked me.

"I'm ok, just a little dizzy. I have to go now," I said.

I kissed her goodbye and I drove back to the trailer to pick up my Uzi, making sure it was fully loaded. I knew I was going to need many bullets that day. "I have to save some bullets for *El Lupe*, but first I have to rescue Juan," I thought.

When I got back to *Lobo's* place and walked in, I saw Juan sitting on a sofa next to him. The bodyguards, five of them, were outside in the backyard smoking. As I got closer, I could feel the cold metal of the Uzi on my right side. I decided to use the automatic since I knew how to fire it at close range with only one hand without wasting any bullets. Holding the backpack with my left hand, I dropped it on the coffee table, making sure never to lose sight of the guys outside and Lobo sitting right in front of me. He was not a young guy, but I knew he was very fast and very alert. I couldn't say the same about his bodyguards. They were clumsily slow. Somehow, by the look on *Lobo's* face, I believed he sensed I was going to whack him. Anticipating his move, before he reacted, I jumped on top of him grabbing his neck. Using *Lobo's* body as a shield; I pulled out the Uzi and shot the bodyguards as they came running into the house, killing them instantly one by one. I screamed at Juan to escape. *Lobo Bobo* got away from my chokehold and, as he turned around to shoot me, I closed my eyes. I knew I was a dead man. Suddenly I heard a shot, I opened my eyes and I saw a bullet crashing into Lobo's mouth. Juan was holding a smoking gun in his hand. He dropped the gun to the floor and walked out. Juan had saved my life. I checked my watch and saw it was 6:15 P.M. I went to the front door and I called Juan. He was outside, sitting down by the *troca* waiting for his strength to come back. I knew from my own experience with my first kill, that he was still fighting the shock and the agonizing stomach cramps.

"C'mon Juancho, we have to take the money and the merchandise, and leave before somebody shows up. I know how you feel kid, but we have to move fast, now."

After killing *Lobo Bobo*, I got three important telephone calls. One from Tarantula,the big boss of the whole drug operation in Mexico, about my promotion. One from *El Lupe* to tell me how sorry he was, and that he wanted to see me about the money. The last call was from Blanca. She wanted to meet with me, but not in the trailer. She would pick me up somewhere by the Elota River. She also sent me an e-mail.

Miguel, I want to tell you that I trust you and I need your help. Now is the moment when I really need it. Now is also the time when you have to trust me, and support me in my decision and my judgement. You say you love me. Are you willing to kill for that love? What kind of existence will I have if you rob me of my future, and take me away to the North. Here in Mexico, women are not authorized to judge men, but they are permitted to forgive them when they need forgiveness. It seems that to pardon and receive punishment is our only mission in this society. A man's life has more value than ours. According to this machista society, a woman's life revolves in curves of emotions. A man's life has larger issues, wider scopes and greater ambitions. I want to see you, to talk to you face to face about this. I'm not afraid to express what I feel at this moment in my life. I'm not afraid to love at all. All I want is to enjoy life, to explore, to be happy. I'll explain all this to you when I see you. I don't worry about the past, I don't care about the future, I only live in the present moment.

Always your friend, Blanca.

After reading Blanca's e-mail, I was a little shocked. "I don't need this, not now. I have too many things to do," I thought. My answer to her was brief.

Blanca, I'm glad you are ok. Let me know when and where we can meet. Love you 4 ever. Miguel

Now you probably think I'm not in love with Blanca anymore, well that's false. I don't see her that often, but I'm still in love with her. I know she's a little crazy for her age. She is only a teenager, but very mature. Ever since she started working at the governor's mansion, she changed. Last year when she was back, after vanishing for a long time without telling me where she went, she seemed to be a different person. She became a little eccentric. Even when we make love, she is like a stranger to me. I have thought about all this, but I haven't asked her any questions. If you really love somebody, sometimes it's better not to know. I felt something cracked inside me.

"Why would I want to be with her if I couldn't touch her world with all of my senses like before? It felt like she shut me out."

A few days after we exchanged e-mails, she came to pick me up in a black sedan with official plates. The driver looked vaguely familiar. There was something evil about him. I instantly disliked the guy. I knew I'd seen him before, but I couldn't think when or where. When he opened the car door for me to get in, he held his right hand tight to his side. I could tell he was carrying a piece. I wondered exactly who he was, but I couldn't remember.

"Hello," he said. "My name is Lagarto."

Right then, and there; I remembered! He was a famous hit man. Well-known for being the best in the trade and really weird.

"Where are we going, *señora?*" he asked Blanca.

"Up the hill" she said.

"Where are we going?" I asked.

"I want to show you where I work and spend most of my time these days," she said.

Seated inside that car going up the hill, sensing already what she was going to tell me, I felt helpless and stupid. I was mad, and I wanted to get out and go back to my place. I wanted to insult her, call her names. I wanted to slap her, punch her in the nose. Instead, I just sat in the car in complete silence, like an idiot.

The governor lived in a sixty-room stucco mansion, surrounded by a white metal fence. When we arrived, Lagarto drove all the way around the property to the back gate, and let us in through a side door.

"You have only half hour, *señora.* I'll be in the garage waiting for you," he said.

When we walked inside the main room, I realized that it would be hard to compare my little trailer with this mansion. I also realized that no matter how good I was at my *negocio,* or how many millions I could make; before our society I would always be just a poor brown Mexican kid. I didn't blame it on racism, not exactly. I didn't know what it was. It was something else. It was something different, so powerful that even today I find it too difficult to compare a white Mexican kid, with a brown Mexican kid like me.

"Let's go upstairs to my studio," she said.

Her studio looked like a penthouse.

"Wow! This is a big deal in your life, isn't it?" I said.

"Of course it's a big deal. It's the biggest thing that ever happened to me."

"What about your feelings?" I asked.

"I'm not about to share my feelings with the whole world," she said.

"Blanca, I'm not your priest. You can stop the bullshit and talk to me. I have some dignity left, you know? Besides, Lagarto only gave us half an hour."

After saying that, I sat down and leaned back on a black leather couch. She looked at me for a long moment. There was a confidence about her now, an assurance that she never had before. The spindly, skinny girl had grown into a woman. Her face bore the imprint of her *Azteca's* forebears, the light brown skin, the arched fine eyebrows, the dark green eyes and the long black hair.

"This won't take long, Miguel. Since you probably know what's going on here anyway" she said.

She bore almost no resemblance to the girl I had made love to for the first time three years ago. At that moment, I wanted to tell her that I felt responsible for everything that had happened to her. For me, for her family and all the other people in power accountable for killing her innocence. It was entirely our fault. It was all of us who banded together and had refused to give her a chance to escape her destiny. Mainly we, the *macho-men*, made her pay a high price with her body, her pride and her soul.

Blanca rose to her feet. She radiated a sense of authority and power. I thought I was hallucinating.

"Miguel, I can't tell you how much I appreciate your coming here today. You are not only my *primo*, my lover and my best friend, you are a very important person in my life," she said.

It was a weird situation. Somewhere in Mexico, in the governor's mansion studio, a very young brown Mexican girl was ready to give a speech to a brown Mexican boy about child abuse, negligence, misuse of power, rape, kidnapping, murder and dysfunctional families, and the boy was ready to listen.

"Miguel, everybody who's anybody in this town comes to this mansion. They drink way too much, *mucho, mucho*, and they talk a lot. I hide behind closed doors and I listen. Your name, Juan's, and *padre* Bernardino's always come up in their conversations. They know what you, Juan and the priest are doing in that church. They are watching you day and night. They know about you and me, your relation with Lobo Bobo and *El Lupe*. I'm sure you are still wondering why I stay here, why I'm doing what I'm doing, and why I stay with Tarantula. When he decided that he wanted me to be his wife, he came over to my house and held me by the hand in front of my mother and warned her about life and death. "*Señora*, I know that Blanca is only a child, but I want her to be mine. I'll move her to my place gradually in order not to alarm or offend your neighbors. If you don't agree, let me know now, and I'll kill her, I'll kill you and your whole family." After saying that, he kissed me on the lips and left. Next day he sent Lagarto to pick me up and he brought me here. I tried to resist but I was forced to stay overnight and lay in bed next to him. He is a creepy old man. He didn't touch me or talk to me at all. He just looked at me for a long while, rolled over and, in less than a minute, he was snoring. With my eyes wide open, I couldn't sleep all night. I could hear my heart pumping with the force of a nuclear bomb. All I wanted to do was to escape, and that idea floated in my head like a mushroom cloud until dawn. When he woke up next morning, he warned me that I was free to come and go as I pleased, but if I tried to escape, he'd kill my whole family.

"Once in a while, I'll ask you to stay over and sleep with me. Only to sleep, no more, no less," the decrepit old freak told me, while smiling in a peaceful manner and kissing me on the cheek. "I was his hostage, and it has been like this for over a year."

I just sat there listening, looking at her in shock. I never expected a story like this.

"You sure opened my eyes about the *pinche* governor. He's not only a sick old man, he's also an impotent. A real piece of work," I said.

"At the beginning I was frightened out of my wits, but after a few months of being a part-time hostage, I got used to it," she said.

In a town where deceit and rudeness was the daily currency of conversation, Blanca fearlessly spoke her mind.

"What about last year? When you got lost? I looked for you everywhere. Where did you go?" I asked.

"I was here all the time," she said.

Suddenly she got up and went to the next room. When she came back, she was holding a baby in her arms.

"I was having my little boy. He's the only reason why I still want to be in this world. Thanks to his love, now I can touch the universe with all my senses intact."

I almost fainted. I felt like I was in this bizarre fog in a very small room, the smallest place in the world, where I could reach out and touch the walls. I could see the baby but I couldn't see his face. I was cold, like there was ice building inside my chest. All the fog and the freezing and the ice disappeared when extending her arms she asked two simple questions:

"Doesn't he look like you? Do you want to hold him? He'll make you feel stronger, you'll see," she insisted.

"Not like this I said, repelling my feelings and running downstairs real quick without saying goodbye. Lagarto was waiting for me by the main door.

"Where to boss?" he said cunningly.

"Far away from here, and fast," I said.

As *El Lupe* strolled towards our *troca*, I saw a black revolver in his belt. I checked my automatic in my right side pocket with one hand, and I smiled at him.

"You sit in the back, Juancho. *Lupe* you sit next to me. We are going to stop by the trailer to get my rifle." I said.

As I drove away, I turned my head and I noticed he was crying. "Why are you crying, *puto*?" I asked.

"Because I took your money," he said.

"Calm down, *Lupe*, we are going to see Tarantula now. Everything will be ok."

When he heard Tarantula's name he froze. He reminded me of a rat. He looked like the stunned rat I saw as a child in my grandfather's silo. I remembered how the rat was paralyzed when the white cat cornered it, impotent before the cat's yellow eyes.

"I should blow your fricking brains out." I screamed. "I split my profits with you eighty-twenty, and after all I did for you; you dare to steal from me?"

"I love you like a brother, Miguel," he said.

"You are not my brother and I don't want your love. I want my money back."

After saying that I left the highway, I made two turns, parked in the lot of a liquor store and got out. *El Lupe*, his face contorted, was shaking like a leaf and crying like a baby.

"I think we need a drink, I'm going to get a bottle of tequila, I'll be right back," I said.

When I came back to the truck, I didn't say a word. I drove off at a normal speed and I took the river road toward our trailer. All of a sudden, *El Lupe* began a conversation and he told me a dozen lies about *Lobo Bobo*, nothing important.

"Miguel, I'm telling you I have been a thief all my life. I mean, I robbed people and drug dealers more than a thousand times, and when they started looking for me to kill me, I'd snitch them off. This way, in some sort of exchange, the police would protect me. I like using my gun and I enjoy killing people. I really like my revolver. It fits right in my hand so nice and all. Let me shoot *Tarantula*, let me do that for you."

Then his appearance started to change and the color returned to his face.

"Now all you need is a drink," I said, handing him the bottle. Driving back to the trailer, I had made the final decision about *El Lupe*. I had to whack the maniac. It was a hard decision but it had to be done. I pulled the truck into a remote spot by the river.

"Everybody out," I said.

Now my palms were sweating. I looked *Lupe* straight in the face, he was still holding the bottle of tequila in his right hand, and I knew that he understood the situation he had gotten into and he would not resist. I drew my automatic.

"You see, *Lupe*, this automatic is for a right handed person, because it kicks the shells out to the right. If you fire it southpaw you might get the ejected shells in your face, and you can lose an eye. So I fire it right handed."

He didn't have a chance to answer. The bullet hit him right between the eyes and blew his head off. Juan breathing heavily instinctively stood behind me.

CHAPTER 5
Blanca Sintierra

My name is Blanca Sintierra. I was born in Sinaloa a few miles south of the Elota River. I live with my brother and my mother in one of the nicest houses in the neighborhood. A stucco ranch painted orange, with a small garden up front, and a big backyard with all kinds of vegetables. I help my mother cook, clean up the house and take care of my brother Juan. I go to school every day and I take Juan with me to make sure he attends all his classes. I also help him to study and stay focused.

For more than two years now, Francisco Tarantula Salinas, our governor, started sending bouquets of flowers and presents to my house. He also started making official visits to my school where he would spend a lot of time in my classroom, looking at me in a very peculiar way. He made me nervous. When I asked him why he was looking at me like that, he smiled, his voice growing warmer. "I want to make sure that they treat you good in this place," he said softly. After he told me that, I was not as scared any more. "Maybe he can be my friend. It will be an adventure." I wanted to tell him that he could be my friend, but young girls aren't supposed to say such things to older people outside of their family circle, and nobody could say something like that to our governor. "I can't tell anybody how I feel. If grandma finds out, she'll kill me," I thought. I was very young at the time, and calling the attention of such an important person made me feel somehow special and, at the same time, gave me a taste of power. My classmates looked up to me and even Mrs. Malamilk treated me special. I was so amazed about the situation that I wanted to talk to somebody about my feelings. For obvious reasons, I couldn't tell these things to my classmates, so I decided to talk to Mrs. Malamilk. When I walked into her office, I felt secure and important. After all, I was the governor's favorite girl in the whole school. I stupidly thought about that while standing still in front of her desk, trying to call her attention, but she completely ignored me.

"Can I tell you a secret," I asked.

"It better not be something stupid, *pendeja*," she said without looking at me.

"It's not," I said.

"Okay, then tell me."

"I would like to be friends with the governor."

Her eyes narrowed. Her eyes always narrowed right before she started screaming and insulting someone. Feeling apprehensive and trembling, I just stood there.

"That's no good girl, and it could be a very dangerous game," she said.

"It's not supposed to be a bad thing, and it's not a game," I responded.

"Since when do you know so much, *pinche cabroncita*? Do you know what happened to the forty-three students reported missing in Iguala? What are your plans anyway?" she asked in a low and angry voice, looking at me straight in the eye.

"I just want to ask him to be my special friend," I answered.

"You better quit saying that," she said. "You are really getting me upset."

She got up, kicked a chair and slammed her notebook on the desk.

"*Pinche* pedophile," she whispered chewing her words.

I didn't understand what she meant by that, and why she got so upset.

"Don't you worry girl, I'll keep your secret. You can go now, *cabrona!*" She said.

I got out of her office, and now I was the one that was mad at her. I knew I deserved better. I didn't understand why she wanted my friendship with the governor to fail, why she refused to help me. He's so nice to me. I don't even know why he's so nice to me, but I like it. I would love to tell everybody, but I can't. The last time he was at my school, he made sure nobody was looking, grabbed me by the shoulders and leaned so close to my face that I could smell his breath, a mixture of tacos, tobacco and tequila. And now Mrs. Malamilk was trying to kill my dream and take my wish away. I wanted to go somewhere else where people could understand how I felt and, like me, believe in hope and dreams. I want to be free, have a nice car and wear fine clothes, be able to live in a beautiful house, and come and go as I please. Maybe it's not a very serious way to say it. Maybe the whole friendship between us because of our age difference is weird and funny. Maybe I should close my mouth, forget the whole thing and avoid the pain I'd have to endure because everybody in town, including Miguel and Juan, will hate my guts. But, at the same time I want to yell out to the world. I want the whole world to pay attention to me. Being the governor's special friend makes me feel important and powerful, like a famous artist, a rich artist. I want to be *la reina* de Sinaloa. Right now, I feel like it might be my only real chance to escape from my house and my family.

As long as I can remember, my house was my prison. The only person that helped my brother and me while we were growing up to search for our dreams was our grandmother. I loved her. I'll always love her. Since I was young I realized that Juan and I were two very lonely children. We were the only two kids in the whole neighborhood that were brave and crazy enough to be willing to leave the house at a very young age. We were the only kids with enough guts and arrogance in the whole *pinche* pueblo to do that. What we didn't know was that there were other kids, millions of them all over the world, who had also left their birthplaces in search of their dream. Most of these kids, from Africa, South America, and the Far East, died in their quest.

I was never afraid to express what I felt. Every time I perceive love, I melt into love. I'm not afraid to love at all. However, because of the abuse and the pain the grownups inflicted on me since I was an infant, I'm ashamed of my past. From the point of view of the victim, I can say that something sad and despicable happened to me, but from the point of view of the fighter that I've become, I can only say that what happened to me was normal. I don't even blame my uncle for abusing me since I was born. If he abused me, it was due to his own domestication, his own fears, and his own beliefs. He had no control over the abuse. He was a victim himself, so he couldn't have behaved any differently. There is also no need to blame my parents for not doing anything to help me. I already figured that then, and now, any nightmare would be better than my reality. But now is the right time to stop the abuse, find closure and, at the same time, take up the opportunity to take revenge. Today, at last, I have all the power, and it's payback time. It's time to free myself from the role of the victim. I have Miguel, Juan and Tarantula, the three of them, on my side. *Ahora es* the best time, and the right time to make my move!

"*Vamos Blanquita*, sing, you can do it, you can sing anything you want," my grandmother said.

I was eight years old and she was giving me singing lessons every afternoon after school. With the guitar on her lap, she sat in the living room watching me sing. The two of us worked long hours on every song until we got it right. Her voice seemed to stick into my brain.

"You are a great singer you know," and she'd get up and squeeze me hard.

Grandma felt like an old friend to me, a friend that was on my side no matter what. "Blanca, if you listen to some of the new pop songs, they are very ingenious, because of how they are produced and arranged, and how they use the verbs. Listening to that new wave of music, I think it will appeal to you and inspire you to get new ideas."

She was always looking for new sounds or styles to help me with my singing. She quit smoking but there was always her silver box full of cigarettes that she kept on the table.

"I would never light up again, they are just my security blanket in a silver box," she would tell me.

She knew about my mother's negotiations with the governor in regard to me moving to the governor's mansion, and she wasn't afraid of speaking her mind.

"If the old man dares to touch you, I'll kill him with my bare hands and I'll take you far away from this lousy place. I already have a plan."

When she told me that, I sensed that she meant it, that she would kill anyone who would try to hurt me. From that moment on, she became my hero.

"We got to stay together if we want to do this together, girl," and after saying that she would sit down very close to me, her voice almost a whisper.

"Look down there, Blanquita, across the river; if you gaze hard enough you can almost see the place where we are going to escape."

"How do you know that, abuela?" I asked her.

"I'm a Toltec. Thousands of years ago, throughout southern Mexico, the Toltec's tribe, their women and men had all the knowledge and the power. They were scientist and artists who formed a tribe to explore and conserve the spiritual knowledge and practices of their older generation. They came together as masters, *naguales* and students at Theotihuacan, the ancient city of pyramids outside Mexico City, known as the place where man becomes God. And I'm part of that family my dear child."

A couple of minutes later after saying that, she put her head on my shoulder and started to snore like crazy. I remained on the sofa next to her in the dark, trying not to think about the governor and his demands. However, it was impossible to get it out of my head, and just imagining being next to that dreadful old man made me feel even worse.

I remember now, that two weeks after that conversation with my grandma, I was at school when the principal Mrs. Malamilk stepped into the classroom.

"May I speak to Blanca in private?" she said.

My teacher gave me the okay. I gathered up my books and followed her out into the hallway. I was a little worried. I wondered if something had happened to Juan.

"What's going on, Mrs. Malamilk?" I asked. She unexpectedly started crying. She was weeping, with these big old whooping tears. I couldn't believe it! This mean old woman was crying like a baby!

"Mrs. Malamilk, what is it? What's wrong?"

She embraced me hard. I have to admit that it felt very good.

"Blanca, I'm sorry," she said. "But I just got a call from your mother. It's your grandma. She's passed away."

"What do you mean?" I asked.

I knew what she meant, but I wanted her to say something else.

"Your grandma is gone," Mrs. Malamilk said.

"It's not possible," I said.

I couldn't accept the truth. I wanted it to be false news.

"Your grandma is dead," Mrs. Malamilk insisted.

That was it. I couldn't fake my way around that. Dead is dead, and the dead don't come back.

I was stunned. I wasn't sad. I was happy for her. My grandma was a Toltec and finally she was with her ancient family and with God. Now she was part of God. At last, she was all spirit. She was not vulnerable any more, but I was. Now I was the most vulnerable child in the whole *pueblo*. I was too innocent to deal with the death of my grandma, so I just ran outside. Suddenly I worried that Juan was going to get killed.

After my grandmother died, my brother Juan changed completely. Right there at the burial, when they lowered my grandma's coffin into the grave, he became a different person. As the box settled into the dirt, he screamed like a wounded animal, turned around and walked across the road deep into the woods. He didn't come back home until the next day. Being without our grandma around the house affected him a lot. He started acting crazy, at home and in school. I had to start taking responsibility for his wild actions. He told me that he was going to start working for Miguel, even though I pleaded with him for a long time not to do it. He made me very unhappy, and to top it off, he made it look like an insult. I forgave him. I know Juan is very smart and I love him. I wish I could have the power to convince him to change his mind and let me help make his life better.

A lot of my classmates had been to a brother's funeral, and a few more had lost their father, an uncle or an aunt in a shootout. One guy's brother died of a gunshot to the head while walking home when he was only in the third grade. All my friends could count their dead in their families by the dozen. I don't want Juan to be one more innocent victim in this violent and crazy drug war. In addition, do you know what the worst part is? The sad part is that about 99.9 per cent of the deaths in our little pueblo have taken place because these criminals are dealing drugs, and in the process murdering innocent people. There are many people directly or indirectly involved in this dirty business. People of every walk of life, poor people, rich people, the police, the generals and the politicians, all the way up to our great *presidente*. Impunity is the name of the game!

According to my grandmother, every single time someone is kidnapped, disappears or is killed in Mexico, we can easily identify the four "virtues" that these criminals that rule the country from the top down, believe in. They promote and cultivate greed, violence, madness and power. Sadly, those four "ugly virtues", like a killer virus, are spreading very fast and infecting our society, and every other society around the world.

The first time the governor sent Lagarto over to my house to pick me up and drive me to the mansion, my mother refused to say goodbye. I watched her disappear into the backyard screaming, "I hate you! It's your fault!" At that moment, I wondered if I would ever see her again. I didn't know what to do or say. I knew my mother was upset and, as usual, would be drinking booze and getting drunk, and acting stupid, sad and mean. I couldn't understand why she was so dejected. I didn't know what to say to her. What do you say to your mother when she is the one who gave the ok in the first place to the governor to take you away, and then she goes into denial? What do you say to her when you don't even know what's going on inside your own body? When you are so confused that you don't have control of your emotions anymore? When you have this strange feeling running down from the top of your head to the tip of your toes, and you still feel sort of sexy? When, disturbingly, you find yourself thinking more and more about the ugly old man with the strangely compelling voice? I guess you do what I had to do. I just walked out of the house without saying goodbye. Lagarto came up and hugged me, slapped me on the shoulder and opened the car door. I sat in the back seat next to a dozen red roses, and I felt important, like I mattered. Those people, like my mother and Mrs. Malamilk, who were so suspicious of my friendship with the governor will soon learn that he's my good friend and cares about me. Climbing the hill, the car was moving fast. I turned around and, looking through the back window, I couldn't see my house any longer, and I felt okay. Very much confused, but okay!

"Now the sky is the limit," I thought.

"I wonder if you know what you are getting into little girl," Lagarto said, looking at me in the rearview mirror as we got closer to the mansion's main entrance.

"This is just the beginning for me. I want to learn," I answered.

The governor was waiting for me by the entrance, dressed all in white. He opened the car door, took me by the hand and smiled. Right at that moment I felt the first stirrings of panic. I just stood there by him, stunned.

"Is there something wrong?" he demanded.

"*Nada.* I'm tired," I said.

While walking past him and entering the house, he rushed behind me. There was a new respect in his attitude toward my persona. I sensed it in the way he looked at me.

"What about dinner?" he asked.

The invitation took me by surprise. I didn't answer.

We had dinner in a restaurant at *Pueblo Bonito* Hotel in Mazatlán. He sat across the table from me, quiet and wary, studying every move I made. When the waiter came to take our order, he asked for a scotch and soda, and I had a coke. We were both silent. As a tribute to my mother's cooking abilities, out of curiosity, just to compare, I ordered her specialty, meat tacos. To my surprise, they were almost as delicious as hers, if not better. Looking at the menu I noticed they were very expensive. For that amount of money my mother could make easily one hundred tacos.

"Are they any good?" he asked interrupting my thoughts.

"Very tasty," I said.

He was chewing his food and wiping his face with a napkin, like a high school kid desperate over his first crush. I was ashamed of being there with him, knowing that it was completely wrong.

"What do you want from me?" he asked, abruptly.

"I don't like owing anyone anything," I added, thinking whether I should stay for the night or leave.

"Let's get out of here," he commanded. "I hear your studies are coming along well."

"Yes," I started to say "thanks to you," then I thought better, and kept my mouth shut.

"You are a good student, aren't you?"

I nodded.

"I want to be the best, to graduate and become a lawyer."
He was paying attention. His face was vibrant and alive. It
reminded me of the face of my grandmother and I realized how
much I was dishonoring her memory. For the governor to be with a
minor in a restaurant, it was part of his accepted life-style, but for
my grandmother to see old men dating schoolgirls was undignified
and it bothered her very much. "They are a sorry bunch of dreadful
and degenerated old bastards." She placed great value on dignity.
Moreover, here I was playing this childish and dangerous game
with this decrepit old man.

"Forgive me *abuela. Perdón* grandma," I whispered.

I felt sad and lonely, and looking for support, I sent a text to
Juan. He answered back right away. I knew that he knew that
something was going on between the governor and me, and that
he was very mad. No matter what happened, I also knew very well
that he would never let me down.

"I know what I'm doing is dangerous, but not if I do it right,"
I thought.

At the time, I didn't know how hard the old man looked
forward to those platonic trysts with me. More than I had ever
believed possible, I had become an obsession to him.

The first time I met my primo Miguel I didn't feel attracted
to him at all. He didn't strike me like a big shot. He was a good-
looking muscular boy, older than me, with a strong personality
and teasing brown eyes. When he said "hello", I still remember the
way he looked at me, it made me feel like a human target. I didn't
know what to say, or how to react to his mixture of streetwise jokes
and flattering compliments. Instead of punching him in the face,
I went home that day completely confused and I spent all night
plotting my revenge. I imagined running him over with my bike
or pushing him under somebody's *troca*. I wished I had a big and
strong friend. I could have sent him after Miguel. I couldn't sleep
that night because I kept thinking about Miguel. I knew he would
be waiting for me in the morning at school. I knew he'd humiliate

me in front of my friends with his lousy jokes. Thinking about all this, laying in my bed, face up in the dark, suddenly I had this warm sensation growing in my stomach that continued down slowly, all the way to my toes.

Next morning after Juan woke up and I made breakfast for him, I put on my best shoes and my favorite coat. Still thinking about Miguel, exhausted and terrified, I headed out to school. Juan, as usual, half asleep and in complete silence, walked the whole ten long blocks, from our house to the school, a few steps behind me. When we got in front of the school, I saw Miguel in the middle of a circle surrounded by my classmates laughing at his jokes. As I got close, they stopped and, in complete silence, they stared at me.

"Hi Blanca," Miguel said. His friends giggled.

"Do I know you?" I asked.

"There are only two hundred students in the whole school, of course you know me," he said.

"Oh, that's right," I said. "You are the boy who tells bad jokes!"

His friends giggled again, but this time, louder. He came closer and gave me a kiss on the cheek. I was happy I might have impressed his friends.

"Sometimes it pays to be a bitch," I thought.

I grabbed Juan by the hand and walked into the school feeling beautiful. Standing by the door as the students were entering the building, yelling at the top of her lungs, Mrs. Malamilk was welcoming everybody, in her own sweet way.

"Hurry up *pinches cabrones!* This is a school not a social club! *Pendejos!*"

Please, don't get me wrong, but no matter how weird she was, I have to admit the old witch had some style!

The first time Miguel invited me to take a walk with him by the river I did not intend to become his girlfriend. However, on that particular day it was as though a thousand devils were conspiring against me. There was a new excitement within me, the exhilaration of embarking on a new adventure, a chance to change my life. For the first time, I understood why my mother clung desperately to men she didn't love, men she hated.

"I have a feeling it's going to be a wonderful day," he said, squeezing my hand.

This was the first time I was walking alone with a boy other than my brother Juan. With Juan we were inseparable. As we grew older, we would walk everywhere together. We would talk about our dreams and our plans for the future. Juan and I were two serious children, determined to spend the rest of our lives together. Now walking hand in hand with Miguel, watching the river flow, I was not the same person. He looked taller and more handsome than ever before. I could feel my throat tightening. Oh, how much I wanted to ask him to take me away from this lousy *pueblo*.

"Why did we ever come to this godforsaken place, Miguel?" I didn't intend to say that, but I couldn't let myself get too emotionally involved. "He would tear me apart," I thought.

"That's a pretty silly question," he said. "I just wanted to be alone with you."

His breath quickened. All the physical needs that had been building up within me, all of a sudden came boiling to the surface.

"Miguel."

"Yes?" His voice was husky. I could feel his male hardness pressing against me.

"Are you going to take good care of me?"

"Yes."

"Then it's all right."

Everything around me disappeared, and I began to explore and discover a world no one had ever possessed but me. I was the first lover in the world, and I gloried in the wonderful miracle of it. His fingers were as light as butterfly wings, moving down my body, caressing my skin. Noticing that I didn't know very well what to do, he guided my hand to softly stroke his chin and slowly drew my fingers inside his mouth. It was like an ecstatic explosion, like falling down a waterfall, making gentle circling motions.

"Close your eyes and enjoy it," he said.

After a long while, when I opened my eyes, we were on the floor naked and he held me in his arms protectively. I was in a soporific state. He snapped me out of it by singing a popular Mexican song he had learned as a boy. He sang it looking right at me, as if he was trying to caress me with each beautiful word. Then he paused and gave me a kiss.

"I'm a woman now," I thought.

I have been hiding in the government mansion from my mother and everybody else for almost three months now. When my belly started growing, it was disgusting. My thinking, breathing and living slowed down, I was in a dream state. I didn't know what to do. From listening to the older girls in school talk about it, I knew very well what it was. At the beginning, I tried to hide it under my coat and my blouse. I also started to wear oversized clothing. It was something that called the attention of my classmates. Around the third month it was impossible to hide it anymore. I started having headaches, and my belly looked enormous. I looked goofy on the outside, but my inside was the worst. It was time to talk to somebody. I decided to talk to Mrs. Malamilk and the governor. When I told him the news, that I was expecting a baby, with his voice always low and wheezy like he was being forced to talk, he asked me to repeat it twice.

"Sorry about that, my child. I'd be more than proud to be the father. Do you want me to take care of business and whack the real father?"

"I don't know who the father is," I lied.

"It's your choice, Blanquita. From now on he's my son, and don't you ever forget that."

I avoided looking at him. I could tell he was breathing with difficulty. There was anger in the moisture of his eyes.

"In this country, you are not worthy to raise your eyes to me. You are nothing. *Nada.* And you tell your friend, whoever he is, that I know everything, and to leave you alone."

He never yelled at me before. He grasped me by the chin and forced me to look directly at him, before walking out of the room and slamming the door behind him.

After the unpleasant experience with Tarantula, the following week I decided to tell Mrs. Malamilk that I had had a little accident and that I was almost four months pregnant. I planned to be as humble as possible and make her feel important. When I sat across her desk, as usual she did not seem to pay any attention to me, looking directly ahead, both hands on her lap. There was a brief silence before she said anything. She just sat there shaking her head, her face in a squint, her eyes narrowed as if she could not bear looking at me, and I already hated myself for what I had done.

"And you call that a little accident, *pinche pendeja?* I don't care who the father is, but you must have an abortion right now, before it's too late."

By the crazy look reflected on her face, I could tell she was very angry with me.

"You have no right to tell me to have an abortion," I said. "This is my body and my baby."

The back of my head was exploding and I was so angry I started to cry, and kept on in ragged spurts. I could not stop shaking. I pulled out a tissue and blew my nose. Suddenly the thought of Juan made me tremble. I could picture him looking at me and shaking his head in displeasure, and I wished I could disappear forever. I was only pregnant, I was not anyone's mother yet, or wife. I was not a real girlfriend to anybody, or a friend. I was barely a sister and, whenever I thought of myself as a daughter, my body felt too small and filthy to live in.

"It's your life, *pinche* Blanca. Do whatever you want. After all, it's your problem, it's your business."

"You are like everyone else, you don't really care, you don't give a damn about me," I said.

"No, this time I'm serious *cabrona!* Whatever you do, you'll be okay. I always knew you were different, and you were going to leave us behind and travel the world. I had this dream about you a few months ago. You and your baby were standing next to your grandma and you looked happy. Moreover, I was happy for you too. Finally, you were free! And I hoped that someday you'd forgive me for being such a witch to you for so many years."

After Mrs. Malamilk said that, I paused a second before answering. If there was something I learned from Miguel after all these years, it was how to concentrate and reach the Zen mode. In this instance I was determined to use it, because I realized that now, more than ever, I needed to have a strong ally like her.

"And who stops you from being free? Freedom has to do with the human spirit, the freedom to be ourselves. You and I suffered all these years of drama for nothing. The belief system that the likes of Zorro Porro and his cronies put inside our minds, is built on lies. Lies that make us feel worthless and stupid, and fight against each other."

"Where do you want to go, Blanca? What do you want to do?" She asked.

"To hide in the governor's mansion till my baby is born. Then I'll try to make my life better."

I stood up and stepped away from the chair, and I offered her my hand. She held it briefly and she stood up as well.

"All your belongings are in your locker," Mrs. Malamilk said.

Again, I felt the blood in my chest, in my face, behind my eyes, and my heart was pounding faster than ever. I left quickly and without another word. Out on the street I noticed the bar on the corner full of people, sitting on the stools and drinking. There was music playing, and men and women looked at me as I passed by them. They looked at my face, my dress, the bag with my belongings under my arm, and as I turned and looked back at them, they gazed away as if I had come to collect something they cannot pay. Placing my left hand on my belly, for the first time in a long while, I felt powerful and strong.

"I'll take care of you my little one, I promise," I said, and I just kept walking.

Parked by the newsstand on the avenue, seated on the hood of the car and smoking a cigarette, Lagarto was waiting for me. I took a quick look at the glossy magazines, a big headline that caught my eye: "A GROUP OF PEASANTS FIND MANY CORPSES IN A MASS GRAVE, BUT NOT THE LOST 43 STUDENTS." All of a sudden, Juan came to my mind and I agonized over the thought of something happening to him.

"Chances are that those forty-three kids are in a big graveyard by now," Lagarto said.

"Greed and death, Lagarto, it's all about voracity and death, nothing else," I said.

As I climbed into the car, I felt restless. I collapsed in the back seat sweating profusely. I looked up. The sky was gray. I could smell the river miles away and I took a deep breath. I closed my eyes and when I reached my Zen mode, I turned to my grandmother in the ever after for advice:

"Grandma I'm pregnant." "Why did you go to bed with him? Why did you have to open your legs, *pendeja*? "I'm not sure, maybe I was in love or infatuated." "Then you should have kicked him in the nuts and masturbated instead."

I opened my eyes.

"I guess my grandmother knew everything," I thought.

"Lagarto, pull up to the main door, and give me the keys and your gun," I ordered.

When the car finally stopped at the entrance of the mansion, I was looking straight ahead through the windshield as if we were on an open road. Lagarto nodded once, and handed me the keys and the gun. I got out of the vehicle and stuck the weapon into the waistband of my pants, covering it with my blouse.

"Good. Now I want you to listen to me. From now on, nobody knows where I am for at least nine months, and I want you to keep this a secret. If you don't do that, you know the consequences." Lagarto looked at me. His eyes narrowed a little, as if he didn't quite know how to take what I'd just said. I turned around, I walked up onto the porch and I opened the door. A warm flush passed through my face and neck, and my mouth went dry. I could not be sure that my plan anywhere along the line wouldn't turn on me. The mansion was not under my control yet. The governor was waiting for me in the foyer.

"Welcome home," he said.

I felt his fingers on my arm. I was ashamed. I knew I was going to be a prisoner in that house for a long time. Yet, I have to do it for my baby. He too, was part of my plan.

To convert the whole top floor of the mansion as my private penthouse and living quarters was Tarantula's idea. It took me only a few hours to move my life from my mother's house to this new place. I was feeling kind of dumb, stuffing my small and humble things into this big and luxurious space, all the time trying to convince myself that it shouldn't upset me so much because, like everything else, it was part of a bigger plan. A plan that, because it was going to take a long time to accomplish, I made up my mind to stop wallowing in my problem and start concentrating instead on the solution. I know I have an advantage, because I'm very young and time is on my side. Since I was born I also knew about life's difficult times. There is always a time to begin and a time to end. I always knew this. I must thank God for each day I'm suffering my pregnancy and my prearranged captivity, because it's always one day closer to the birth of my son.

The days, the weeks and the months went very fast. The servants would bring me breakfast, lunch and dinner any time I desired. I organized my own time schedule. Get up early in the morning, go for a walk around the compound listening to music on my iPod to keep me moving at a good pace and, at the same time, keep me from thinking too much. This was the most beautiful mansion in the state. It was filled with antiques, priceless tapestries and beautiful paintings. In the grounds, there were guest cottages, stables, a tennis court, a private landing strip and two swimming pools. Everything was at my disposal. Because of the baby growing inside me, I made sure I ate all my meals to keep my body well fed and nurtured. Tarantula would come upstairs three or four times a week to spend the night with me, and discuss my future and my son's.

He would lay down next to me and place his hand on my belly. I felt the tears come, and my stomach twisting up.

He would talk to the baby for hours. His conversation was more of an indirect interrogation to me than a speech to the little person inside my womb.

"I thought I'd check on you, boy, see how you're holding up," he said. "Do you think that, once you are born, they will try to find you and your mother, to take you guys away from me? Or do you think she'll try to escape by herself?"

My belly kept growing and in a few weeks, I was going to be a mother. It was nearly impossible for me to get any sleep. With the old man next to me talking nonstop all night, nearly every night, plus what I already had in my head, I tossed and turned most of the time, listening to his voice. I was having nightmares. "The first nightmare for everyone is being born," my grandma used to tell me. "Just think about it. When you are in your mother's womb you are happy, content, well fed, warm and comfortable floating around, doing nothing and, suddenly, for no reason, you get shoved and pushed, squeezed and pulled, until you are out in this bright noisy place called the world. That's why the *pinches* babies cry like crazy. As soon as they are born they just want to go right back in, the little *cabroncitos!*"

It was a day of bright sun, too warm for my taste, and I felt funny. So I decided to take a shower. I walked down the hall naked into the bathroom. The sunlight came through the bathroom window overlooking the river. The light was too bright, so bright that it made me feel dizzy. The tension due to my pregnancy building up for months had driven me deeper into exhaustion, more than I had anticipated. I was drifting off and ready to pass out at any moment. I shut the door. I got in the shower and closed my eyes.

"Breath in, and breath out, and push, *cabrona*, push!"

I was coming back to my senses and, before opening my eyes, I felt the wet floor of the bathroom on my back and I knew that I had fainted, and I knew the voice that was screaming and the person behind it. Mrs. Malamilk, resting her palm on my forehead, was yelling at the top of her lungs. She was so close to my face that I was able to hear her breathing. She was telling me to be careful, to be very careful, and in her voice there were still signs of her anger and disbelief, like the last time she spoke to me in her office at school. I also sensed her fear for my well-being and my baby's. I took a deep breath to speak out, but Mrs. Malamilk was placing her index finger on my lips, ordering me to be calm. She retrieved a wet towel from the bathroom sink and put it under my neck. I heard somebody in the background mentioning something about scissors.

"Bring them to me," she said. "You keep breathing and pushing, girl. Don't stop!"

Mrs. Malamilk was looking down at me but her eyes were on the task between my legs. She ordered Tarantula and the servants to step away. They obeyed. She sat on the floor beside me and touched my face, called my name and asked if I was awake. I closed my eyes and smiled at her. She began to weep and said nothing. She simply wept.

Tarantula and Lagarto, lifting me gently, covered my body with a blanket and took me down the corridor to my bed. Mrs. Malamilk, seated on the mattress, holding my newborn baby in her arms, glanced at me. The baby holding first the fingers of one hand, then the fingers of the other, his little arms folded in front of his chest; looked happy and beautiful. He's more to me than innocence. I smile and I think about Miguel, and I can't repent now. My body had become stiff. The muscles of my stomach, my neck, back and legs as tight as if bound with an iron chain. A burning pain jumps up and down from my vagina to my upper torso.

The window is open and the sun is shining over the grass. I feel in my hands the pounds of his tiny heart and, in Spanish, I whisper to him, the fruit of my love.

"Hola mi amor, bienvenido al mundo!"

"Blanca, I want you to stay in this room until I say otherwise, all right? If you have to go to the bathroom, I want you to ask me first," Mrs. Malamilk commanded.

CHAPTER 6
The Delivery

Miguel stretched out his hands and slowly pulled the canvas to show the merchandise. Somebody snapped his fingers sharply and, at the sound, everyone turned around. Smiling pleasantly Tarantula, the governor himself, approached the *troca*.

"Who let the dogs out tonight?" he joked.

Miguel's eyes narrowed, he laughed. I knew that laugh. I also knew the smell of death. I started shaking. He stared the old man hard in the eyes and said:

"The dogs are here now, let them be. It will be a sacrilege not to feed them."

After Miguel said that, he punched Tarantula in the balls and he fell to his knees, like a sack of potatoes, his mouth and jaw flapping open. He then kicked the unconscious old man in the head and, grabbing his arm, threw him inside the *troca*. He dived head first under the pickup truck and started shooting at the *gueros*, knocking them down like big black bowling pins.

"Shoot, *pendejo!* Stop looking at me! Shoot, *cabrón!* Shoot!" he yelled.

I ran ahead towards the house, hoping to take Blanca with me. I tripped on the front steps, knocking loose one of my sneakers. The first shot coming from inside the house pierced my right ear and I fell backwards, yelling in pain and shooting back at the house. I had blood all over my neck, Miguel was hiding behind the *troca* and waiting for the right time to get inside the house. He looked at me trying to keep cool, and he made a gesture telling me to stay down. I knew that the box with the dynamite was on the back seat of the *troca*, and I wanted to get it and blow the *pinches cabrones* all the way up to the sky!! I let out a loud scream and I started shooting. Miguel holding his M-16 with both hands stayed his ground, shooting nonstop, and everybody was backing up. There was blood all over the place. My arms and my legs were a storm of electric nerves. When I reached the main entrance there were these two guys shooting at me. I dropped to the floor and I shot both of them in the chest. The blast sent them back-pedaling eight or ten feet, and they fell dead on their side. Miguel was already by the door, close enough to hand me a stick of dynamite.

"There are six guys in the back of the house. Just blow them up, and let's go!"

I wasn't quite sure how to use the dynamite. When I saw the six guys hiding behind a wall with their backs to me, I lit the fuse, counted until ten like my grandpa taught me, and then threw it their way. It hit the wall, rebounded and landed next to them. The huge bang blew them to pieces. The glasses from the windows popped and exploded all around me. A bloody head with the eyes still wide open bounced at my feet. I wasn't screaming any more. I was crying. Miguel came around with the *troca* and picked me up.

"Let's go, Juancho, we have to get the money and get out of here!"

"What about Blanca? We have to take her with us!"

"Lagarto ran away, and took Blanca and the baby with him. She's not here."

"I have to go back and look for her!"

"We can't waste any more time! We're going to get killed. You can't protect her forever."

I was starting to understand. Miguel was my teacher. I had to add my hope to his hope. I had to multiply hope by hope. Take my hope somewhere else where other people have real hope. I was carrying the burden of my family, especially my sister's, for too long. I didn't know where she was or what she was doing. Maybe I just didn't want to know.

"Did you kill Tarántula?" I asked.

"No, Juan, I believe he escaped with Lagarto and Blanca!"

"*Viejo hijo de la chingada!* Fucking old prick!"

"Forget it, Juancho! We'll get him next time! Now let's get the money and fly!"

Before I had a chance to enjoy our win, Miguel ordered me to stay by the porch as a look out while he went inside to get the moneybags and load them in the *troca*. Watching Miguel at work, I waited patiently and I counted fifty-five black moneybags.

I can't remember any more who I killed or how many, or what they looked like, which is significant of the state of mind I was in. After loading the truck, for some unknown reason, Miguel drove around the whole property, a lugubrious place now filled with dead corpses. The spectacle nauseated me. I wanted to get back to my trailer as fast as possible and be by myself.

"Take a good look," Miguel said. "The main thing is that we finished them off."

I agreed. Secretly I nourished the hope that Miguel had killed Tarantula, and we would look for Blanca and would be able to find her. Then the three of us would escape to the North.

"Next time you'll be able to do as you please," he said, as if he was reading my thoughts.

When we got to the trailer, a heavy mist had descended over the river. We walked cautiously. The old bricks at the entrance were slippery with moisture. As we reached the door, the light of the moon broke through the clouds. Slowly, in silence, we turned around to make sure nobody was following us. I opened the door and we walked in.

"Check the bedroom," Miguel said, "don't put the lights on and make sure to look under the bed."

Strange house this trailer. To get to any room you had to walk through every other room. I had to pass a row of three identical metal doors placed in the center of the structure to get to the bedroom.

"No one here, Miguel," I said.

"Ok, let's put the money away. Just tell me what you would like to eat. You can have anything you want."

"I'm not hungry," I said.

It was pitch dark now. Miguel sat on a chair by the window watching the *troca*, with the M-16 on his lap and ready to shoot. He didn't move.

"Go outside, Juancho, and hide under the truck. If somebody shows up, we'll have him under crossfire."

The fog was thick outside and it made the trailer appear to be under a white cotton blanket. I heard a car go by twice on the asphalt along the highway and waited for the engine to gear down, and see the swing of the headlights through the trees. That didn't happen, and so I waited. Lying under the *troca*, my eyes were half-open, and my heart was beating in the grip of my hands, in the squeeze of all my fingers, except one, and it was a pained effort to keep that one from pulsing against the trigger. I was thirsty and I wanted something to drink. My mouth had opened a bit. I turned my face to the side and I stood in that position for a long time.

"Wake up *cabron!* As a look out, you stink! What's wrong with you?"

Miguel's voice woke me up. He sounded so much like himself. His voice was stronger than ever.

"I'm sorry." I said.

"I'm sorry? That's all you have to say, *pendejo?* Because of you, we could be dead!"

I took a deep breath and got up. Miguel was quiet for a second.

"Please don't talk to me like this, Miguel."

"Like what?"

"Like, don't call me a *pendejo.*"

"I didn't mean it that way. I'm just trying to protect you, and protect myself. If you die, I die."

"I can't die."

"Why?"

"Before I die, I have to go to the North to see my friend Barack."

"You are really crazy!"

"I'm not!" I said, "and you are coming with me!"

"I can't, I have a business."

"You call it a business?"

"Yes!" He blew his nose. He was quiet, just long enough for me to answer.

"You can't go on like this forever, Miguel."

He didn't answer. I thought about Blanca and Tarantula, and wasn't even mad any more. After all that had happened, I didn't feel really anything, just dried up and hollow. But I couldn't get Blanca out of my mind. Maybe what she was doing was serious business. My sister certainly thought it was. I suddenly understood that, if every moment during a delivery was serious shit, then every moment of my life was very serious as well. I was past telling Miguel about all my plans to escape to the North, past asking for any real help from him, but I could ask him this:

"We killed everybody. We have all the money and the dope. What now?"

"We can't stay here for too long. We must take everything to the church and store it in the basement," he said, "and hide in there for a while."

"What about *padre* Bernardino? Should we tell him what it's all about?"

"*No, realmente no*. We don't have to tell the *pinche* priest what's in the bags."

"You mean, he has no fricking idea?"

"No, Juan, he's too busy fighting Zorro Porro and all the members of his band of corrupted public officials. He has his hands full and his life is in constant danger!"

The church of *La Cruz*, curiously enough, is a sad place even in full sunshine. Like all the architecture of the Mexican churches, there is never an ounce of personality in their structure. Sadly, they all look the same to me. *Padre* Bernardino was sitting at his usual place on the opposite side of the altar, waiting for us.

"I want you to park in the back kids, under the trees" he said, "I'm sure that Zorro Porro and his band of criminals are looking for you, by land and by air. Now kneel down children. This one time I want you to pray with me. We need God's help. The three of us need him to come down here, now more than ever.

We kneeled down next to the priest, not knowing what to do or say. Luckily, he started to pray.

"Oh Jesus, do you suffer more than other men? Just how do you suffer? Christ! Oh Christ! How do we suffer? Just how, can you tell us? Can you help us?"

Looking at the cross and listening to Father Bernardino pray, I was thinking if there was any way somebody could explain to Miguel and me just how to comprehend what makes a man believe in God. There are so many little things to ask God for, like for example food for little children. In addition, will he have the patience to listen to all of them, until the end? Or religion is not for empty bellies? Here in Mexico kids like us are treated like animals. We would be much better off if we were two monkeys in a zoo. For the two of us, what does matter now is that we still have a name and we are alive, and that we are free to escape to the North before Zorro Porro and his killers find us.

"Dear God, bring us peace and have mercy on us," Father Bernardino was saying.

"Yes, if God exists, he should come down, that would be an act of mercy here." Miguel said.

"We really need God to come down and visit Mexico. If there was a God, he would not allow all the evil that is happening in this country. There is nothing in Mexico but the monotonous excitement of violence and torture. Violence and torture is our middle name. Man-torture-man. In the middle of all emptiness, where even the beat of eternity is faint, there is this curse called torture and violence. This is the cornerstone of Mexico's drug war. The rock on which the tomb of the womb of our country is built, this is Mexico's drug world, its end and its meaning, its beginning, its evolution, its goal and spawn," he said ending his prayer. *"No te entiendo nada pinche cura,"* I thougth.

Finally, Father Bernardino went silent, got up and shook our hands. "There is only one word to remember, kids, as you pass in and out of life, and that word is love, don't you ever forget that," he said.

He let us out through the side door of the chapel and we got into the *troca*. Miguel drove to the back of the church. There were these huge trees all over the place. They were not just old trees they were tall and green, brown and big. Some of those trees were seventy feet tall and more than five hundred years old. They were older than Mexico. Some of them were alive when Pancho Villa was in charge and when Emiliano Zapata was doing some good and massive killing around the country. It was June and it was hot, global warming hot, and crazy. It hadn't rained in almost ninety days. I noticed about a dozen vultures flying circles up in the sky.

"Look up Miguel," I said.

"C'mon Juan. You are the toughest kid in Mexico. Don't tell me that you are afraid of those lousy birds!"

"It could be a bad sign, *primo.*"

"Bad sign my ass, *cabron!* Just help me unload the merchandise and the money!"

He threw the first bag with such force against my chest that I ended up falling backwards on my ass. The moneybag was on top of me and I couldn't move.

"If I had a monkey with a face like yours, I'd shave his ass and teach him to walk backwards," I said angrily.

"I once took a shit that looked like you. Then I took a bigger one. And then it looked and smelled even more like you!" Miguel said, and he laughed out loud. *Juazzzzzzz!*

"Kiss my ass!" I yelled back.

After we finished unloading, we sat in the basement, which was maybe ten degrees cooler than the rest of the church, and read books, watched TV and played video games. Father Bernardino came at dark to bring us some food and drink.

"I really hate to do this," he said, "If it were up to me, I'd send you two and everybody else to the North. But it's not up to me. So we are just going to have to wait it out and do our best here, okay? You play it cool and stay cool no matter what happens, okay?"

"Okay *padre.*"

Miguel and I both agreed to that. We knew we had a long wait.

After almost ten days in seclusion, we didn't feel like playing games or watching TV anymore. We just sat still watching the walls and dreamed about the Elota river, the mountains and wide open spaces.

Early Sunday morning Father Bernardino came downstairs.

"The governor and his entourage are coming at ten. They want to have a service to celebrate the governor's second term in power. I have a bad feeling. Whatever happens now, you must stay down here. You must not come into the church."

Father Bernardino looked directly into our faces and, slowly sat across the table. He appeared to be close to making some sort of decision. He was half smiling as if he didn't know if the situation we were in was a joke or not. He looked back and forth from me to Miguel, then back at me again. I noticed that he looked vulnerable and confused, his two pale lips parted, his forehead furrowed.

"Being a priest means everything to me, but I also have my own personality and my own voice, and I'm not the typical *curita de pueblo* addicted to suffering. Here in Mexico there are conflicting agreements that go against the people, and the Mexican people agree to help each other suffer. Mexicans are addicted to suffering.

Their addiction to suffering is nothing but an accord reinforced every day because they are afraid. This is like a symbolic death wish, which kills the mind without harming our physical body. Here in Mexico we need a great deal of courage to face Zorro Porro Neto and his gang of criminals. We need to be very strong. There is no need for you two to be religious or go to church every day. I can see that your love and self-respect are growing and growing. You can do it. You can be next to God. If I did it, you can do it also. Do not be concerned about the future, because the future is yours. Keep your attention on today and stay in the present moment. Just live one day at a time. Today I'll be facing these criminals with only God standing by my side. Today is the beginning of a new dream, my dream, your dream, and Mexico's dream. I wanted you kids to know that."

The world outside the church ceased to exist. We were aware that Zorro Porro Neto and his gang were pillaging Mexico and at the same time they were looking for us. However, the danger Father Bernardino was going to face in less than an hour overshadowed all of that. He moved away from the table, not sure what to do. He waved goodbye, nodded his head gravely, turned around and slowly, climbed the staircase to the main altar.

"This time he's going to need all the power of Heaven and all the strength of the saints."

"Some big *cojones tiene el cabron!*" Miguel said.

"Yes! He won't give up! He has some balls!" I said.

After that exchange of words, we kept silent. No more words were spoken but a wave of hot fury crouched inside my chest. The feeling in that basement was the feeling of a rock when the fuse is burning in toward the dynamite. Time went by very fast. The whole church seemed hushed and expectant. We heard the footsteps of hundreds of people on the street and upstairs as they arrived. Miguel stood up and stretched lazily. He did not look at me. My hand tightened on my silver revolver. We heard Father Bernardino giving mass. I couldn't understand what he was saying.

Halfway through the sermon we heard five shots. The shrieks were deafening. We just stood helplessly holding our guns. The people were flowing out to the square. The cries inside the church grew weaker. In the distance, we could hear the siren of an ambulance getting closer.

Right at that moment we knew that Father Bernardino was dead and there was nothing we could do about it!

CHAPTER 7

The Escape

Anita, her husband and her five children, Faustino, Ava, Kayla, Lucas, and Melanie, lived in a pleasant little house right across from the church. Anita was a good-looking mature woman, nearing fifty. Her husband, an ancient, dried, bald man, a relic of a past generation but still in good shape, was nearly ninety. He drove an old Chevy pickup truck. The battered truck had the image of Pancho Villa mounted on his horse painted on the rusted hood. It was long since anyone had remembered that his name was Francisco Villa.

During the week, Anita worked in the church's office. It was her duty to answer the telephones and all the e-mails. She also fed the chickens, dressed Father Bernardino and put her four children to bed. Faustino her oldest kid, her pride and joy, the one she called "the pride of my life," was away studying at the Escuela Normal Rural Raúl Isidro in Iguala. Father Bernardino helped the family with their expenses, and gave the kid a gold crucifix as a going away present for good luck. The priest was happy that Faustino wanted to become a teacher and improve the living conditions of the community.

Anita's body looked perfect for a mature woman and a mother of five. She conceived Faustino, her first baby, when she was thirty-one, her second at thirty-four, the third at thirty-five, and the others at thirty-nine and forty years old. Anita kept her own private agenda and this way, she was not only busy at the beginning of the week but she was also very busy with making certain preparations for the entire week, and the weeks to come. Once a month she went to confession. It would be interesting to know what sins she confessed and when she found the time to commit them. After confession, she would come down to the basement to bring us food and clean up the place. Anita was a quiet woman, somebody we could trust one hundred percent. As far as she was concerned, we were never there hiding in that church. She promised to keep the secret to the extreme, as if we didn't even exist. For Anita, life was never too complicated. If there were problems, she would usually lay those problems in the arms of The Virgin of Guadalupe who, Anita knew, had more knowledge and time for such things than she did.

On the night of September 26, when she came down to the basement to see us and ask for help, she behaved with a great deal of dignity. She smiled and smiled when she should have been mourning. Nevertheless, she couldn't help that, that's the way she was. She was a kind and happy person. She was a natural. That day we already knew what really happened to the forty-three students in Iguala and she didn't. Faustino, the pride of her life, was among those forty-three students that were reported missing after the local police, working with a local drug gang, abducted the students and then turned them over to these killers. We knew those criminals well. They were a band of psychopaths. They were *Los Mandriles*. They would do all the dirty work for *Lobo*, Zorro Porro Neto and *Tarántula*. Sometimes they worked as informers for the DEA. They were the worst bunch of brainless, vicious and destructive killers in the whole Mexican Republic. Knowing *The Mandriles* well, we also knew that Faustino and his other forty-two fellow students were tortured and surely already dead.

"I just want to know how he is, where he is and what he's doing," Anita said. "When I read in the papers that they keep finding human remains all over Mexico, I don't want to believe it's him. I have to believe he is alive and for some reason they haven't turned him over yet. I know that only you two can find Faustino and bring him back to me alive."

She spoke, as would a young girl, a new bride. Abruptly, she stopped, as if she had suddenly realized the futility of all she was saying. I thought perhaps she was disappointed at the situation but then I saw her smile, looking up at us and still cheerful with hope as she shook our hands and went back upstairs. When she shut the door behind her, I leaned over and said to Miguel, "We must do something about this *primo*, we really have to."

"You have a good heart, Juancho," Miguel said, "but don't forget that, right now, this woman is refusing to see what really happened to her kid. Eventually she'll find out he's dead. That's the Mexican way. Luckily very soon all this horror will be behind us."

For Miguel and me, the bags of money piled up in that basement had become the symbolic center of our friendship, the point of trust about which our lives revolved. It was a great feeling to know we could trust each other. In our mind, the money had long ceased to be currency. It's also true that, from time to time, we had dreamed of how many things we could buy with that money - a big house, a nice car or a jet plane. After a while we lost the conception of its legal value. Now our aim, our personal mission, was to give that money back to the Mexican people, decent people like Anita. I looked back once at the bags of money piled up against the wall, closed my eyes and I could hear my grandpa talking to me.

"It's far worse to defraud the poor than it is to take liberties with the law."

After Father Bernardino's assassination, we couldn't hide in the church's basement for too long. We could feel the eyes of Zorro Porro Neto and his gang of killers going through the walls and the windows and the roof looking for us. Miguel looked at me and I saw that his eyes had become fierce as a tiger's. In his face I saw horror and indignation that could not be simulated. His chin stuck out and, as he sat on the floor, his whole body weaved a little, like a rattlesnake aiming to strike. I didn't realize he loved Father Bernardino that much. I began to cry. Miguel put his arm around my shoulder. It was dusky in the basement and the smell of incense coming from the main altar scented the air. Outside, the big trees whispered softly in the breeze. I wondered how bad it was going to be today. We had been in a big mess before, but this time it was much worse.

"Don't cry, Juan. Now we have to plan our escape. We can't stay here any longer. Crying or giving up is out of the question. We have to talk to Anita and Francisco," Miguel said, "as soon as possible."

"Tomorrow I'll do it," I said.

Mondays and Tuesdays, Francisco Villa drove his *troca* across the street and into the church's yard. He parked by the back entrance and started working in the garden. The motor of the lawn mower coughed with effort, making enough noise to wake us up. At the end of the day he'd trim the big trees and, after loading the branches in the back of the *troca*, he'd drive up the hill to the local dumpsite to unload the cargo. The next morning when, true to his duty, he came down to the yard, I was waiting for him.

"You are up early," he said, picking up the lawn mower from the back of the truck and, without any effort, placing it on the ground.

"I need to talk to you," I said.

He wiped the sweat on his brow.

"First let me do my job, so it doesn't get too late."

"I have to talk to you now."

"Talk about Faustino?" He motioned over his shoulder, "do you want me to call Anita?"

"Yes! And we need your help guys."

After watching Francisco go across the street toward his house, I went back inside. Miguel was already up.

"Where did you go?" he said, "I started breakfast while you were out."

"I don't feel like eating at all."

"I hope you don't mind if I do," he laughed, "today is going to be a hard day Juancho."

"It doesn't look much worse than it did yesterday."

"That's because you have no idea about my plan and how we are going to escape."

"Anita and Francisco are coming here right now, so you'd better get your act together!"

"I think I can manage that."

Cautiously, Anita and Francisco made their way down the steps and came inside the basement. She was wearing a white straw hat, a red skirt and a light green sweater that accented the color of her eyes. In the morning light, they were almost like calypso, reminding me of the color of the mountains by the Elota River. As Francisco moved around her in his white t-shirt and old blue jeans, holding her hand and kissing her on the lips, he looked ten years younger.

"I hope you guys don't mind if I give Anita a kiss. I kiss her all the time. I'm so in love with her."

Miguel pulled out his chair and indicated for them to sit down. Anita let Francisco push the chair in for her, and watched him take a seat next to her and sit down as well.

"Yesterday morning I tried to place a police report about Faustino's disappearance," she said, "but Toro Lopez the officer in charge was already drunk and tried to rape me."

"I hope you don't mind if, the next time I see that *pinche Toro*, I go ahead and kill him," Francisco said angrily.

"We can take care of that for you," Miguel said.

"You don't have to. I'll kill the *cabrón* myself!" Francisco insisted.

"We don't live around here, so it would be easier for us to whack the son of a bitch."

Anita laughed. She was pretty. She looked even prettier than the day before.

"It feels good to be so important," she said.

Miguel poured some coffee and, after finishing serving it, without any hesitation, he told them about our plan to escape, the whole operation, the money, the drugs and all that had happened in the aftermath, including our relation with Father Bernardino and our private war against Lobo, Tarántula and Zorro Porro Neto. When he finished, Anita seemed to be studying us.

"Any idea what you are going to do? Where are you going to hide?"

"We assume our best option is to escape to *El Norte*," Miguel said.

Anita seemed not so sure about that but she said nothing. Instead, she reached for her coffee.

"Well, no matter what happens, I think you are doing the right thing. To find Faustino the pride of my life and bringing him back here to me alive and well."

Miguel didn't say anything, but then he didn't have to. The fact that they realized that we needed their help was more than enough. They knew a lot about suffering and they understood our suffering as well. Help was all that we wanted from them or anyone on that particular day and, though we met Anita and Francisco only a few weeks before, we sensed that somehow they already knew us better than most people did. Maybe, we thought, probably better than anyone.

After we finished our meeting, Francisco fished the keys from his coat pocket, went outside and got into his truck. From the backyard Anita, wearing my blue jeans, my shirt and my baseball cap, playing the lookout, waved as if wishing him good luck. Francisco looked over his shoulder and began backing up the truck to the basement door. Though we were not sure what to expect, Miguel and myself started to load the moneybags and the drugs as fast as we could. We didn't know when *Tarántula* and his gang would show up and we didn't want to be caught in the act.

Francisco motioned to the moneybags. "Do you need a hand with that?"

Miguel shook his head. "Thank you man, we can manage. They're not that heavy."

The operation went smoothly and, in less than two hours, we were done. Miguel took a small step backward and jumped into the truck bed, hiding under the moneybags. Wearing Anita's red skirt, the green sweater and the white straw hat, I sat next to Francisco in the front seat of the truck. He pulled the truck up to the side of the big trees and switched off the engine. After taking a moment to prepare his old self and take a breather, he got out and started covering Miguel and the cargo with huge tree branches. He moved as if he were twenty years younger. When Francisco pulled out onto the main road, everything with regard to our operation was going perfectly. I saw Anita in the rearview mirror, still wearing my clothes, entering the church by the side door as we planned. That's why, when I saw Lagarto standing on a ladder over the main road painting a telephone pole, looking over the church, I started to worry.

"If we can make it to the city limits," Francisco said, "we'll be fine."

"I saw Lagarto, their hitman, on top of a telephone pole, watching over the church."

"Anita knows very well what to do," Francisco smiled, "As you guys planned, she went in dressed like a man and she'll come out dressed like a nun. No sweat. She'll be okay!"

After being on the road for more than one hour, my throat was dry. I could feel the ache in my back from sitting in the same position like a woman for too long. I shifted in my seat and I wondered how poor Miguel was doing in the truck bed, buried under the moneybags and the tree branches. We have at least three more hours' drive to get to Iguala. Our final destination was the burial site. *The Mandriles* had at least half a dozen secret mass graves with unknown occupants, barely concealing the extensive toll that organized crime, corrupted police officials and politicians had taken on the Mexican people. In Mexico, death is a personal matter, a national sport, arousing sorrow, despair and fervor, for inspiring beautiful songs. Funerals, on the other hand, are like social functions. No decent Mexican citizen goes to a funeral without first polishing his *troca*, and wearing a *camisa negra* and black boots. He makes sure he sends flowers with the proper card attached, to prove his presence. A dead man may be loved, hated, mourned or missed but, once he is dead, he becomes the main ornament of a happy and formal social celebration. Submerged in my thoughts, suddenly I was awakened.

"Get ready," Francisco said, "I think there is a road block."

Parked in the middle of the road I could see a police car with the lights blinking and a cop standing behind it pointing a gun at us. He raised his hand and threw it forward.

"You, the driver, come out with your hands up," he said, "lady, you stay in the truck."

I looked around not realizing he was talking to me. I pulled my silver revolver from under the skirt placing it between my legs. Francisco walked slowly towards the policeman.

"Come closer, old man, I want to take a good look at your ugly face."

Watching Francisco make his unsteady way up to the police car, the cop noted that his eyes narrowed a little, as if he didn't know where he was or how to handle the situation.

"Have you been drinking?" He asked, pointing the gun at the old man's face.

"No officer, I never drink in the morning."

"Turn around, grandpa, and put both hands on top of the car," he ordered.

Francisco leaned against the car with his hands, and they were both very quiet. I saw the cop handcuffing him.

"Get in the back seat and don't move, *pinche viejo!*"

He looked over my way and gave me a weak smile. As he got closer, I could see that his uniform shirt was wrinkled and sweat-stained under the arms, and his pants were too big and dirty. A rush of anger seemed to go through me. I wanted to kill the cop. "That fucker just wants *dinero*. He probably does this all the time. He makes money off people's problems!" I thought, as he was getting closer to the *troca*.

"You don't have good news for me, do you officer? I asked faking my voice.

"I don't have good news for anybody, *mi reina*," he smiled.

Now he was standing by the passenger window so close that I could smell his breath. He grabbed his crotch, and slowly licked his upper lip. I acted like a real lady avoiding any eye contact. I had my right hand between my legs holding my silver revolver.

"You look so beautiful with that white hat," he said, "take it off bitch!"

In one fluid motion I took off the hat with my left hand and threw it at his face, and, with the finger on the trigger, I raised my right hand from under the skirt and shot him once in the heart. With a panicked look on his face, he fell backwards. He was dead before he hit the ground

"What was all that about?" Miguel laughed, "I thought you and the cop were in love!"

"You just stay put and hide in there until we get to Iguala, *pinche primo*. We don't need any more surprises. Now I have to get Francisco and keep going."

I walked over to the police car. Francisco sat still, conscious only of his own heart beating, and the air entering and leaving his lungs. It seemed to me that he wasn't quite sure just where he was anymore. I took the handcuffs off and helped him out of the car.

"The guy you just whacked was *Toro Lopez*," his voice was calm, "I told you that he was all mine."

"Sorry Francisco, I had no choice. It was him or us," I said.

Then a voice came out of him, but it wasn't his really. It was more like an approximation of a sound. It was not the same voice anymore, like something broke inside him. He was in a trance. He didn't know from where he'd come from or where he was.

"Faustino, my baby, was born in the garden of love. Those are the best kind of babies, because all those babies are born to do good things. He is my baby and the baby of my Anita. He is the pride of her life. When she married me we knew already about Faustino, even before he was born. At the time she was very beautiful and young. Her eyes were bright, she had a nice body, and her hair was long and shiny. Soon Faustino was born. There is nothing as great as having a baby. That's why we must find Faustino and kill his captors. It's not good letting these criminals get away with murder. It's much better to kill them all. I can't stand the sight of them anymore. That's why I wanted to kill Toro myself."

He sat at the wheel with his head bowed. I watched him knowing, that he was mentally ill and in bad shape. He needed time to collect his thoughts, so he could drive.

"Let's go. They're after us," I said.

"Do you mind if I give you some advice?"

"I guess not."

"Keep your head down. They have snipers all over the place."

"What about you?" I asked.

"They don't shoot old people. For those fuckers, we are not the enemy."

The day passed quickly. The old truck roared through the highway, and I could see the cars and big trucks going south for towns like Iguala. Francisco was still very quiet behind the wheel and, even though I was in his truck, it was so familiar for me to sit on the passenger's side of the *troca* that it almost felt like Miguel was driving.

"So where are we going, Juan?"

Without waiting for me to answer, he looked at me, rested his right hand holding a pistol on his knee and turned left, driving past a bunch of small trailers on a grassy hill. He reduced the speed a little and took a dirt road away from the highway.

"This is *The Mandriles* neighborhood. Now we are in nowhere land," I said.

"It is?" He asked.

"I would never lie to you, Francisco. Let's find a place to bury the money and the dope."

We drove deep into the forest and stopped by a clearing in the countryside. Miguel jumped out, stretching his limbs, jumping up and down like a mad man and doing push-ups to boost his circulation.

"At last! We made it! I couldn't stand it anymore!" he said, "Let's find a place to dig."

Francisco unloaded the shovels and the pick axes from the back of the truck, and we started digging. We had to work fast. We had only seven hours before dawn.

"Hey, kids! I found a leg bone!" Francisco called out.

"Keep digging! Don't stop! Once we are done, then we can study anatomy." Miguel said.

Soon came other fragments, a rib, a knee bone, five cracked skulls. Nevertheless, we just went on digging, doing our job, trying to mask the heartache, the stench and the horror.

I looked across the mass grave, and I saw that Miguel and Francisco had paused and, like me, were staring at the human remains. We stopped digging for a moment. The sky was full of shadows. In the silence of the night, we could hear the wind humming steadily.

"I wonder what kind of people could do something like this," Francisco said.

"Because they are animals," Miguel answered.

"Why? I mean, who are they?"

Instead of answering, Miguel reached for a bottle of tequila in his back pocket. With deliberate motions he opened it. After taking a big swig, he handled the bottle to Francisco.

"You might need a drink," he said, "Go and get the moneybags. We have to unload and bury the whole cargo before daybreak."

With the full moon hovering among the clouds, the air had a luminescent quality, as though particles of light were suspended in the dark. For a moment, standing there deep inside that dark hole, I sensed I was at a funeral and the dead people were calling my name, pleading for their soul. I knew I couldn't do anything for them.

"I found Perlita's bracelet and Faustino's gold crucifix," Miguel said, stepping away from the grave, "They are both dead and both of them were buried here."

I looked down at his hand that was holding the two shiny items still covered with dirt.

"I have to tell Francisco," I said.

"Shh," he put his index finger close to his lips. "No you don't, *pinche pendejo!*"

I was mad at Miguel for a moment. Then I realized that he was right. As much as I hated keeping the truth from Anita and Francisco, the sad news would have hurt their feelings more than just about anything. I noticed Francisco unloading the moneybags and watching us. I waved at him.

"Hey, Francisco," I shouted, "let me help you."

"What are you waiting for?" he asked, throwing a moneybag my way.

It took the three of us about five hours to bury the whole cargo in that big hole. The worst part was to gather all the human remains and load them in the back of the truck. It was crazy and sad. We had to pick up the bones one by one, and tenderly set them up next to each other on the truck bed. We then put all those *huesos* in a plastic bag marked: Iguala-September 28-2014. It was our own way to say good-bye to the dead.

When Miguel was closing the plastic bag with the bones inside, Francisco turned to him and said.

"Put those things away, please. I don't want to look at them."

"Francisco," Miguel said, leaning on a shovel. "You must take these bones to the Prosecutors office, and make sure they give them to the Argentine and Austrian team of forensics. Only to them."

When we finally finished, we were tired and hungry. The sky above us, was beginning to clear, the air was growing warmer. We took off our gloves, remaining silent for a moment. Francisco looked puzzled. Miguel patted him on the back and gave him a melancholy smile.

"Francisco," he finally said. "Thank you for everything. I can't imagine what it must have been like for you to keep your cool while digging all night in that grave, and having Faustino in your mind. There is no way we could have made it without your help."

Francisco watched him soberly, his hands trembling.

"I know you do Miguel. It was the worse time I ever went through."

"You make it sound so simple," I whispered.

"I'm still hoping that, thanks to you guys, Faustino will come back home safe."

"I wish we could find Faustino and have the chance to meet him," Miguel said.

"I take things one day at a time. In a situation like this, when a loved one is kidnapped, it's the best thing to do. When I wake up in the morning, I tell myself that I only have to be strong for one more day, and the next day my son will be home. I play it over and over in my head, to avoid going insane!" Francisco said, flashing a quick smile.

"I'm pleased you take it easy, Francisco, but don't forget that, right now, *The Mandriles* roam this area killing anything that moves and Zorro Porro's men are after us. We must get away from here as soon as possible, before we all get killed," Miguel said.

Francisco got behind the wheel and we drove off. Looking at Miguel sitting next to me, I was holding my question about where we were going until we were way on our way. Soon we were riding out of the town of Iguala, taking a shortcut to Mexico City. The road was crowded with late afternoon traffic, so we decided to avoid the D.F. altogether and made our way onto the main highway heading north towards Sinaloa. Earlier, we had decided to go to our trailer and get some things to make our crossing to El Norte a little easier. Rain was beginning to fall. I rolled down the window and let the wind blow the rain onto my face. Francisco started driving faster. I felt restless. I was sweating in the truck but I was also soaking wet by the rain. I could smell the river. I was used to that smell, the way a normal day smelled to me. What I really wanted to do was drive the *troca* all the way up to *El Norte*, non-stop, and never come back again.

"Give me your name, kid. What's your name?" the cop shouted.

A patrol car had pulled up. Francisco and Miguel looked down hiding their faces. The young deputy whose face was alert and wild, stepped up to the truck, his hands on his hips, and nodded his head in the direction of the truck bed.

"What are you carrying in the back boys?"

"Just tools," Francisco said.

"Step out of the truck and show me, *abuelito*," the policeman said.

Breathing with difficulty, Francisco got out shaking his head. He was very angry. His lips moved as if he wanted to say something. He continued shaking his head. I saw his hands trembling and I was afraid the old man would drop dead at any moment. I didn't see clearly where the cop was standing, but I moved closer to the truck door and pushed it open with such a force that surprised me. I heard a bumping sound and I saw the policeman falling backwards. Next thing I saw were Francisco's hands fixed on the cop's neck, lifting him from the floor, the cop's feet kicking and dragging beneath him. Francisco shook him once, twice, repeatedly, the head of the cop jerking backward and forward. It seemed that there was no end to Francisco's fury and strength. The cop now on the ground had dropped his hands, and with his mouth half open full of saliva he was not moving anymore. Sitting upon the dead cop's chest, Francisco paused for a moment before releasing him. He got up, kicked the dead guy once in the head and gave me a wacky smile. There was that tightness in his face again, like when he was standing by the mass grave in Iguala. Maybe he was really going mad or something.

"Are you ok?" I couldn't help asking.

"Yes and no," Francisco said, looking down at the dead cop. "This one was for Faustino."

Miguel was standing by the side of the truck, embracing his M-16 close to his chest, looking cool and composed. He took two steps forward, taking a good look at the dead cop lying on the ground.

"One more lousy cop dead," he said. "No big deal! Besides, I had you guys covered all the time." *Juazzzzz!* He laughed.

Now, after that violent act, a dark feeling started to take over me, like when I was in the basement of Father Bernardino's church and I couldn't escape. I felt fatigue and confusion, and a deep feeling in my heart that perhaps what I just saw before me was a dream. Francisco was standing next to me, not moving, and he began to weep silently, turning his face from side to side.

"*Orale cabrones!*" Miguel shouted. "Let's get moving! We still have a long way to go!"

We got inside the truck and Francisco started the engine. The day had gotten brighter and I could already smell the Elota River. As I pushed my silver revolver into the waistband of my pants, I knew I was on my way to *El Norte* and that I was ready for a good fight. I don't know if it was that I was too tired or because I had fallen asleep in the truck before we reached our trailer, or because I finally realized we were going north, but for the first time in a long while, when I opened my eyes, I had a joyful feeling about Mexico.

"Turn off the lights now and park around the back," Miguel said, interrupting my thoughts, "Juan and me, we walk the rest of the way."

Walking together in the darkness, listening to the sounds of the night, it felt like we were kids again. Kids as we were before carrying out so many killings, before all the madness and everything else started piling up on my conscience. I almost sensed that all the digging in that mass grave had purified me, and given me the right to have hope and start over. Standing by the trailer's front door, behind a pile of wood, I saw this man and somehow I knew he was waiting for us. It was a hot night, and Miguel's forehead and cheeks were shining with sweat as he carried his rifle under his right arm, holding a *machete* in his other hand. He knelt down and pointed the M-16 directly to the guy's head.

"I'll take him or you take it?" he whispered.

"I'll do it myself. Give me the *machete!*" I said.

With the *machete* in my right hand as I got closer to the man, I became aware that even standing up, he was sound asleep. I just hit him hard on the head and, without making any sound, I placed him gently on the ground.

"What do you think you are doing?" Miguel said, taking the *machete* from my hand and pushing the blade deep into the man's throat.

The guy's legs started twitching and jerking on the grass. There was a lot of blood on the ground. Standing by the dying man, Miguel was smiling like an idiot. I felt mad and frightened all at the same time.

"Get inside and get the stuff Juanchito, and make it snappy. We have to keep moving."

I walked into the darkened trailer. It was a small and pitiful dump. I couldn't remember clearly what I was looking for. I went directly into the bedroom and I took our fake ID'S from the night table drawer, and my army boots and Miguel's bulletproof vest from the closet. From under the bed, I pulled a wooden box containing my old silver revolver and a bunch of letters from my mother. I heard a car passing by on its way by the river road. Suddenly I realized that Zorro Porro was still after us and there was no more time to waste. I put everything into a backpack and I walked out.

"That was fast, kid!" Miguel said, "Now, let's burn the fucking place down!"

After pouring gasoline all around the old trailer and setting it on fire, we left the place about eleven o'clock that night.

"Our first stop will be Ciudad Juarez, and of course we have big plans," Miguel said.

At a distance we could still see the smoke and the flames reflecting in the sky.

With my eyes closed, listening to the soothing noise coming from the engine, I was falling asleep when, all of a sudden, the noise changed to a frightening rattle, as if the clutch, the rear end, the differential, the carburetor, and all the nuts, bolts and ball bearings would drop out any minute.

"What's happening now?" I shouted.

"The *pinche* radiator. We have to stop for a while," Francisco said.

We had been advancing by slow stages, stopping every forty or fifty miles to let the truck cool off and add some antifreeze. Everybody was passing us by, heavy trucks, old *trocas*, motocycles, skooters and even a bunch of ugly looking indians riding horses.

"It's better this way, because we don't look suspicious" Miguel said, smiling. "Who would want to stop two dumb looking kids and a crazy old man in a dilapidated *troca?*"

We were on a stretch of an open and inviting highway ahead. Francisco stepped on the gas, determined to reach Juarez before dark. When we got to the foot of a mountain pass, near town, the radiator began to boil over and, for the fifteenth or twentieth time that day, we had to stop. Sitting in the truck, we had to wait for the engine to cool off again. An old drunk that was hanging by the side of the highway started talking to us.

"For the next twenty miles, this is the worst spot on this highway. And I mean pretty bad," he said.

"I'm not worrying about whether the road is dangerous or not, but whether the water will boil over before we can reach the top of the pass," Francisco said.

Francisco tried to find out whether it was a long climb or a short steep one.

"There ain't any part that's not dangerous," the drunk kept repeating.

"That means nothing to me because I have no other way to go."

"Of course, it's just as bad going down," the drunk said. "It's only five miles to the top. If you get over it, you'll be alright."

I knew he was very drunk, but I didn't like that "if".

"What do you mean?" I asked, "Is it so terribly steep?"

"No, it's not that steep, it's tricky," he explained, "People get frightened when they find themselves hanging over the cliff. That's when all the collisions happen."

I watched the sun rapidly setting and I wondered if the old truck would hold out all the way to Juarez. I touched the hood to check out how cool it was. It was still as hot as a boiler ready to explode.

"Well," Francisco said, "I think that there are no more than seven miles of descent."

Climbing to the top of the hill, the *troca* was making a terrible racket, a real Mexican racket. It sounded like some mariachi singer screaming with pain over a dead lover's body. The signs by the side of the road all warned to us to go slowly. Instead, Francisco stepped up on the gas and we were climbing too fast. When we got to the top, I looked at the gauge. It read 180 degrees.

"Hold on tight *muchachos!* We made it to the *pinche* top! Now we are going down, *cabrones!*" Francisco screamed happily.

I didn't have much time to reflect on the fantastic view. We started to go downhill, rolling very fast. Francisco was trying to work the brakes around the sharp curves, almost to no avail. I thought we were actually flying. Finally somehow we made it all the way to the bottom. Francisco slowed down almost to a standstill. The *troca* was shaking like a leaf. A cloud of white steam coming from under the hood was covering the windshield. To make things worse, nearing Juarez it seemed suddenly as if we had come upon a hot house. The smell in the air was overpoweringly unpleasant. Just as we arrived with our smoking *troca* into what looked like a parking lot, to make things a little more complicated, an old man in uniform rushed out to the middle of the road and ordered Francisco to pull over.

"Stop right here and put your brakes on please," he said quietly.

"So we are in Juarez," Francisco said.

"Where did you guys come from?" the old man asked.

For a moment I couldn't think, and Miguel came to my rescue.

"Come from? Come from where? What do you mean?"

"Are you Mexican citizens?" he asked.

That question seemed thoroughly absurd after all we had been through. I almost laughed in his face.

"Yes, we are Mexican citizens," Miguel said.

"Your radiator is leaking, do you know that?"

"Yes," Francisco answered angelically, shutting off the motor, climbing out and opening the hood to have a look at it. The cloud of smoke hit the old-timer right in the face and he started coughing

"Where are you bound for now?" he asked, still coughing.

"Ciudad Juarez. Is it very far away?"

"Just a few miles down the road."

As Francisco was pulling out, the old man stopped him again.

"Before you go, can I see your license please?"

Next to me I saw Miguel holding his pistol and ready to shoot the old guy at close range. Lucky for us, Francisco was not one of those panicky people who gets into an attack of hysteria for any reason in the middle of nowhere. He just handed the license to the old guy.

"Francisco Villa!" The old man cried out happily, raising his right hand and making a military salute, "I'm at your service! Pleased to meet you sir! Have a good trip!"

"*Viva Mexico!*" Francisco shouted, taking his license back and replying with a military salute of his own.

We left the old man standing in the middle of the road, scratching his head and whispering to the sky.

"Francisco, what was that all about?" asked Miguel.

"I'm a Toltec and my family's last name is Villa. I'm the last *viejo chingon* of my generation to stand up and fight for freedom. In Mexico we are not free anymore. We are a completely domesticated society. It's very tragic when we don't even understand what freedom is and why we are not free. I refuse to accept it. That's why I'm a class apart. Do you understand what I'm saying? *You pinches pendejos.* " He shouted.

"Francisco," Miguel laughed, "I think you are exaggerating."

"Why? Because the belief system that was put inside your head, is based on lies?"

"Don't get upset Francisco," I said, "Miguel is just an illiterate wetback!"

"Sure, you are the bright and shining *pinche* Mexican star, Juancho," Miguel said, "but if you don't behave and stop breaking my *cojones*, I'm going to kick your ugly *culo!*" *Juazzzzz!* I started to laugh, and laughed aloud, and Miguel laughed. *Juazzzzz!* and Francisco laughed too. *Juazzzzz!* We couldn't stop laughing. We kept laughing as Francisco drove into the downtown area of Ciudad Juarez and headed to the local motel's parking lot. Francisco pulled all the way to the far side of the lot and parked. He turned off the engine and the lights, and we just sat there quietly, gazing into the rearview mirror, sitting in that *troca*, knowing that *Zorro Porro* was after us. The silence was frightening.

"What are we doing here?" I asked.

"We are staying at Perlita's sister's place, just ten blocks down the avenue," Miguel said.

The *Chinga Dores* Motel was located on the outskirts of town, right across the street from a truck stop. The side streets around the motel were deserted and there was hardly any traffic. I saw only a few cars passing by. Downtown Juarez was its typical sleepy self. I saw a big black dog sprawled by the motel entrance. He raised his head from his paws each time a person walked into the motel lobby. He looked as if he was making a mental note of all the people checking in. The only storefront light was from the topless bar next to the motel. There was garbage all over the place. A gust of wind lifted some papers and made them dance on and off the sidewalk until they landed on the street. Miguel shook his head, looking at the empty streets and dirty sidewalks.

"Reminds me of the end of civilization," he said.

"It sure feels like that, *primo*."

For some reason I was whispering. It didn't seem to fit what we were doing or where we were going. Miguel nodded and we walked on. When we got to Perlita's sister's house, there was a small light on in what seemed to be the living room, but other than that, the house was dark. Miguel walked to the front door. We followed him. We walked quickly, still clinging to the cover of darkness and avoiding the glow of the streets lights.

"When I told her we were coming, she became very agitated," Miguel said. "She was very frightened."

Before Miguel had a chance to knock, a young woman opened the door, as if she was expecting us right at that moment.

"I'm scared," she said. She was trembling.

"Is everything ok?" Miguel asked.

"Hurry! C'mon in," she said, and walked quickly into the living room.

We followed. She was blond, about twenty years old, a very good-looking young woman. She walked with her shoulders hoisted as if she was trying to keep from getting a bad chill. She turned abruptly and started pulling down all the window shades, not even stopping to look back to see if we were right there behind her.

"What is it, Dorita? What's going on? Why are you so scared?" Miguel asked.

She turned to him slowly. "I know they are out there! They are after you, and they have my sister Perlita!" She shouted and laying her head on Miguel's shoulder, started to cry.

I could always tell from the way other people looked at Miguel and addressed him that he commanded great respect. Just in the relatively short time he had been in the house, I could tell he was in charge and Dorita looked more relaxed already. "Did Miguel's power come from inner strength or inner madness?" I thought.

"Can I have a glass of milk?" Francisco asked. "My ulcer is killing me."

Dorita smiled at him, opened the refrigerator door, took a container of milk and placed it on the table. Francisco sat down, shook the container and started to drink directly from the carton.

"Mind if I join you?" she asked.

"Anyone is free to sit anywhere he or she wants," Francisco said.

"I can tell you are upset about your son, Faustino," Dorita said.

"If you are referring to his disappearance, of course I am."

"Did you know I saw him the night before all that happened?" She said.

"You saw him, that same night?"

"We made love the whole night."

"All night long?"

"Yes, it was the night before his confrontation with the police. Did he ever tell you about all our daily meetings with the students at the *Escuela Normal* in Iguala?"

"No," Francisco said.

He nodded and continued drinking his milk. I saw the way he was looking at Dorita across the table. There was that tightness in his face again. I suspected that, one way or another, he would try to find out more details about Faustino's disappearance from her. To me, he looked upset and surprised at the same time. I watched Dorita sitting at the table, next to Francisco, noticing again how beautiful she was. I could tell she was very nervous, finding Francisco's behavior oddly disgusting.

"Relax, Francisco," I said, "we must rest now."

"Juancho is right. We must rest," Miguel said, "Tomorrow at six in the morning we have a five hour drive to Nogales."

Three hours later, I couldn't fall asleep. Looking up at the ceiling, I laid awake on a blanket on the living room floor in the darkness, thinking about Zorro Porro Neto and his gang of criminals looking for us. However, this was not what kept me restless. It was my friend Barack and the letter I had to write to him before crossing the border to *El Norte*. All these thoughts increased the speed of my heartbeat. Unable to rest, I got up and took my laptop into the bathroom.

CHAPTER 8

Ciudad Juarez

THE FIRST LETTER TO BARACK

Ciudad Juarez, September 29, 2014 (2:09AM)

Dear Barack:

It's two o'clock in the morning and I'm sitting here on the toilet in my friend Dorita's bathroom in Ciudad Juarez which, by the way, I just realized is as oval as your oval office in the White House. Moreover, to be honest with you right now, I do not know how I am supposed to begin a letter like this. I don't know you in person but you seem to be a very nice guy. All I know about you is that you are the first black American president, the mero-mero, the big boss of the great Gringo-Land. We never met or exchanged emails, text messages or letters before today. I know about you through the news when I see you on TV, the social media and newspapers. I know it's not the same as meeting you in person. I wish I could be able, right now, to talk to you face to face but, due to the place and the situation I am in at this particular moment in my life, I can't do that just yet. So here I am, struggling for words, trying hard not to think in Spanish when I write to you in English or vice versa, and wondering if anything I write to you will reach your heart. I tried to call you many times but it was impossible to communicate with you over the telephone. You are so far away from me. I wish you could hear what I have to say. I am still trying to make sense of the world we live in, and that is part of the reason I'm writing this letter. I know that our leaders here in Mexico have told you many things about my people, but I think it is about time that you knew the real story from the perspective of a brown Mexican kid, a kid like me, since we are millions, and growing. My heart feels as if it is bubbling instead of beating. The words are bunching up in my head, pressing at my brain, urging my fingers to type, like a voice inside me screaming to tell you about my ideas and my plans once I get to Gringo Land. You have to understand that there has always been so much arrogance about you gringos, that we little Mexicans have grown to detest you, so I figured that you and me together could try to revert back to the old ways, when we use to love each other. I know we can work it out. What I most appreciate about you is that you do not pretend to be somebody you are not. That is why, out of admiration for you all these years, I have been talking about you all the time and telling everyone in Mexico that you are my best friend. Please let's keep this secret just between you and me. When I tell you all this, I am not trying to pressure you in any way to let your guard down and just let me walk into your country as a happy tourist. I know it's up to me to try and conquer the wall in order to see you. I guess what I'm trying to say is that I have changed and, little by little, I began to think there is something about you that's worth climbing the wall for and crossing the border to shake your hand.

My mother, just like me, used to talk about you all the time and I can only imagine how many letters she must have sent you also. She loved you as a special friend, the same way I love you, but I'm sure you know that. What you might not know is that, before I became your friend, I was not entirely convinced about you and your Gringo Land kindness and integrity. As you well know, here in Mexico most of the people are influenced *and manipulated by crooked politicians and a corrupted media machine, determined to brainwash them into having a negative opinion about you and your wonderful country. I wish I could tell you that this ugly situation is going to change soon, but I can't. For kids like me to survive here in Mexico, it's very hard. Nobody cares about our generation. Mexico is not a country for young men. It's amazing to realize how cheap our life is. They just kidnapped 43 students in Iguala and we know enough not to expect justice or mercy for them. Only an act of kindness from you and your government could end this vicious circle of crime without punishment that's been going on in Mexico for centuries. Kids like me have been humiliated, tortured and reduced to the level of a wild beast. Who cares? Nobody! Specially, nadie in Mexico, or outside Mexico. Not even God knows what we suffer, what we go through. There's no language to convey it. It's beyond all human comprehension. As a friend, I beg you to do for us, what God himself wouldn't do. To help my people and make our leaders stop the impunity and obey the law. Otherwise, the whole country will fall apart and, next time you come to Mexico, we will be barking like wild dogs.*

"Open the door, *pinche cabron!*"

The shouting and the knocking at the bathroom door shook me up.

"Open up! I have to take a leak!"

Miguel was yelling at the top of his lungs. Not totally awake yet, still sitting on the toilet with the laptop on my knees and staring down at the screen, I said, "I'll be right out!" I closed the computer and walked out.

"Get your stuff together, Juancho, we have 344 miles to Nogales," Miguel said.

After having breakfast, we walked back to the motel's parking lot. Francisco and Dorita had gotten up much earlier and were standing by the side of the *troca*. The old man was bending over under the hood and had his ear close to the motor, like a doctor examining a weak lung. Dorita, holding a backpack and smiling timidly at us, looked very happy.

"Found out what's wrong yet?" Miguel asked.

"No," Francisco said.

"What's up with the girl?"

"She's coming with me," the old man said. "She's going to help me find Faustino."

"Not very convenient but understandable," Miguel said.

Miguel smiled at everybody and shook his head. He stared at me, and then he smiled in such a chilling way it made my heart stop and start again. He kissed Dorita on the cheek, took her hands and hugged her. She hugged him back, but without any enthusiasm.

The big black dog was out in front of the motel, as usual. He raised his head and, wagging his tail, he approached our group when we paused at the entrance of the lot. I patted the dog on the head and the dog followed me. With his eyes open wide and cheerful; he kept wiggling his tail.

"Zorro Porro is getting closer! Everybody get in the truck and let's go!" Miguel said.

We all jumped in. Francisco drove out of the parking lot down Main street, cruised through downtown Juarez and continued driving very slowly all the way to the highway. Looking in the rearview mirror, I saw the big black dog jumping in the back of the troca.

Francisco put the truck in high gear and finally made his way onto the highway, heading north. He turned on the radio and a DJ was offering a free trip to Cancún. His voice sounded idiotic and full of good cheer. Thank God, Francisco switched him off and rolled down the window. By the clatter coming from the engine of the old truck, I could tell he was picking up speed. I was hoping that I would be able to have time to finish writing the letter to Barack before our crossing to the other side. Lately, I was overwhelmed with concerns. I felt as if I was in a downpour of question marks, rushing from the cover of one answer to another. I sat there in the truck next to Dorita and Miguel, thinking about what Miguel and I had decided. Somehow, some way, we were going to get to *El Norte*, and that was a good thing. Something that, if my Grandpa was present, I was certain he would disapprove of, for sure.

"Don't go too fast, Francisco." Miguel said.

"I don't think they are looking for us this far north kid,"

"You never know," Miguel said, "I don't trust those *pinches cabrones!*"

"Leave it to me, Miguel," Francisco said, "the trick is not to do anything that deviates from what they think is the normal routine."

"The police would probably make up posters with your face on it and put them in post offices," Dorita said. "It was all they did when I reported that my sister Perlita was missing."

"Whatever," Miguel said, "but, no matter what, no cell phones, okay?"

The time passed quickly. The *troca* roared through the highway on our way to Nogales. I saw the gauge moving slowly up to 180, which worried me a bit. I remembered what happened on our way over to Juarez when the *troca* overheated several times.

"I think it's going to boil over," I said.

"I don't think she'll boil," Francisco said, "*trocas* here in Mexico act temperamental, just like people. Don't worry, Juan."

Francisco slowed down to fifty miles an hour. He scratched his head and ruminated a little bit. I heard a funny noise coming from the engine.

"I don't think we'll have any more trouble," he said, looking at my face, "but just to make sure, when we get to Nogales, I'll take it to a mechanic."

We had a friendly conversation about the slaughter going on all over Mexico, and about the kidnapping of Faustino, his son. We were just entering the desert that lies between Juarez and Nogales. Animals and birds rarely cross that empty space.

"Don't worry," he said, "we'll get to Nogales in good time. If not today, we'll get there tomorrow. This is Mexico. Time makes no difference."

We got to Nogales that same afternoon. The first thing that struck me was the presence of lots of people waiting for us, people who were angry and who were all, including the octogenarians, fed up with Zorro Porro Neto, his policies and his cronies. Everybody knew Miguel, and they wanted to shake his hand and talk to him. It was hard to follow the conversation because everybody was talking at the same time.

Except for Dorita, there wasn't an attractive woman in the whole group. The men looked like hard workingmen, excluding nine or ten who looked like aged revolutionaries. Seated at a long table, as we ate, they became more discursive, more argumentative.

"Who will fight?" an old timer asked. "Is there no one left in the world who's not afraid?"

Everybody at the table grew silent.

"*Nadie*? No one?" He asked again.

Miguel drew himself up.

"Juan and me, we are not afraid of anything or anybody!" he shouted.

For a long moment the people sat still, holding their breath. The old man broke the silence.

"Am I going mad? Or something is wrong with my hearing?" He said. "You are not afraid? *Verdad*? I believe I heard that you two *pinches pendejos* are escaping to *El Norte*."

"I can't believe that you and Miguel are going to *El Norte!*" Dorita said.

Sitting beside me, she looked up in silence. I could hear her muted sobs. Her eyes were filled with tears and unspoken anguish. I stood up and opened my arms. Instinctively Dorita rose, trying to stop her tears. We embraced, holding each other for a long, long time. I saw Miguel sitting across the table, holding a glass of beer and watching us soberly.

"Keep all of that love for later on, *pinches cabrones!*" he shouted.

"Please, Juan, take me with you!" she whispered in my ear.

"I can't believe Miguel is jealous," I thought.

By eleven o'clock it was all over. The old timers, sleepy and tired, went to bed. In the kitchen, one of the younger guys was playing beautiful and romantic music, serenading Dorita. The big black dog was looking at me from under the table, begging for food. I gave him a piece of bread. He almost ate my hand.

"What are you planning to do with that dog?" Miguel asked me.

"Give it to somebody before we cross the border."

"Does he have a name?"

"Yes, *Perro Negro*"

"*Perro Negro*, that's it?" Just *Perro Negro*?"

"Yes, *primo, Perro Negro*," I said, "as a tribute to our former boss in Sinaloa. Remember him?"

"How can I forget? We whacked the fricking guy, didn't we?"

I saw Dorita coming out of the kitchen. She was carrying a bowl with a piece of red meat to feed *Perro Negro*.

"I hope you don't mind," she said, talking to the dog, "do you want to eat now or wait a little while?"

The dog caught Dorita off guard. He jumped up and swallowed the whole thing in one single bite. Standing up, with the empty bowl in her hand, watching the dog in shock, she looked very pretty, even prettier than I realized a few hours before.

"You didn't have to do that," she yelled to the animal.

Miguel turned back towards the doorway of the house.

"What's wrong with you, *pendeja*?" he yelled. "The damn dog doesn't know what you are talking about! All right, whatever! I have had enough for today! Good night everybody, I'm going to bed."

That night in Nogales, as I laid in bed staring at the ceiling, trying to figure out what the old timer had meant when he made the comment about both of us escaping to *El Norte*, I decided not to pay too much attention to that subject. On that particular night all I wanted to do was to finish my letter to Barack, and my mind was one hundred per cent fixed on that. Somebody in the next room was watching TV and the noise distracted me, but only for a moment. I got up, took my laptop, walked into my oval office, locked the door, sat on the toilet and continued writing the letter to my friend in the North.

Nogales, September 30, 2014 (3:00AM)

Barack, I'm sorry that I'm writing to you while I'm on the road, but you must understand that Zorro Porro Neto and his gang of killers are after us and won't give us a break. In reality these savages are devils concealed in human flesh.

Can't stop, not even for one minute. We have to keep moving. We must cross the border and see you before we get killed. I know that, not long ago, Zorro Porro Neto called a press conference and mentioned to you and the world that we are the worst criminals in the land, but to be honest with you, we are not as bad as he made it seem. If you consider how I grew up, it will make your hair stand on end. As a child I never had the opportunity to choose my own beliefs, however I had the good fortune that my father died before I was born. So when I finally came into this world, I had one less problem to deal with, one less person to bargain with while I was growing up. Unlucky for me, the persons I had to cope with were my mother and my sister, and let me tell you, it was not an easy task. It was more than enough. I know that you perfectly understand what I'm trying to tell you, because I'm certain that when it comes down to dealing with women in the family, you are a guy that has a lot of experience in this particular subject. I was born practically with two brains. Okay, so that's not exactly true. I was essentially a very bright baby. My brain was fast, so fast that it worked like a jet engine. My way of thinking was weird, sometimes serious, sometimes poetic, most of the time very funny. It seems more accurate to say, I was born with the power of knowledge. To *rehearse the story of my life in this letter is not my purpose. Besides, my short life is not so very unusual. In a moment of weakness, in the moment when it seemed that every man's hand was turned against me, I crossed the line into this world that I'm living in now. Living in this other world, each day that passed made it more and more difficult for me to go back and rejoin society, rejoin the herd. Crimes born of necessity soon led me to commit crimes of sheer bravado. While working with Miguel, after my first killing, I committed purely gratuitous crimes, like an athlete would do exercises just to keep in shape. My world of course is the school of crime par excellence. Until I went through that school I was only an amateur. In my world, friendships are established fast and deep, often in less than one minute. Just a kind word, a look, a pat on the back would be sufficient to do anything to prove one's loyalty, to a person or to a gang. In my world, even if one wants with all his heart and soul to go straight, when that critical moment comes, when it is a toss-up between believing in society or believing in one's friend, one will choose the latter. Very early in life, my mother and me had a taste of the Mexican justice system and, after that experience, I know enough not to expect justice or mercy from it. But, at the same time, I can never forget an act of kindness shown to me in a moment of great need, from people like Father Bernardino, Anita, Miguel and Francisco. You need a very strong will in order to adapt to my world and the codes you must live by. In my world, among us we have codes, unbreakable codes. That's why, of all things, I decided to visit you. You have to understand that, deep down in my heart, there has always been pure veneration for you and the principles your country stands for.*

Sitting on the toilet in the dark, totally concentrated on my writing, the bluish light from the computer screen reflecting on the walls of the bathroom gave me a sedated sensation, like floating in a cloud. Suddenly, I heard somebody turning the doorknob trying to get inside.

"Who's out there?" I asked.

"It's me. Francisco!"

"It's three in the morning. What do you want?"

"I have to pee, *pinche cabrón!*"

"At three o'clock in the morning? Are you nuts?"

"When the prostate calls, there's no way you can ignore it! I have to go right now or I'll pee in my pants!"

"The prostate? What are you talking about, Francisco?" I asked.

"The prostate gland, Juan," he laughed, "sooner or later you'll find out kid! It's the law of nature!"

As soon as I opened the door, he smiled at me, shook his head and, holding his flabby dick in his right hand, hurried into the bathroom slamming the door behind him. I never realized anyone could have that sort of desperation just to take a leak.

"I guess older people behave differently," I thought and I went to bed.

Next morning, everybody looked happy and rested. Hunched slightly over the wheel, Francisco was very quiet and self-contained. His eyes were bloodshot. It was his eyes which gave me the sensation that he was beginning to go totally mad. When I questioned him about his eyes, he replied, to my astonishment, that the condition was due to his enlarged prostate gland. Again, for the third time, I noticed that tightness in his face.

"Once, I almost lost my sight," he said. "I started taking *peyote* and they've improved."

While driving on the highway, our conversation lasted several hours. Miguel was rather surprised to see me talking to Francisco so earnestly. That morning, before leaving the house, he had been rather hesitant about letting him drive all the way to Mexicali, because he looked as though he was weary and nervous. To top it off, when *Perro Negro* jumped in the cabin of the truck, happily wagging his tail, he slapped the dog in the head and threw him out.

"Get in the back! You stupid dog!"

"Are you okay, Francisco?" Miguel asked.

"I'm good kid! I just hate that *pinche* animal!"

We were already by the *Rumorosa* area. Looking out the windshield into the sunlight, I saw myself as someone who wanted not only to help, save, and protect everybody in my group, but at the same time to make the world safer for kids like me, and to make it right once and for all. "That's something I have to write to Barack, about," I thought. I lowered my head and looked at the thick and dirty carpet on the floor of the *troca*. I tried to remember the floor of Miguel's yellow *troca* when we used to make deliveries around Sinaloa and whack some *cabrones* at the same time. I remembered driving up the hill by the Elota river on our way to kill *Lobo*. I remembered our trailer, the mountains and the river flowing, everything resembling a white mix. I don't know why, at that precise moment, I also remembered my video game remote control, backwards on my lap, the back-window of our trailer wide open, the screen and the sunlight shining on my face, and me, firing my silver revolver.

"How much longer do we have to go, Don Francisco?" Dorita asked.

I perceived Francisco sitting straighter at the wheel, as if he had just slipped a heavy pack of bricks from his shoulders.

"Calm down, my child, we are getting closer," he said. "To your right, behind those mountains, is the *Laguna Salada*."

"Can you stop somewhere? I have to pee!" Dorita said.

"Good idea, girl! I have to go myself!" The old man said.

"Okay, *pendejos*!" Miguel said, "let's do it at the next rest stop. I'll keep you covered."

When we reached the rest stop, by the side of a mountain range, Dorita and Francisco got off the truck and went their separate ways. After taking no more than twenty steps, the old man turned around and began to urinate. I saw Dorita disappearing behind a big boulder. *Perro Negro* started barking, jumped off the truck and ran after her. We heard yelling and cursing, followed by a shot and a man's voice calling our names.

"Miguel, Juan," he shouted. *"Zorro Porro Neto* wants you two to come with me!"

Suddenly we saw Dorita standing by the boulder, a big dude holding her by the neck, using her as a shield, and pointing a gun to the back of her head. He was waving at us.

"Put down your weapons and come closer," he demanded, "if you don't want to end up like your pinche dog! *Cabrones!"*

"He shot *Perro Negro!"* Dorita cried out.

"Step forward, Juancho, and give me your revolver," Miguel whispered, while tossing his MR-16 on the ground.

The thug directed his attention to me.

"Stop right there, *culeao,* or I'll kill this *pinche vieja!"* he warned me.

With my arms up, I kept walking. I knew it was the first time that Miguel had to use my revolver. The video game in my head continued repeating itself every two seconds, the sound of the microchip, as automatic and insincere as lies. Now this was the real thing. This time it was not a video game, not child's play. I kept walking and I felt like vomiting. I just kept walking towards the guy. He took a shot at me. The first was a warning shot, the second was deliberately aimed at my head, luckily for me, he missed. It was a miracle, since the distance was less than twenty feet. Then a third shot. By the sound of the third shot, I knew it came from my revolver. It was just one shot. One single bullet that entered Dorita's right eye and exited below her left ear, hitting the guy right in the throat. The man, and Dorita, already dead like two drunken straw dolls, stumbled backwards. They hit the big boulder and slid to the ground. I was crying, I couldn't move. Francisco, petrified, still holding his flaccid pecker with his right hand, in shock with his eyes wide open, was looking at us. Step by step slowly, like a zombie, he started walking towards the *troca.*

"I need an answer, *cabrón!"* I demanded.

Holding my revolver straight at his side, Miguel's eyes were fixed on mine. It took him a long time before answering my question.

"A single shot, Juan," he said, "a single shot to save your life. That's all I had. A single shot fired by someone not used to handle your *pinche* revolver. Now get in the fricking *troca*. Zorro Porro and his clowns are closing up on us. We have no time to waste!"

After seeing Dorita and the dog die right in front of my eyes, there was a heavy pause, like a silence in the air, broken only by Miguel's voice giving orders.

"Could you please stop complaining Juancho, and help me hide the bodies," he snapped viciously.

After hiding the bodies, covering them with rocks and bushes, I glanced at Francisco, who was already sitting behind the wheel, his face reflecting his rattled nerves.

"Hey kids! Why are you wasting your time burying that smelly dog? he shouted.

"*Perro Negro* was not an ordinary dog," I shouted back. "He had authentic human eyes."

"I'm no judge of dogs," Francisco answered. "One thing you have to be in agreement with me, the pinche dog was a constant pain in the ass!"

"No matter how much or how little you know about dogs, you must admit that when *Perro Negro* looked at you with his soulful eyes, the feeling he gave you was that he was sad because nobody in his whole freaking dog life, except me, had the intelligence to recognize him as a human being and not just as a dog!" I said.

"Soulful eyes?" he laughed. "You mean to tell me that *Perro Negro* was the reincarnation of some dead human being who was condemned to crawl about on all fours in the body of that ugly animal?"

"What do you think, Miguel?" I asked.

"I don't know, Juancho! I could never look at *Perro Negro* in the eyes for more than a few moments," he said. "The stupid dog would bark at me!"

CHAPTER 9
Mexicali

THE FIRST LETTER, PART TWO

We left the rest stop late in the afternoon. Looking at the old man, it felt like I was waking up from a long and painful dream realizing the stupidity of our fruitless private war. I became conscious that our wretched temerity, our ferocity and our tenacity were a sad joke, just a shameful tale with not even a genuine cause worth fighting for. It was time for us to quit. It was time for both of us to get out of the delivering business forever. For the first time in a long, long while, I sensed that at last we had won the right to be completely free, to finally climb the freaking wall, and cross the *pinche* border to Gringo-Land. It was a good option, a great idea and the right thing to do.

"Francisco, we have to get to Mexicali as soon as possible. Let's all take a deep breath now and forget what just happened, make sure nobody is following us and let's finish our plan in peace," Miguel said.

"This is all desert, this entire area," Francisco said. "There is always some vegetation, it's not just sand, you know. It has brush on it and there is soil if you can bring water to nourish it."

"It sucks to be a farmer in Mexico," Miguel said. "They are all so poor!"

Miguel and I had driven along that road before. It was a deserted road and there were only eroded hills around it. Being on that familiar road unsettled us in mysterious ways or rather, for unknown reasons, we became very agitated. I did not remember having ever stopped in that rest area before, and yet I could have sworn that I had not only been there but, for sure, we had whacked somebody there at one time. It was not a clear memory. I did not remember the big boulder or the mountains. What I felt was a vague but a strong apprehension that something big was going to happen to the two of us. I was not sure what.

"*El Norte* and Barack perhaps," I thought.

When our journey to *El Norte* began, we were in high spirits. Now, after all that had happened, it was a nightmare. The beginning of an endless nightmare, I should say. It was still four more hours to get to Mexicali. We were in open country, the traffic almost nil, the air was hot and the *troca* was doing fine. The palms of my hands were bruised, my arms were in pain and I was so angry about Dorita's senseless death, that my head was ready to explode. Francisco continued driving at a normal speed. I looked at the gauge's needle. The temperature was 180.

"It must be the radiator again," I said.

Francisco took a deep, nervous breath. Drops of sweat were running into his eyes and snot was running down his upper lip. I could tell he was getting angry.

"I don't give a shit about the radiator", he said. "Right now I have much bigger problems to take care of! Zorro Porro is chasing us, and I have to deliver the bones to the Argentine forensics and find my son."

"Keep going Francisco. You have been doing fine up to now. I need you to keep your sanity. We are getting very close to the wall. Let's stick to our original plan. Let's not throw away our only chance to be free!" Miguel said.

Nevertheless, things changed, as things always change, when I got this e-mail from Blanca.

Juan, after learning what happened to the forty-three students in Iguala, I decided to contact you. I know I can't call you and I don't know if you are going to get this e-mail on time, but I'm praying that you are ok. I know it was selfish of me not to go with you to El Norte, but I suppose that you two understand why I decided to stay behind. If you are reading this, it means that you are alive and well. The reason for this note is to warn you not to climb the wall by the site you originally planned. Once you arrive in Mexicali, just drive to the corner of Lopez Mateos Boulevard and Altamirano Street. I'll be there on the lookout for you guys to give you more instructions on how to get over safely to the other side. I don't want you to think for a moment that I have forgotten about you. Rather, I'm going to use my contacts to help you escape. I'd like to think it's possible for you to attain your dream and meet Barack. If you want to know the truth, that conviction is the only thing that helped me make it through all these years without you. If I close my eyes, I can still see you walking to school next to me, smiling, with the sunlight flickering on your face. As I write this note, I know that I love you as a brother and my best friend, and I miss you already. I'm sure you'll be always in my heart. You are my everything.

Love-U-Blanca

I showed the email to Miguel. I expected him to go crazy, but he was calm.

"Don't answer that email," he said. "Let's meet her first and see what she wants."

We arrived in Mexicali at nightfall. The moon was out and it seemed to me that it was bright enough to drive without lights. Like a big mirror, I could see the reflection on the mountains. Everything seemed quite normal. I saw a black SUV coming from behind that slowed up alongside our *troca* for a few seconds, speeding up and passing on the left. I noticed the Sinaloa plate shinning in the moonlight. Just to make sure there was no danger, we hung on their tail, with our guns at the ready, for about four miles up to the town entrance, before slowing down, and turning our attention to the road signs for directions. As Francisco drove down the dusty boulevard, the town grew vast and sordid, like a huge lighted swamp. The heat was so dense you could touch it with your hands. I saw a group of young *maquilladoras* on their way to work, laughing and playing while crossing the street; looking like a bunch of happy and domesticated schoolgirls. I could make out the dilapidated factory building through the *troca's* rear window, looking like a jail but we weren't close enough to tell if there were steel bars on every window.

"Why do these beautiful girls have to work in this horrible place?" I thought.

"The whole atmosphere of Mexicali is Mexican, but it's not Mexican," I said.

"To the left," Miguel yelled, without pausing to reflect a second.

"Are you sure about it?" Francisco asked, his head swinging over the steering wheel.

"Absolutely! You just keep going to *Plaza Constitución*. That's where we get off."

Francisco stopped between *Bravo* and *Azueta* streets, about three or four blocks from *Altamirano* Street. Miguel practically jumped from the *troca*. A gentle breeze from the north rattled the trees, and scattered leaves on the street and the sidewalk. A few couples were in the plaza at dark. No one noticed Francisco's dilapidated *troca* with Pancho Villa painted on the hood as it parked by the curb. Curiously enough, *Plaza Constitución* was a gloomy place, especially at night. I had never found a park in Mexico that filled me with anything but sadness or boredom. I would rather sit by the side of a mountain, the sea or a riverbank, than in these so call "breathing spaces", amidst the stench of asphalt, chemical fumes and gasoline. After I got off the truck and we started walking towards *Altamirano* Street, I thought of my sister waiting for us and in the mess she was in. Maybe I was mistaken, and for her to be with Tarantula was absolutely serious business. Now, walking next to Miguel on our way to see Blanca, I was totally confused. Suddenly I understood that I should take my own life seriously as well, to better understand the world and learn how to solve the problems I was facing.

"Not much of a park, is it?" Miguel said.

"That's why they call it a *plaza, pendejo!*" I laughed.

Blanca was waiting for us at the corner of *Lopez Mateos Boulevard* and *Altamirano* Street. Her shiny black hair, her big green eyes and her native features were a perfect match. She was wearing a long white dress, almost transparent, and white sandals. Her breasts were small and brown, like those of a young girl. When she saw me, she ran to my arms screaming my name. I embraced her and smelled the perfume of her skin, like when we were children. It was music to my ears when I heard her soft voice saying:

"Juanchito, *hermano!* I'm so glad you are alive! *Estas vivo!*"

Lagarto, standing by the black SUV like a rabid guard dog, with the driver's door open and the radio tuned to a station playing *mariachi* music, was watching after Blanca.

"Do you remember me, *pendejos?*" he shouted.

"Lagarto! What are you doing here?" Miguel asked.

"For the humble amount of three million dollars, Blanca asked me to help you. From now on we are *carnales!* Or, if you prefer, just call me your private facilitator," he laughed.

"I didn't have a clue about that," Miguel said. "And you, Blanca. You never said anything."

"After that night when you and Juan stormed Tarantula's compound and killed everybody, I had no choice but to take my baby and escape," Blanca said. "Lagarto helped me to hide for a while. When things cooled down, I had a meeting with Zorro Porro, and he allowed me to go back and live in the governor's mansion."

"You had a meeting with Zorro Porro? And made a deal, just like that?" Miguel asked.

"It's a long and complicated story, Miguel," she said. "He wasn't easy to handle, but I'll do anything for my baby boy!"

"I knew you were weird, but not that you were this fricking crazy," Miguel said.

"I don't think I need to be stigmatized anymore. Everybody, even me, deserves a second chance," she said.

Miguel shook his head.

Blanca stared into space with an inscrutable expression and the hint of a sad smile. I could tell she was very angry. I had adopted quite an indifferent and neutral attitude during their conversation, but I decided to say something, just to say something. Just to break the ice.

"That explanation, of course, lies in your mental state," I said.

They looked at me as if I was crazy and completely ignored my statement.

Blanca explained to us her plan in detail. It was very simple. According to her, she had access to all government files and she gathered as much background information as she could about these two cops. They were ex-FBI agents. They had met at the Border Patrol Shooting Club where they had been members for over ten years. They weren't close friends, but they had spent time together and occasionally had dinner. Both of them were security specialists which in the border patrol, meant they did everything from motel watching, to shaking people down for drugs and money, to polygraph exams. They were not bright but, for half a million dollars, they were more than willing to help us get across the border without any problems, passports and working visas included.

"You'll meet them later tonight to coordinate everything," she said.

Suddenly, Miguel smiled and grabbed Lagarto by the arm. I was scared, terrified. I knew Miguel's killer smile very well.

"Lagarto, tell me the truth. What's the real deal with you? Why, the three million dollars?"

"Miguel; Blanca is the one paying the bribes, not you. She doesn't want you guys to go across the border like two lousy wetbacks and get killed. I have my contacts. I know everybody that's anybody. I know every crooked politician and every corrupted cop in Mexico, and on the other side of the fence. I even know our *presidente* very well. The whole country exists for this man. There is scarcely a single action up in the *pinche* republic not to protect him or to give him pleasure. He has his own house within the presidential palace and one hundred servants who keep him company wherever he goes. I worked for him and Tarantula for over ten years, and I am lucky I could escape alive, since you have a contract with them for life. The only way you can live or get away from his inner circle is in a wooden box. If you have a chance to escape, like I did, he'll send his hunting dogs with their double-barreled shotguns after you, and they'll chase you down forever. I have to hide and watch my back at all times. I know how he is and I still fear the guy. He never forgives or forgets. He never gives up. I remember that Zorro Porro's routine never varied. Like a good and crooked politician that he is, he rose late, precisely at twelve noon every day for a hot shower and then went to the dining room of the presidential palace where there'd damned well better be some *huevos rancheros* and plenty of tequila. A *Ley* 925, of course. While he ate, he greeted each one of his colleagues in crime with a healthy good morning, *macho to macho*, as they drifted in and out of the room. Like a pack of wild hounds, they were sleepy-eyed and anxious to return to their duties where they could continue torturing and murdering innocent people. For all of them, it was a great way to start the day; being able to meet their boss and get his blessing. The longer the motivation speech, the more hyperactive they became. *Zorro Porro* knew how to handle these crazy beasts and how to keep them under control. They would practically lick his feet if they were asked to. Zorro Porro is used to having power. He loves power. He was only fourteen when he organized ten uprisings against the central government and lost them all. At the time he already had ten male children by ten different women. Very early in life, all his sons learned how to resist authority, and the inside out of the drug trafficking business. He has survived two hundred attempts on his life, forty-nine ambushes and twenty bombings. He lived through a dose of rat poisoning in his coffee, enough to kill a horse. *Zorro Porro, hoy por hoy*, is the most feared man in the whole pinche Mexican Republic. And you, two little *chingones*, had the balls to challenge him? Right now, I feel like I'm talking to two dead kids walking. If you guys want to die of old age, the sooner you cross the border the better! Zorro Porro is untouchable. A murderous thirst consumes his heart! Look what happened to the forty-three students in Iguala. Your life in Mexico has no value at all. And you'd better put that inside your little empty heads, *pendejitos!*"

We listened to Lagarto's speech in silence. Discussing Zorro Porro's ways was a debate that none of us needed to be reminded of, especially at that moment. All we wanted to do was to get the hell out of Mexico, and fast!

It was already ten o'clock when we went back to Plaza Constitución to pick up Francisco and follow Blanca to the house she had rented on the outskirts of town for our meeting with the two cops. The place was not the best. It was dark and poorly furnished. We washed, ate meat tacos and drank Mexicali beer, while waiting for the two policemen to arrive. I grabbed my laptop and went into "my oval office", the bathroom, to take a *caca* break and try to finish Barack's letter, not exactly in that order.

Mexicali, October 1, 2014 (12:00AM)

Barack,

> *We are already in Mexicali and I believe we are going to cross the border tomorrow, with the help of two border patrol officers. They are providing us with forged passports and visas. Barack, my friend, between the two of us, it's hard for a kid like me to understand how these two officers, a symbol of law and*

order, who presume to protect your country and uphold the law
of your great nation, are associated with a criminal like Lagarto
and taking half a million dollars in bribes from him. I know how
things work out in Mexico with our corrupted police and the
famous Mexican mordida, but I never expected something like
this could go on inside your police force. I'm shocked. Deep in
my heart, I know this must be a mistake, or maybe part of a
wider, top-secret security plan designed by the FBI, the CIA, you
or your top administration officials to protect all your citizens.
When I finally meet with you, I'm sure you are going to clarify
everything for me. Like I said before, I have pure veneration for
you and the principles your country stands for, and that's what
motivates me to leave everything behind, including my lindo y
querido Mexico, and cross the border to see you. If any of those
who had criticized you so much in the past, only knew, how hard
you work to protect your fellow Americans, and the values and
democratic principles of your great country around the globe.
They would realize that, thanks to you more than three quarters
of the American people are living today on a level of security and
subsistence far above the norm. You are the one who has achieved
the great goal of American manhood: to be successful. I'm sure
the American people would support you and your policies for a
much better world, instead of unjustly attacking you. I'm still
trying to make sense of it myself and that's part of the reason
I'm writing this e-mail, hoping to see you real soon and try to
use my talents to help you. I think that I'm safe in saying that
your talents and mine lay in the same direction. I'm opening up
to you in a way I never have with anyone else. But it wasn't just
your talents that moved me. It's everything you are, your courage
and your passion, the commonsense wisdom with which you view
the world. I think I sensed these things about you when I saw
your face for the first time on the cover of Newsweek. You are a
rare kind, my friend, you have qualities to be a great leader. I'm
a lucky kid for having a chance to come to know you in person.

I hope you are doing well. As I type this e-mail, I feel free already. After I meet with you, I honestly swear that I'll change, that I'll never do anything wrong again in my whole life. I love you Barack for what you are and for what I feel we have already shared. You are my best friend. In a few days I'll see you in Washington and I want you to know that you already became my vision. Juan

P.S. Hopefully, I'll be in Washington in a few days. I know how busy you are. But if you have a chance just write me back and let me know date, time and place we can meet.

Like it happened in Nogales, I'm sitting on the toilet, concentrating and thinking about Barack. I'm trying to make this whole thing a spiritual experience, when, in response to frantic calls from Francisco, I had to stop typing the letter, wipe my ass and open the bathroom door to let him in.

"Is your prostate bothering you again, uh?" I asked.

"Yes!" He shouted, "my *pinche* prostate and your fricking dog!"

"What are you talking about?" I said. "*Perro Negro*, my dog, is dead! Remember?"

"I'm glad he's dead!" he yelled back. "But before getting shot he ate all the bones!"

"That's terrible! I'm sorry he did that to you," I said.

"He didn't do it to me! He did it to the forty-three missing students! That was the only proof I had for the Argentine and the Austrian forensics to help find out what happened to those kids. I feel like your fricking dog ate my son together with his forty-two friends!"

The old man pulled up the zipper of his worn out and dirty blue jeans, and turned away from me. I touched his shoulder with the intention of embracing him, and he farted. A slimy one, a greasy smelly one that sounded like it was half-solid. "This must be The Weapon of Mass Destruction the gringos were looking for in Iraq," I thought.

"Don't touch me, you stupid kid," Francisco yelled.

My heart broke in forty-three pieces, one for each student that disappeared in Iguala. I started crying. Francisco started crying too, and I could tell he hated that. He wiped his eyes, stared at his wet hand and screamed. I was sure everybody in the house heard that scream. It was the worst sound I ever heard. It was pain, pure excruciating pain.

"Francisco, I'm sorry," I said. "I'm sorry."

He stopped screaming with his mouth, but kept screaming with his eyes.

"I have to go and see Anita. I'm going to drop dead if I don't leave," he said.

I stayed in the dark, standing by the bathroom door for a while. Francisco walked away. I stupidly hoped that he would turn around and forgive me if I stayed still a little longer. However I had to get moving and go to the meeting with Blanca, Miguel, Lagarto and the two cops. I knew that I would never see Francisco ever again.

CHAPTER 10
The Border Patrol

When Miguel and I walked into the small living room, Blanca, Lagarto and the two cops were sitting at a round white table, waiting for us. I tried to relax but I couldn't. The tall cop with the crooked mustache called my attention. He sipped a Mountain Dew, tapping the floor with his boot. He looked like he was about to say something important but kept silent. He just looked at us, from head to toe. I wanted to ask him what he thought he was staring at. The other deputy was short, fat and ugly. He had a big pimple on his forehead and was chewing gum. He waved the tall deputy over and whispered something to him, and then he turned around and smiled. I looked at Blanca. She seemed very tired. On the table in front of her, there was a black leather briefcase. Lagarto smoked a cigar and drank from a can of beer, his golden forty-five in his holster. His long fleshy face was red like a ripe *chile poblano*. I noticed how big his chest and biceps were. He reminded me of my uncle and I didn't like it. I went over to Blanca and hugged her.

"You look pretty sad, sis. What's up?" I asked.

She held me for a long, quiet minute.

"I'm very upset about the whole situation. I wish you would listen to me and stay."

"I have to see my friend Barack. He'll fix everything for us, and for Mexico. Soon all of this will be behind us," I said.

She straightened up, taking a tissue, and wiped under her eyes. I sat across from her, next to Miguel, feeling a little hopeful that our plan might get worked out after all. Her tone was gentler now. "Lagarto and these two officers will help you cross the border," she said.

"Nice meeting you kids! My name is Max Whevon and this is Dick Lesser, my partner," the tall cop said. "More than anything, I want to make something very clear to you. I want you to know that we are the law, and we must get along with the traffickers, the crooks, the killers and even decent people, which is not an easy task. Most of the time we make very grave mistakes. We kill innocent peasants, rape their women and get into partnerships with the killers from the cartels. Still, we are not at all like some other border patrol officers who are involved in the trafficking of human beings and selling drugs, which is an unpleasant fact here, and on the other side of the line. We are two real patriots risking our lives to protect our homeland from the evildoers, at all times! Do I make myself clear? Take it away Dick!" He said, gesturing at the other cop to talk.

"Hi, I'm Dick Lesser. I'm at your service, boys! You must not say a word to anyone about anything we discuss here tonight. You are not just Lagarto's friends, like Max just said. We are the law and we don't want to do anything that would hurt you," the fat short cop laughed and then turned serious again. "I'm convinced that you two are good kids and I would kill anybody in order to protect you, as long as I get paid. I know you used violence in the past because you had to, not because you wanted to. You had been threatened and provoked. You had no choice but to act accordingly. I identify with your quest. Do you get my drift?"

He thought for a while, looked at his cell phone and took a call.

"It's late. I have to be getting home, my husband is waiting for me," he said casually.

"Me too, it's been a long day," Max Whevon said. "We can pick you up tomorrow at twelve noon. No need for you to drive kids. We'll take care of the transportation."

Miguel and I looked at each other. We had made a long and difficult journey by *troca* to get to the border. We had already overcome many hurdles and now we had to deal with these two cops. As it was, one of them had a husband instead of a wife. They didn't look too friendly. Each of them had a rifle in his hand and a revolver in his holster, and probably a couple of hand grenades in their pants' pockets. They were armed to the teeth. They were the law. We both knew very well the kind of law they were talking about, the law that shoots first and asks questions later, the kind of law that stares at you through the barrel of a rifle. I could tell they were two killers, men who hunt down human prey for a salary. Looking at them, I could tell they were unfit to associate with human kind, even with two pathetic misfits like us. As long as I live, I shall never forget those cruel, ash-gray faces and those cold, man-hunter's eyes.

When Blanca walked both deputies to the front door, Miguel confronted Lagarto.

"Lagarto *cabrón*! Evidently you got two real meatheads to help us cross the border. I'm sure they are only good for banging on poor people's doors, killing unarmed wetbacks, beating up women and kids, and kicking over trash cans," Miguel said.

"I don't know what you are talking about," Lagarto said, somehow unsteadily and without sufficient conviction. "They are my friends and I trust them!"

It was Lagarto's eyes that betrayed him. They fluttered and dropped, and darted away quickly before returning to look at Miguel, then dropped again, all in an instant but with plenty of proof that we could see right through him. His breath was short, like gasping for air, and his shoulders jerked ever so slightly. We knew he was lying. However, there was no way we would go back to Sinaloa. No matter what, we had to take a chance and cross the *pinche* border. We had to keep going. In Washington, Barack was waiting.

After the two cops left, Blanca locked the door and came back to the living room. She opened the briefcase. She seemed utterly preoccupied, and sat motionless for a long time before touching the dollar bills with the tips of her fingers and closing the case.

"Lagarto, we have three million dollars here, and we still have a lot of things that need to be discussed," she said.

"You already know the story," Lagarto said.

"Yes, I know, but there is more to it than that." She said. "I want to make sure these two cops can be trusted."

"You are beginning to lose me," he said.

"I'm speaking about Juan and Miguel's safety."

"Ah, yes, of course. Max and Dick are one hundred percent reliable. They are two professionals. I work with them all the time."

"Lagarto, we have been friends from the beginning, haven't we?"

"We are the very best of friends, Blanquita."

"If this is how you treat your friends, then lucky for me I'm not one of your enemies."

"That's not funny."

"Of course it's not funny, it's grotesque."

"Why do you ask stupid questions, when you already know the answer?"

"I don't need you anymore, Lagarto."

"Since when?"

"As of, now! I know you are still working for Zorro Porro Neto."

"You are out of your mind!"

"No Lagarto. If anything, there is too much on my mind. But you know I'm right, and you know that better than anyone."

"It might not be so easy to get rid of me, Blanca, and you know you need me. You are stuck with me!"

"No Lagarto, you are wrong. Everything is over for you now."

"You are a *pinche cabrona*! You are a goddamned *hija de la chingada*!"

"And you are a fool. A miserable and *pinche* fool!"

Lagarto jumped up and took a step towards Blanca, pounding his chest in anger.

"Why don't you shoot me now and get it over with?" he screamed. "I'm your friend!"

He then took another step, and another, daring Blanca to kill him. A moment later, in a flash, he was up against her. Without hesitating, she took the golden forty-five out of Lagarto's holster, grabbed him by the collar and yanked him to her feet. Lagarto didn't resist. Like a tame dog, he was on his knees, like begging to be killed. Holding the gun in her right hand, she landed the first blow on Lagarto's face with such brutal force that it knocked him unconscious. I could see Lagarto, out cold on the floor, and Blanca continuing the brutal assault, kicking the guy in the head, as if it was a soccer ball. There was blood all over the floor. I couldn't tell for certain whether he was dead or alive. Suddenly she stopped.

"Miguel, Juancho, take this piece of garbage to the basement. Make sure he's dead. I'm going to wash my hands now."

She turned off the lamp in the corner and left the room, not even bothering to give Lagarto a last look.

I put my ear against his mouth, listening for the sound of Lagarto's breath. He was still breathing. He was alive.

"He's alive!" I said.

"It won't be for long," Miguel said.

My heart felt heavy, like oppressed. My breathing became difficult. I feared I was going to get ill. I couldn't believe what Blanca had just did. What I just witnessed was not a mixed-up dream. I was awake. The reality was that Miguel and I were carrying Lagarto's body to the basement. With a movement of his head, Miguel, urged me to just throw the body down the stairs. When we did, I wanted to laugh at the absurdity of Lagarto's body, still alive, tumbling down the steps. I was beginning to get nervous. Blanca and Miguel, they did not seem to be joking. They could kill people in an explosion of temper and this was quite the contrary to my normal reactions. I had always felt edgy in the presence of anyone who would kill people for pleasure, with the mysterious exception of Miguel.

"This is absurd," I said.

"This is not a matter of putting two and two together. This is about surviving. This is about you and me, *pendejo!*" Miguel yelled at me.

Judging by the way they acted after Lagarto's assassination, it seemed like Blanca and Miguel had talked about killing him way in advance. I felt betrayed and angry with both of them. Being left out of their plan, now could escalate to being left out in the future, and carry other grave implications. Their attitude scared and worried me. I didn't want to live the rest of my life the way I had for the last three years. Blanca came back to the living room, holding a tequila bottle and a couple of glasses. She was feeling good, as if she was finally in control. She saw Miguel and me sitting side by side waiting for her. Her presence somehow changed the room, as if anticipating the way she was feeling. Miguel's face was calm. He turned around to say something but, when he saw Blanca's eyes fixed on him, no words came out of his mouth. All he did was stare at her.

"Is he finally dead?" she asked.

Miguel shook his head, his eyes never leaving hers.

"*Pinche* Lagarto is dead for good! You'd better believe it!" he laughed.

"That sounds great! Do you want me to open the bottle?"

Blanca rose and went over to the table to retrieve the brief case with the money, then she sat beside me. I noticed Miguel watching her with almost wary fascination. Blanca smiled as she reached for my hand. As she did, I could feel that she never realized that she didn't know as much about me as she thought. Both of us had the same look in our eyes that we had had in the past, when we were two innocent kids and would get together over the holidays and joke about some of the mischievous things we did at school. Both of us had changed. It was only just a couple of years after she moved in with Tarantula that I realized that she had altered her behavior, that she was not my best friend anymore.

"I'm not sure you two need a drink just now," I said.

"Why not?" Miguel asked.

"Tomorrow we have to cross the border with Max and Dick, and we need to be alert!"

"You're right, Juan. To be honest with you, I question their intentions. I don't trust them at all," Miguel said.

Blanca leaned back on the sofa and took a deep breath, fingering her tequila glass with her free hand and rotating it in circles.

"In the beginning, I guess I was afraid these two cops weren't for real. I didn't trust them either, but desperation can do strange things to people and, before you know it, I closed the deal with them. I don't know, it just seemed the best way for you guys to go to *El Norte*. I didn't see the point of you two jumping over the wall. It was just too dangerous."

She paused for a long while, choosing her next words carefully.

"You also have to realize that you guys are not the same kids you were back then. Juan, you were only seven years old and you, Miguel, only thirteen when you started your own business. I'm not even sure now if either one of you is ready to go through with something like this. I mean, this is like playing in the major leagues. What will you do if something goes wrong once you are on the other side? In *El Norte* they have different rules, different codes. *El Norte* is not like Mexico."

"I know we can handle it!" Miguel said.

I could tell that Blanca was skeptical about that but she didn't argue with Miguel. Instead, she shrugged.

"Maybe you are right! Who knows? Maybe you two are more than ready to conquer *El Norte*. But I still don't want you to take a chance. I need to make sure you guys are safe!"

"Blanca, I don't really care if we are safe or not anymore! I just want to leave Mexico as fast as possible! I must go to Washington and meet with my friend Barack!" I shouted.

"Juancho, *por Dios!* What did Mexico do to you? Are you a Mexican or a *gringo*?" she asked, angrily.

"Blanca, I love Mexico. Just for a minute, suppose you were I and you were living in Mexico and you were not content to remain in Mexico for the rest of your life. Suppose that, every day, when you go to bed, the names of some fantastic cities in Gringo-Land were tinkling in your head all night long. Naturally, if you go to bed with the names of big cities jingling in your head, you would dream some fantastic dreams. Sometimes you might find yourself dreaming with your eyes wide open, not certain whether you are in bed or standing up on a sunny Sunday morning on the corner of New York's Fifth Avenue and 59th Street. However, most of the time, when you had hoped to close your eyes and give yourself up to the most delicious dream sensations, you find yourself wrestling again and again with the Mexican nightmare!"

"You should see some of the things I have to put up with in this country, but I don't care! There is nothing else I would want to do, or any other place I would like to live. This is a fabulous country! For me, Mexico is like a gift from God. I love it!" Blanca said, proudly, her sweet voice filled with excitement. "It has everything anyone could ever want. I never get tired of it!"

"Nice, very nice sis, I'm sure you are proud to be a Mexican and all that but no matter what, Mexico will never belong to you! Mexico is not yours and it will never be! Mexico belongs to the likes of Zorro Porro Neto and his friends!"

"You are wrong, Juancho. A little part of Mexico belongs to your sister. She's married to the very wealthy. She has power and she knows how to use it," Miguel said.

"I'm sure that to have power is a great feeling, however I still choose freedom. Freedom is closer to happiness. Freedom makes you stronger!" I said.

I looked out the window and saw the mountains battling the clouds. They collided with one another, like blind birds smashing against a wall. The three of us together in that house seemed to me as though we were at a frontier, where two different worlds were fighting for domination. Aside from that, our conversation went smoothly and easily, and lasted for several hours. At all times, I observed the expression on Blanca's face. She still approached each situation and each new experience exactly the same way like when we were kids. Wherever we went, when we were children, Blanca would talk to anybody, the homeless people, even the gays who were talking to invisible people. She saw gay people as magical. She had no use for all the gay bashing, *machismo* and homophobia going on in Mexico. However, at the same time, she could kill somebody like Lagarto and not assume she was a *pinche* murderer.

"Listen," she said. "I know you have heard this before. We know white people are not to be trusted. If you pay them good money, they will kiss your *culo* and do anything you ask them to do. Trust me, Dick and Max will help you cross the border!" she said.

"Right now, we don't have enough time to analyze or discuss this," Miguel said.

Listening to them, I felt helpless and stupid. I felt too Mexican, like a real Mexican, a big tough *macho* man. Way too tough for any kind of emotion. I started rambling and letting it out.

"We Mexicans have lost everything. We lost our land, our heroes, our language, our songs and our dances. We lost each other. We only know how to lose and be lost, it's more than that. We are so distraught by the whole world and we feel so betrayed, that we murder our own people just for kicks, just for the hell of it."

"You're still healthy and alive, Juancho. Please, stop preaching! Tomorrow you are going to *El Norte* to see Barack. You don't need to call me in the middle of the night. As long as you are able to meet Barack, I'll be at your side eternally. You don't need to say goodbye or good luck! Just continue being who you are. I'm sure you will not miss Mexico a bit!" Blanca said.

"Juancho, *pinche cabrón*," Miguel said. "It's costing a lot of money and planning to get across the border to fricking Gringo-Land. Trust me we could die if we don't take care of business. So, *por favor*, keep yourself focused on our task, and stop the whining!"

I wanted to punch Miguel in the face. I wanted to punch him in the nose and make him bleed. I wanted to punch him in the eye and make him blind. I wanted to kick him in the ass. I wanted to kick him in the balls and make him pass out. I was angry. Miguel just looked down at me as if I was a piece of crap, a loser.

"C'mon Juanchito, be cool. I'll protect you," he said, and smiled. He knew me. He knew I was afraid, and he also knew that he would probably have to fight for me. I wanted to hate Blanca and Miguel. I wanted to blame them for my troubles. I wanted to blame them for my dead dog and for what happened to Francisco, but I felt I couldn't blame them, because Miguel and Blanca are like my twin suns around which I orbit. My world without them would explode like an atomic bomb.

"Go to bed, Juancho," Miguel said. "Tomorrow, at twelve noon, Lagarto's friends, those two meatheads, are picking us up to go to Gringo-Land! You know how these pinches *gringos chingones* are. Even if it is just to screw you up, they are always on time! You'd better be wide awake and ready to go, *pendejo!*"

Next day, I got up at ten o'clock in the morning feeling like a ghost. Well, that's not exactly the right description. I mean, if I'd been walking around like a ghost, I might have been scary. So no; no, I wasn't a ghost. That made me a nothing. Zero. Zilch. A *pinche nada*. And I know you are thinking that maybe I'm magnifying my state of mind, and okay, maybe I'm overplaying my case. Maybe I'm exaggerating. So let me tell you a few good things that I discovered that morning. First, I learned that I was shitless about going across the border escorted by two corrupted cops. No matter how old you are, if you have to leave your country forever, it hurts, it hurts the same as if a loved one suddenly died.

Blanca was already up and waiting for us in the kitchen. Her movements were leisurely and deliberate, a little too much so, it seemed to me, to be genuine. Perhaps she was trying to conceal her nervousness; perhaps she was ashamed of revealing her real emotions. She handed Miguel the black leather briefcase with the money.

"Put this thing away please!" she said. "Just let me know what you would like to eat. You can have anything you want!"

The two cops showed up exactly at twelve noon. They were dressed in gray. Somehow, they looked taller and a bit heavier than the night before. With pale skin and tired eyes, they had the appearance of someone who had been drinking all night long. It was an odd sight, these brutes standing next to Blanca. To me she was a real dame, a royal girl. As we approached them, and we got up closer, I didn't like the way they looked. Very early in my life I regarded all policemen as idiots and, I had to admit, I never trusted them. I still remember when I was eight years old and I told my grandfather I wanted to become a cop.

"When you become a cop, you're not a man anymore, you become a coward. Besides, if you are stupid enough to want to do that, I'll kick your sorry ass!" he told me.

After saying that, he spat on the floor and walked away. He was fuming.

"Well, what have we got here?" Max Whevon asked, disrupting my thoughts.

Holding his rifle under his left arm, he patted Miguel, trying to find out if he had any weapons on him. All the while, Dick Lesser had his right hand on his gun.

Miguel let out a loud shriek and he almost tripped while trying to back up.

"Don't touch me! *Pinche maricón*! You son of a bitch!" He shouted.

"C'mon now kid, cool down. What's going on?" Max said. "We are a team now, and we must stick to the rules. You two are not allowed to carry any weapons to the other side."

He knew very well what was going on. Miguel hated him, looking directly at the cop, with his head up, his eyes wide open staring at him, waiting for a chance to attack. I knew that look. It happened all the time and every time he came face to face with a cop.

"Cool it, *muchacho*," Dick Lesser said. "Especially tonight, when the wetbacks from all over Mexico are heading north before the grape and lettuce farming season begins. They often make a detour by Mexicali to jump on a cargo train. There is a fence and a ditch they have to cross to get to the tracks, and that's where we are actually patrolling the area and waiting for them. Since we are wearing a uniform, when they see us they have a chance to turn around, go back to their village, and avoid been shot or arrested. They know damn well we have to do something official to stop them from boarding the train."

"Did you know that foreigners like you, preventing people from boarding a cargo train, is a crime in this country?" Miguel said.

I saw their faces grow pale with anger. It was fun knowing they were afraid of Miguel. I kept him calm and at enough distance to avoid physical confrontation. I would have loved my friend to go toe to toe with these two *pinches policías*.

"Okay guys, stop the nonsense! Let's go!" Dick said laughing. "We have to carry out the OWB."

"What do you mean by OWB?" I asked.

"Operation Wet Back kid! We selected a good damn car for our trip! It's a good and reliable American made vehicle," Max Whevon said.

The car they selected for the trip was a black Buick Le Sabre. Neither of us knew anything about cars. Since we were born we only knew about *trocas*. In my humble opinion, all things considered, if you were going to compare a car with a *troca*, the car has a lot of weak points, especially the Buick which, next to our yellow *troca*, looked too feminine.

"Okay boys, get in! We have to get moving!" Dick said.

We said good-bye to Blanca for the last time. We got into the back seat of the car, rode north on *Calzada Adolfo Lopez Mateos* for about ten blocks and suddenly we drove up a hidden pathway.

We couldn't go very far because a red pick-up truck was already parked, blocking the driveway to the house. On the rear window of the *troca* there was a very big and colorful GOOD NEWS! GOD IS LOVE! bumper sticker.

"Everybody get out!" Max ordered.

We got out. Miguel was carrying the black briefcase, and both of us squeezed past the pickup and the Buick. As we got into a clearing, I saw a huge house and an old man on the front porch sitting on a rocking chair, looking at us, with a can of diet coke in one hand. He had a long boring face and, hanging from his big nose, a pair of huge eyeglasses. He was only wearing a pair of yellow Bermuda shorts. On his chest, like a red tie, a big scar stood out from what seemed to be old and successful heart surgery.

"Hello Henry!" Dick shouted.

"You're early," the old man said.

Dick motioned to his friend and introduced us.

"Miguel and Juan, these are the two Mexican kids I told you about."

Henry smiled, nodded to us, and drank from the can of diet coke. A gold ring, with the Star of David on his index finger, caught my eye.

"I'm sorry you kids had to come all the way up here, but I needed to talk to you in person," Henry said.

He pushed the screen door open with his foot, his back to us.

"Come in, children, come in. *Mi casa es su casa*," he laughed.

I inhaled deeply and looked at Miguel. He was standing next to me, holding the briefcase tight against his chest. I felt a tickle in my fingers as I let the air out of my lungs. Right at that moment, my tickling fingers and the whole me missed my silver revolver.

"Miguel," I said.

"Yes?"

"We are screwed!" I whispered.

Henry turned towards me as if he was surprised I had said that. He smiled, and came over and hugged both of us. He stepped back and looked at me with his hands on both my shoulders. "I know how you feel kid, these are shitty times in Mexico, and you can't trust anybody!" I'm your friend. Better yet, I'm a Jew and, in this instance, I'm also your broker! So lean on me boys, the anger, the resentment, the bitterness, the desire for recrimination against people you believe have wronged you, hardens the heart, deadens the spirit and leads you to self-inflicted wounds."

"Are you a Mexican Jew?" I asked.

"Yes, kid, forever!" he laughed. "I'm eighty per cent Jewish, twenty per cent Mexican and one hundred per cent about money!"

"Henry is the guy who controls both sides of the wall. He knows very powerful people. In the past he's worked for two American presidents. Right now he is the one who decides who is coming or going across the border!" Dick explained.

"And for all that, I only take a humble thirty per cent cut!" Henry said.

"Okay," Miguel said, staring at Henry and the cops. "From now on do we have to deal with you or with these two meatheads?"

"Like I said children, I'm just your broker. You pay me my thirty per cent right now, in cash, and I put everything in motion. When you get to Arizona, you pay the balance, three hundred and fifty thousand dollars, also in cash, to officers Max Whevon and Dick Lesser, as per their agreement with Ms. Blanca Sintierra. As the saying goes in my old country, a deal is a deal, is a deal!" Henry said, as he stood up, took the brief case from Miguel and proceeded to take the money for his services.

"*Gringos chingones!* I feel like I'm being robbed," Miguel shouted.

A voice came out of him but it wasn't his really. He was very angry. I knew that deep inside, he wanted to kill all of them. The way everything was happening around us, things were exceedingly clear to him, the kind of pristine clarity you can only get in the center of something big and reckless and on a path of its own. He realized he was not in charge anymore and that made him feel bad. Instead, I didn't care about the money or who was in control of the situation. My only concern was to cross the line, to go across the border and get to Washington real fast to see my friend Barack.

"Oh well kid, if that makes you feel better," Henry said, handing the briefcase with the money back to Miguel. "You are dealing with Henry the Big K. Why don't you just give it to me?"

I looked at him, like I wanted to believe what he said but I didn't, not completely. His eyes were giving him away anyway, those small black eyes magnified by his big eyeglasses that almost glittered with the dark uneasy light. I had never seen killer eyes like that in a grown up person before.

"I don't want to fight anymore!" I said, taking the briefcase from Miguel. "We'll pay you for your services. We keep our side of the deal and you keep yours."

"Son, you have no choice but to pay the price," Henry said. "If you stay in Mexico, Zorro Porro and his gang are going to kill you, I'm going to kill you. We are all going to kill you. You can't fight us forever!

"I don't want to fight! I just told you, I don't want to fight anymore!" I shouted.

"Don't bullshit me, kid! I know everything about you! You have been fighting since you were born," he answered. "You fought all the drunks and the drug addicts and the cartels all over Guerrero state. You kept your dream alive, and now you want to cross the line to take your dream and go somewhere where other people make their dreams become a reality; I respect you for that!"

It took me a while to count the money. My hands shook as I handed the bills to him.

"Hey boy, calm down, it's just money! Lousy green stuff, no more, no less," he said. "I learned the value of money and power when I was very young, a young boy just like you, growing up in Brooklyn. I remember one Sunday morning when there was a party at the local synagogue. I saw my mother with tears in her eyes, screaming at the top of her lungs. "Henry, your father has resuscitated!" I had never met my father before. He was standing next to my mother like a tame old dog, smiling affectionately at me. He patted me on the head and suddenly started talking: "My boy, you must study and be the best. You are very ugly and, because of your ugliness, nobody will love you. You must attain power! Once you have power, everybody will depend on you. Go to school, Henry, don't waste your time, don't you ever fall in love. You can always buy women and their love included. Henry my son, power is the answer to everything and everybody. You don't have to be good or bad, just be powerful. With power you can induce everybody to love you. They will love you, not for who you are, but for what you represent. After that speech, my old man kept silent and I never saw him again, but I took his advice very seriously. That's the way it was all my life kid. Too bad the old man forgot to tell me that fulfillment and power don't mix. That happiness doesn't have a price tag!"

As he put the money away in his desk drawer, he placed his right arm around my shoulder and gave me a big brown envelope.

"How often do you get to meet a decent and educated gentleman like me?" he said. "Open it!"

While I was opening the envelope and reaching inside, he glanced down at my trembling hands and started laughing. When I saw what was inside, I felt a sudden lightness in my chest and heaviness in my two legs. I wasn't certain if it was a mistake or if it was for real. I was holding in my hands two brand new American passports, one for Miguel and one for me. I was embarrassed about my fear and my doubt. The two passports looked real and smelled like fresh ink. Before I cleared my throat to thank Henry, he stopped laughing and said:

"They are better than the originals. They were made the old fashion way. They were designed in Brooklyn and printed in Israel!"

My first thought was to call Blanca to let her know what was happening. I wanted to tell her that we finally had our passports, that we were out of danger and that we were in a secure location. I sat down. I wanted to be alone. I was not feeling that great, dealing with these kinds of people. I was also thinking about Francisco again, his sad eyes and his crooked mustache, his beat up old *troca* with Pancho Villa painted on the hood, driving off in the middle of the night, to keep searching for his son Faustino. I had been thinking of him on and off since that last night in Mexicali when he farted, a greasy smelly one, a silent killer, and called me stupid. I keep seeing that dark need in his face as he left to go back to Sinaloa to be with his lovely wife Anita. I imagine both of them now, hand in hand, supporting each other to keep searching for their dead son, even if it was just to keep their hope alive. These were the thoughts that were haunting and disturbing me. I was not feeling like the free and fearless kid I used to be anymore when I was growing up in Sinaloa. I was feeling once again like a man, imperfect, insecure, power hungry, dirty and paranoid and, worst of all, feeling as though both of my hands were tied up.

CHAPTER 11

The Crossing

As we walked out of Henry' house and around to the car, Max had already started the engine. He waited for us to get in before getting up to full speed to enter the *Calzada Adolfo Lopez Mateos*. He lit a cigarette and drove north. The day had gotten brighter but I had the slow-blood sick feeling you get with a hangover that probably would last all day. I also had that old dark mood which started to open up inside me. I could smell the stench of death inside the car. The Buick slowed down and stopped by the control booth. One of the *La Migra* agents leaned his face out of the small window, looked at the four of us, came out and slowly proceeded to check our passports. Meanwhile Dick stepped outside the car and walked up to the cop, just to greet him and shake his hand. The cop smiled, vigorously shook his hand and handed the passports back to Dick, saying something about "senior officers knowing everything." When we were passing the gate for official vehicles only, I noticed a group of Border Patrol agents joking and having fun, harassing a bunch of peasants while holding them against a wall. I had never been at the border before. What I knew about it came from stories people told me, stories about poor ignorant people believing a coyote's promise that, at any second, the reality to cross to the other side would be in their grasp, and never noticing how he was betraying them. Still, against all odds, these sorry peasants followed their dream at the cost of starvation, death, humiliation and ridicule. I looked at the wetbacks' faces and noticed the shadows playing on their features, brown skin and black eyes flecked with fear. I felt sorry for those poor souls. Most of them were my country men, my *carnales*. That's when I knew I had to start somewhere and take action. However, in a country the size of Gringo-Land, I also knew I had to be very careful in handling and executing my plan. That's why to get to see Barack as soon as possible was a must!

"Okay boys," Dick yelled from the front seat, interrupting my thoughts. "Welcome to the United States of America!"

I nearly dropped dead when he said that. I even jumped out of my seat, I was so excited, I really was.

"Are you sure?" I asked him.

"Yes kid!" he said laughing out loud. "Do you want to get out of the car and say hello to the people or say something?"

"Finally, we are inside the fence now!" Miguel shouted..

"Hey kid! Don't get sore about it! You are in the land of the free! Enjoy it!" Dick said.

"Who's sore? Miguel said. "Nobody's sore!"

I nodded because Miguel was looking right at me, and I wasn't sure what he was talking about. The thing was, though, I didn't feel much like concentrating. I felt too tired and, at that moment, all I wanted was to get to Chandler and fast!

"All right. Cool down, children. Listen to me for a minute now," Max said. "What you kids are doing now is very special, and it's also a horrible moment in your lives. No matter what now, you can't fail. This whole arrangement is designed for people like you who, at some time in their lives, are looking for something different, looking for a change, something Mexico couldn't supply you with. You gave up the fighting and the hope. Lucky for you, you gave it up before getting maimed or killed. You two are bright enough to know that to die even for a noble cause is stupid. So relax, we have two hundred and thirty nine miles to go to Chandler. Enjoy the moment."

"Children, before I forget," Dick said abruptly, turning around in the front seat. "Remember, when we drop you off in Chandler you pay us our money and then we part ways. And whatever happens in the future, we never met."

"Why exactly in Chandler?" Miguel asked.

"We found it on the internet!" Dick said, grinning.

"So you found this town on the internet?" Miguel was shocked.

"No," Max said. "Dick is just trying to be funny. We chose Chandler because we don't want the sheriff of Maricopa County to see us with two brown Mexican kids like you in our car. He would report us for sure!"

"I thought that everything was already arranged," Miguel said.

"Not with this guy," Max said. "He's full of shit and not to be trusted! Just to give you an idea how fucked up he is, he claims to be Italian and eats spaghetti with ketchup! He's worse than a desert rat! You don't want to get to know José Zapallo kid, I can assure you of that!"

"He's not only a crazy son of a bitch, he's also a CPA, you know, a constant pain in the ass!" Dick laughed.

I looked over to Miguel who was staring out the window.

"Look at the sky," Miguel said. "It doesn't look sacred like it does in Mexico."

I laughed. "I suppose not. Maybe we should run back to the sacred Sinaloa sky, right now!"

"Look, Juancho, an omen!" Miguel said. "Those birds up in the sky, they are Eagles!"

He was right. We had left the border just a few minutes ago and there they were, a flock of huge bald eagles, plodding slowly and steadily to the left of the car window, out and away into the vastness of the Arizona blue sky. How do you count the hours of this kind of travel? How do you define a mixture of loneliness, anger, anxiety and pain? As soon as we left Mexico behind us, it was as if our great country had never existed, as if we had had an amnesia attack. Suddenly, in our little brain, Mexico was a mere dream of a republic amid this all-engulfing ocean of mountains and grassland, home of millions of displaced kids like us, aimlessly roaming the land, eventually fleeing to *El Norte* to escape all the misery and the suffering.

"An omen?" I asked. "Here? In Gringo-Land? I don't think so." Miguel's eyes had this strange faraway look, as if he had been hypnotized.

"Omens are omens, *pinche cabrón*! No matter where you are!"

The Buick driven by Max moved out onto the surprisingly thick weekday traffic. The road in Gringo-Land was now a major highway and Max had to brake for a disabled car that was holding up a line of heavy trucks. He cursed and slammed the steering wheel with both hands. Suddenly he sped nimbly and dangerously past them all, narrowly avoiding side sweeping other cars as he ducked back into his rightful lane at the last possible moment. Dick started laughing.

"Don't laugh at me, you faggot!"

"I'm not laughing at you, Max!" Dick said. "I'm laughing at these two fricking brownies in the back seat talking about eagles and omens!"

"Instead of looking for omens, these little pricks should give thanks that we didn't kill all their ancestors when we really had the chance to wipe them off the map!" Max said.

"You two are kind of *pinches maricas*, aren't you?" Miguel asked, angrily.

I couldn't believe Miguel was so nice to the two cops. Even though he called them *pinches maricas*, he was, well, he was actually polite. I knew very well that, in a different situation, he would shoot them in the head, cut them in little pieces and feed them to his pit-bull for lunch. It was amazing how he controlled his temper. Through the rear view mirror, Max stared hard at Miguel. I noticed that he was dangerously angry.

"Okay, Miguel," Max said. "Where did you learn this fact? Are you gay or something?"

"No amigo. I'm not a *puñal*," Miguel said. "But I'm sure your partner can tell us the truth. After all he's the only one in this group who claims to have a husband!"

"Uh, actually," Dick mumbled, and suddenly went pale. "When I was only a child, I was seduced by a priest. He was tall, black and, at the time, the most powerful man in America. His braids, wrapped in silver rings, were legendary. Of course, he did care about me, and the other twenty or thirty kids he also abused in the same school. He mostly made fun of me, for some reason. I never understood why he called me Tricky Dick as a tribute to an old and famous president. He was a sick man with a sick sense of humor I guess. For me he was like a God. Moreover, even though I was only a child, the night when I stabbed him fifty times in the chest and neck with a kitchen knife, looking at my hands soaked in blood, I knew I was doing something wrong, and I also knew that, from that day on, I'd be one of those guys who, no matter where I'd go or what I'd do, somehow, I would always be surrounded by evil people."

Listening to Dick, I felt sad for a moment. Then I realized that Dick was a cop and maybe he was bullshitting us to make up a conversation, or just playing with our heads.

"Hey, partner! Why do you have to get so personal with these two kids? Are you planning to tell them the story of your life?" Max said.

"Nope," Dick smirked. "I just put myself in their place. To be raped when you are a child, is a horrible experience. It feels like an open wound that never heals. Pedophiles, especially priests, should get the death penalty!"

We stopped under a railroad bridge to get some gas. We got out of the car to stretch our legs and grab some burgers at a greasy joint across the street. As we walked inside there were these four white dudes standing by the counter. We couldn't understand what they were saying, but we understood perfectly when one of them said.

"Hello girls."

We just ignored them. At the same time, we felt threatened because they gave us the finger and kept harassing us, and everything they said after that we knew was offensive, as if they were trying to start a fight. Let me tell you, if you want to start a fight with Miguel Meromero, my *primo*, very bad things can happen and fast.

"*Yo no hablo inglés, gringos maricones!*" Miguel shouted in Spanish.

"Are you a boy or a girl? What are you going to do? Are you going to hit me, or blow me?" a big and despicable fat dude said, clutching his balls with both hands.

Back in Mexico, we were Miguel and Juan, the most feared and respected dynamic duo in the whole Guerrero State, almost like Batman and Robin, but without the sissy customs. Out here in Arizona, nobody knew who we were. For these creeps, we were just two sorry wetbacks invading their country, and they had the idea that an exemplary lesson; like beating us up right then and there, was the order of the day. In the meantime, I'm trying to keep Miguel away from these *pinches cabrones* and also trying to make a quick getaway. However, the four of them, are already lined up and surrounding us, and I'm suddenly lying on the floor face up. My nose is bleeding. Semiconscious, I realize that somebody punched me in the face and that there was no way we could avoid a confrontation.

"*Levántate y patéale los huevos al gordo!* Kick fatso in the balls!" Miguel yelled at me.

As he was saying that, he lifted me up by the arm and grabbed a plastic knife from the counter. As he ordered, I kicked the fat son of a bitch with all my might, right in the balls. He bent forward with his mouth and eyes wide open, desperately grasping for air. Smiling, Miguel jumped forward and, in a flash, stabbed him in both eyes with the plastic knife. The creep fell on his knees, screaming like a wounded beast, his eyeballs hanging from the bleeding eye sockets.

"I can't see! I can't see!" the poor soul cried out, while crawling around the floor, like a dog chasing his tail.

"Good for you, fat pig!" Miguel shouted, while grabbing another plastic knife from the counter and facing the other three *pendejos*. "Who's next?" he asked, smiling pleasantly at them.

The other three dudes were not moving, like in a trance, they were frozen, looking at their friend still bleeding and screaming in pain, soaked in blood, turning and crawling on the floor. When they saw Miguel holding the plastic knife and approaching them, they ran away like sewer rats.

"Run, *putos*, run!" Miguel yelled at them. "From now on, I'm not running anywhere anymore! I'm here to stay! I'm not the chased any longer! Now I'm the chaser!"

"Jesus Christ!" shouted a man coming out of the kitchen. "You crazy *putos*! Was it necessary to poke the poor guy's eyes out just to prove who's more *macho*?"

He had a long black ponytail and a big belly. He looked like a mixture between a Mexican Indian and sumo wrestler. He was wearing an Arizona State t-shirt and white pants. He had oil, grease and food spots all over his clothes. Looking at his face, I could tell that he wanted to get rid of us in a hurry. He walked us through the kitchen to a back door into an alley.

"Go to the left, it's only two hundred meters to the railroad tracks," he said. "Get lost and don't you ever come back here again! If you do, I'll call the police!"

"Thank you, brother!" Miguel said, trying to shake his hand.

"Brother? Brother *de la verga, cabrón*!" he shouted.

"Keep your *puñetera* hand in your pocket! Just get out of here, *pinches pendejos*!" the dude said, while slamming the door in our faces.

We walked out of the alley at a normal pace, went around the railroad tracks and back to the car in exactly six minutes. Max and Dick were already inside with the motor running.

"What did you do?" Max asked.

"Nothing," I said.

"You did nothing?" He insisted.

"We had a lousy burger that tasted like garbage!" Miguel said.

"Next time, try *Mc Moco!*"

We heard the police sirens and saw about seven police cars, with lights flashing, going into the parking lot of the restaurant. Max turned around looking at us with a poker face.

"They reported on our radio that a guy was stabbed in the face in that joint!" He said.

"Are you sure?" Miguel asked. "We didn't see anything!"

Dick didn't turn around, he just sniffed.

"Yeah, man you two smell like a fricking burger. For sure, you guys were in there!"

"Maybe it happened before or after we were in there," Miguel said.

"Oh, that's right," Max said. "You are the kids who can't figure out your ass from your head! Anyway, it's not our problem. In twenty more minutes, we'll be in Chandler and then you're on your own. And frankly, once you kids pay me, I don't give a flying fuck whatever happens to you!"

When we arrived in Chandler, it was already late afternoon. Max parked the Buick on a dead end street. I noticed these two Mexican kids working in a garden, and loading branches and black plastic bags into the back of a *troca*. Inside the car we were handing the cash to the two cops and waiting for them to count it. I saw that the two Mexicans were looking at us. After Max and Dick finished counting the money, we got our guns back.

"Thanks for the ride," I said.

"You bet."

They looked at us; they laughed and buzzed away. We walked up to the corner. We could still see the red taillights of the Buick fading out in the distance until it disappeared out of sight. What we didn't know was that, at that same exact moment, they were calling sheriff José Zapallo and telling him about these two armed and dangerous Mexicans kids, walking around Maricopa County carrying this black leather brief case loaded with money.

I reached for my cell phone in my back pocket and called Blanca. I didn't even let her say hello.

"We are in Chandler already," I said.

"Where in Chandler?" she asked.

"They left us, on a dead end street."

"*Policias cabrones, hijos de la chingada!*" she said. "Get out of there as fast as you can, and go to Chandler Boulevard and Arizona Avenue to the Center for the Arts. My friend Sammy Kabronisky is waiting for you guys by the front door. You can trust him one hundred per cent! Juan, by the way, it's very important to keep the calls short, no more than fifteen seconds! Ok?"

"Okay," I said and hung up.

I turned around to call the two Mexicans, but Miguel had already beat me to it.

"Hey, *carnales!*" he yelled at them. "Do you want to make two hundred dollars?"

Sammy Kabronisky was waiting for us at the front door of the Arts Center, seated at the wheel of a white BMW convertible. He seemed very composed and sophisticated, as we were getting off the dilapidated *troca* full of garbage bags and three branches. We said goodbye, hugging the driver and his companion, as if they were family. I saw the expression of shock on Sammy's face, and I almost cracked up.

"I didn't expect you so soon," Sammy mumbled. "Get in."

Sammy had grown up in the nearby town of Gilbert and he knew every enforcement officer, every sheriff, every prosecuting attorney, and all the political leaders in Arizona. Nevertheless, suddenly he didn't seem to know what to do with Miguel and me, these two "magnificent" brown Mexican kids now in his custody.

"I have two backpacks in the trunk. You should get rid of that briefcase and put the money in there," Sammy said. "By the way, my fee is two hundred thousand dollars."

"Can you clarify something for me?" Miguel asked. "Are we in the land of the free, or where we actually are, is in the *pinche* land of the fee? Every move we make here in Gringo Land, there's a *pinche* fee, and we have to pay for it!"

"That's not funny," Sammy said.

"It's not supposed to be funny," Miguel said. "I'm just telling it like it is!"

A thought came to my mind.

"How come Sammy knows that we are carrying money in that black leather briefcase? Is he a visionary, a psychic or another *pinche* traitor?"

CHAPTER 12
Phoenix

The drive from Chandler to Phoenix in Sammy's BMW was a breeze. He drove fast. There was practically no traffic on the highway. When we arrived at his house and settled down for the night, right there he demanded the full payment of his fee in advance. Looking out the window facing Camel Back Mountain, there was that feeling that trouble was coming. There was tension in the air. It felt as if Miguel and I had been taken for a blind ride. It was as if negative and positive ions clashed before a storm. What we didn't know yet, was that sheriff Zapallo was after us, and our money.

Next morning when we got up, Sammy was already dressed and ready to go out.

"I need to see your passports," he demanded.

"No way," Miguel said. "Not for free! We paid very good money for them!"

"All right, wise guy," Sammy said. "Stop fucking around and you'd better listen to me!"

He walked over into the living room and sat on a folding chair. He pretended to be angry, trying to make Miguel shut up, but Miguel stood his ground and looked up at him with humorous defiance, ready for a confrontation. That's the way my *puto primo* was, a kid with lots of guts, el *meronísimo pinche cabrón* with two big *cojones*, two *cojones* bigger than the whole Mexican Republic.

Sometimes, like in this case, he could react like a crybaby and be a real pain in the fricking *culo.*

"*Primo,*" I said, trying to calm him down. "What's wrong with you?"

"I'm tired of these gringos *cabrones* taking our money!" he shouted. "From the moment we stepped on this side of the wall, all we've been doing is paying bribes! I feel like we've been taken hostage!"

"Okay kids," Sammy said calmly, turning his back on Miguel. "You are dealing with the Government of the United States of America, the most powerful country in the world. You'd better realize, sooner rather than later, that you are not in Mexico anymore. As of now, it's a complete different ball game. This is like playing in the Major Leagues. You are dealing with very powerful and dangerous people. Don't be so arrogant. You'd better change your attitude right here and now, before it's too late, if you really want to come out of this situation alive! For starters, like I told you before, I need your passports, to get you an ID."

"How come we didn't get those documents directly from Henry?" Miguel asked, angrily.

"Henry didn't give them to you because he's too cheap. Greediness is in his blood!"

For me, it was somehow suspicious that white people were interested in seeing some brown Mexicans kids coming into their country, just like that. For them, I think it was sort of like watching Mexican hunting, as if it was some sort of a sport, a video game or some kind of entertainment. I felt exposed and primitive, like a wild animal.

"Weird," I said. "Henry seemed like such a nice person."

"Don't get me wrong," Sammy said. "Henry is a good guy and very well educated. He worked as an adviser to two presidents. In those days he was the only person negotiating war, peace and every coup d'état that was going on around the world. He was the main man. A very powerful son of a bitch and a big shot!"

"Then how come a big shot like him ended up taking bribes at the Mexican border?" Miguel asked.

"Every man is a mystery. Each one of us is a mystery, and Henry is no exception. He is an extremely weird man. You never know what he's up to!"

"Maybe he's still working for the government and all this bribe thing is just a cover up. According to my grandpa, drugs, human organs, weapons and oil are the most profitable businesses in the whole world. They go hand in hand. To manage all that traffic and all that money, the Mexican border, strategically speaking, is the right place to be," Miguel said.

"Where did your grandpa learn all those facts?" Sammy asked.

"I don't know," Miguel said, giggling. "Not in school, right? We all know there are so many amazing things to learn in school!" *Juazzzzzz!*

"Okay kids." Sammy said. "I have to go now. Let me have those passports. Remember not to go out or answer the door. No telephone calls, please! I'll be back in six hours!"

Sammy's place was a huge red stucco house built on the side of a mountain range. It had large windows with white shutters. Big cactus plants and big boulders surrounded it. In addition, let me tell you; there are plenty of rocks and cacti in Phoenix. Everything seemed to be big in Arizona, houses, cars, people, cacti, rocks and mountains. Even the bribes we had to pay every time we met someone were way too high for my taste. Inside there were high wooden ceilings and Persian carpets. In the living room, there was an enormous bar with a big mirror practically covering the whole back wall, and a white grand piano, an extremely large white leather sofa, like two white elephants standing in the middle of the room, surrounded by pastel-colored paintings all over the walls, which reflected the bad taste of the owner. Following Sammy's advice, we stayed inside the house, away from the windows. I noticed that Miguel was getting angrier by the minute.

"Things are going to get better soon, *primo*," I said, just to calm him down.

"I don't know about that. Here, inside the fence in Gringo-Land, people are too complicated. To top it off, we are not in control of the situation anymore! We don't even have a *pinche* idea when are we going to get to see your good friend Barack!"

"I know, I know, but I think we have to outsmart them, we have to integrate. We have to blend in. We have to act white."

"Screw that!" he shouted. "As far as I'm concerned, I'm a brown Mexican and that's what I am! Not even God working overtime, together with the *Virgen de Guadalupe* can change that! The white people can kiss my brown stinky ass!"

"Besides that you stink, they'd never do that! I'm telling you, *primo*, you have to act white to make your life better and be successful in Gringo-Land."

"The people back home, they don't call me Miguel Meromero for nothing!" he yelled.

"Miguel," I said, "I don't understand what you're trying to get at!"

"Well, in the early days when we started our business in Sinaloa, our community, Father Bernardino, Perlita, Blanca and all our friends were our only protection against predators. We survived because we trusted one another."

"So?"

"Here you can't trust anybody! Brown people, like you and me, get banished."

"You mean brown people like you!" I said, laughing out loud. *Juazzzzzzz!*

"And you!" he answered, cracking up. *Juazzzzzzz!*

"All right then," I said, "so, you and me we are a team of two: The Brownies Dream Team!"

Suddenly I had the urge to hug Miguel but unfortunately, at the same time, he had the sudden urge to stop me from hugging him.

"Don't get emotional, Juancho! Don't be a girl now! Don't act like a *pinche vieja, cabrón*," and taking a step backward, he turned down my embrace.

"Even brown Mexican kids, like the two of us, are afraid to show their emotions," I thought.

While waiting for Sammy to come back to the house, I decided to bend the rules a little and call Blanca anyway. I went into the bathroom and I dialed her number. I wanted to ask her a few important questions. I knew I only had fifteen seconds, tops, for the call. Her phone only rang twice.

"*Mande!*" She screamed, at the other end of the line.

"Sammy is charging us two hundred thousand dollars for two lousy ID's!" I said.

"He is also driving you all the way to Washington," she answered.

"That's it?" I asked.

"He's arranging your meeting with Barack at the Kennedy Center, and that's also included," she said abruptly.

"He didn't say anything about that."

"Come on, Juanchito, stop worrying. We are trying to do something major over there. You're in very good hands. Trust me," she said. "How's Miguel doing?"

"Anxious," I said.

"I know. He can't be inactive for too long. He's a warrior!"

After saying that, she just hung up. I looked at my cell phone. Our conversation had lasted exactly fifteen seconds.

"She's not fooling around, this is serious shit! This is serious business. Blanca certainly thinks it is," I thought.

I suddenly understood that, from that moment on, every second of our new life in Gringo-Land should be taken very seriously as well. At the same time, because of that, I had this sinking feeling that I was becoming less and less Mexican by the hour. I didn't like that! I didn't like that *pinche* feeling at all!

When Sammy came back to the house, it was already dark outside. His appearance when he walked through the door was worrisome and really scared me. He looked physically and emotionally exhausted. There was also some sort of nervousness in the way he behaved. Like a reaction to post traumatic stress of some kind, like a frightened soldier returning from battle. When he finally spoke, his tone was light but I could perceive the anxiety underlying it.

"I'm sorry I'm so late. I had a difficult day."

"What happened to you?" Miguel asked. "You look like you just saw a ghost!"

"A Spanish girl was killed by the police right in front of me."

"Why? What happened?" I asked.

"She was selling oranges and lemons on the street, without a license."

"What?" Miguel shouted. "She got shot, just because of that?"

"There was a scuffle and she threw lemons at the police," Sammy said. "I guess the officers felt threatened."

"How old was she?" I asked.

"About thirteen years old. No more than that!"

"There are some sick bastards in uniform out there!" Miguel said.

"It's more complicated than that Miguel," Sammy said. "You need to go through each case, one by one, and in detail. It takes time to reach the right verdict."

"I know, *pinche* Sammy! I know very well how complicated it is to stand with your hands up facing a racist cop with a license to kill, pointing a gun directly at your face, not knowing what his verdict is going to be! You don't know if he's going to let you live or execute you like a dog! I know the feeling! I've been through that, and I'm so lucky I'm still alive!"

"Maybe it was her mistake, I said. "She struck them with lemons instead of oranges!"

They both looked at me as if I was crazy. Sammy raised his brows meaningfully.

"Juan, you are so intelligent! It was so clever of you to figure all that out."

Miguel was fuming. "How could you say such a stupid thing like that? You're a moron!"

"I'm sure you guys heard this before. We all know how much white people like chocolate, ice cream, pancakes, sweets and diabetes. Like the popular saying goes: lemons are sour; oranges are sweet. It's up to you to figure it out! Now let's talk about our trip to Washington, after all, that's what we're here for! Right?"

Nothing I was saying about the girl killed by the police made any sense. It was offensive and stupid. I was at risk of having my ass kicked by both of them. However, the idea was to distract them and make them stop arguing, which I did.

I could see that Miguel was still irritated. As he got older, his good humor was fading, almost as fast as his appetite. We were supposed to be on our way to Washington. Instead, we were still in Phoenix, Arizona, locked up in a big house way up by the side of a mountain.

"I'm worried," Miguel said, pouring himself coffee. "I feel we are wasting our time here."

"Pack your bags," Sammy said. "We are going to New York very early in the morning."

"New York? Are you sure?" I asked.

"Yes! I have a meeting at The Human Rights Watch Headquarters on Fifth Avenue."

Sammy seemed quite sure. He was scared but he was unlikely to make an error about something as important as my meeting with Barack in Washington. Besides, logic dictated that Blanca's plan was perfect. Unlike human emotions, logic could be relied upon. Logic is never wrong. Blanca planned the whole thing. She outsmarted Zorro Porro Neto and his gang, not Miguel and me. Blanca was brilliant, a virtuoso in her craft, a craft she learned with Tarantula, the Governor. In terms of pulling off the plan of our escape, she had taught me everything she knew. We wouldn't even be in Phoenix if it weren't for Blanca. How strange life could be sometimes, a humble little girl from Sinaloa, beating the big shots in power, on their own turf and at their own game.

"Today, José Zapallo's deputies followed me all the way up to the house. By now, I'm sure he's trying to get a warrant to search the place," Sammy said.

"Can he do that?"

"Of course, he can! He's a con artist, stupid and quite crooked. He's a psycho too!"

"He might be a stupid cop, but I'm sure he knows on which side his bread is buttered. I'm sure we can bribe him! The Mexican *mordida,* in the land of the fee," Miguel said.

"Not with this prick! He's a sadist and he's desperate for money. He'd kill everybody and take it all! Not that your two hundred thousand dollars wouldn't come in handy but, more than anything, I love to be alive and I plan to keep it that way!" he added with a grin.

José Zapallo was not a bright man. After all, he was just a sheriff. He knew all the politicians in the State of Arizona really well. He had classified information about their public and private life. He had wisely blackmailed some of them and, twisting some arms, he also got generous contributions from others. He diverted considerable resources to catching illegal immigrants, and other vicious thieves and criminals, well, only some of them. He knew that the majority of those thieves and criminals in the state were among his friends and contributors. During his long and prestigious career as sheriff, his obsession was to stop those impertinent young "brownies" crossing the border from Mexico from invading and taking over the country.

"For heaven's sake! This is obscene! They are taking over our homeland! We don't have much time! We must stop them now, before it's too late! We need stronger laws! At this moment, I'm talking about the defense of our country, our institutions, our way of life, things that we take for granted but must be defended, whether Mexicans, Muslims or any other group of people who invade us. They are all running away from something ugly, and they denigrate anything and everything they touch. Anyone crossing our borders illegally should get the death penalty!" he screamed to his deputies.

His four deputies, three mature men and a much younger dude, all of them bored stiff, looked uneasily at him. A few hours before, José Zapallo had planned with them to kill and rob the two Mexican kids, leaving them dead by the roadside. He knew their names and their physical description. He got all the information from two highly decorated Border Patrol Agents, Max Whevon and Dick Lesser. According to these two cops, they tried to stop the kids before crossing the border but the two young Mexicans escaped. These two honorable guardians of the peace had classified information. The two kids were already in Maricopa County carrying drugs and money. They were heavily armed and dangerous.

"How cynical can you get?" the youngest deputy thought. Then he spoke.

"What on earth are you saying boss? If by any chance we catch them alive, we just shoot them in the head! For those wetbacks, we are the death penalty, aren't we?"

Zapallo let out an angry squeal. "You don't shoot nobody without my approval, you imbecile!"

"That's two negatives boss!" the young deputy chuckled softly.

"Are you all right, deputy? You want me to kick your ass now or later?"

The three other deputies started to laugh. Zapallo nodded.

"Sorry guys for treating you like this," Zapallo said. "I just learned at the last minute that Sammy Kabronisky had changed his plan. They plan to leave for New York City tonight. As a con artist, he is quite brilliant. Interpol has been after him for over five years. I want you to get ready for tonight. We'll meet by Camel Back Mountain at eight. Everybody must be on time. Don't forget to bring your rifles. It's hunting season! After we finish with them, we can go out to dinner. Spaghetti with ketchup, it's my treat!"

We left the house at three in the morning. We exited through the back door of the garage and walked by the side of the mountain. It was a long walk, well over three miles. The mountains around us began to take on a frightening aspect. The magic I felt the first day when I arrived had disappeared. Behind every boulder in every ditch, there could be a potential danger. It began to rain.

"It never rains in Phoenix at this time of the year," Sammy said. "Watch out for the snakes!"

"Snakes in uniform? Or the ones that rattle?" *Juazzzzz!* Miguel laughed.

It poured. Every clearance, every ditch, was now an enormous puddle. Everything had changed around us. I began to feel that we were heading into an ambush. A continuous sheet of rain fell slantwise on our faces, slowing us down. The three of us kept walking. My silver revolver, stuck in my pocket, was getting wet. We kept silent. After half an hour, the house was already out of sight. Sammy's plan was very simple and to the point. Stay away from sheriff Zapallo and his deputies, who for sure were looking for us all over the area. Get to a back road by foot, where he had previously parked a rented car, and drive all the way to New York City.

"We are almost there boys. Let's walk all the way down to the road now," he said.

We started our descent. Around us, the towering mountain ranges, shining under the falling rain, looked completely red, like strawberry ice cream without the cone. Slowly, gradually, we walked down the path. I can't describe the emotion that such scenery produced in me. Me, Juan Sintierra, the brand new Mexican pioneer on foot, surrounded by the huge mountains of Arizona, trying to claim what belongs to my people. Holding my silver revolver reverently in my hand, I pointed to the sky and saluted the Creator.

"Maybe God would be kind enough to get me to Washington, and put Barack within my reach so that I can shake his hand and salute him in person," I thought.

"Stop! And get down!" Sammy whispered.

We heard heavy, uneven footsteps coming from below, male voices, and saw flashlights illuminating different stretches of the hillside. I looked down, gulped and grabbed my silver revolver with my right hand. Miguel laid down in the mud, belly first, with his MR-16 aiming at the lights. To say that I felt intimidated and scared would be an understatement. I took cover behind a boulder next to Sammy. With his index finger, he gestured to me not to shoot and to keep silent. The voices kept getting closer.

"God works in mysterious ways," I thought. "In this instance, it seems he has inherited some land in Arizona and wants us out of the way!"

The sound of the first shot roared like thunder bouncing off the sides of the mountains. There was a brief moment of silence and then the shooting started again. A barrage of bullets ricocheted all around us. The pieces of rock kicked a few feet in front of Miguel. He moved backwards, deeper into the trench, and fired back. Sammy and me jumped about four feet up in the air and hid behind a bigger boulder. The rain was falling harder now, affecting our vision. Way down, I saw an obscure figure, wearing a white cowboy hat, climbing up the hill. I grabbed my revolver and, as usual, my finger started tickling. I aimed low and pulled the trigger, one, two, three, four shots. My hand was not shaking this time. Somebody cursed and I saw a dark figure, with the white hat still on, falling sideways, splashing into a ditch head first. Now the white hat was floating next to him. He was not moving anymore.

"One down, *carna*l! Good eye, Juan! Good eye!" Miguel shouted.

Alert and attentive to any sound coming from down below, we didn't move from our position. The rain didn't let up. Soaking wet, we waited for them to make the next move. Even if we couldn't see them or hear them, we knew they were hiding somewhere by the hillside, ready to take our money and kill us all. We waited for more than an hour. A strong wind started to blow. The wind and the falling rain dancing on the rocks, were the only noise in the whole fricking mountain. Nothing was moving.

"We have to split up and get down," Sammy whispered. "Go and tell Miguel to cover us. I go first and then you follow me. I go left and you go right, in three hundred seconds. Get it?"

"Three hundred seconds, I got it!"

I had to crawl over the right side of a boulder to reach Miguel's position. He was lying on the ground, face up, looking at the sky. His face was all wet and full of mud, his arms holding the rifle folded across his chest. He just laid there in the trench, looking at me with his eyes wide open. For a minute, looking at his face, I thought again of my friend Barack.

"What's going on?" he asked.

"We are going down," I whispered. "We need you to cover us. Sammy goes left, I go right."

Who's going first?"

"Sammy. In exactly fifty seconds," I said.

There were about six hundred yards of solid rocks and bushes to go before reaching the car. It was necessary that we had an absolute union of ideas and signs on our part, in order to kill the cops and escape to New York City. It was not about solving the theorem of Pythagoras or rocket science. It was all about being smart, knowing how to count to three and making the right decision to avoid the bullets. In addition, be almost invisible and extremely shrewd when pulling the trigger. That was exactly what we did.

"Go now!" Miguel said, and started shooting.

I ran a few yards down the mountain and shots rang out all around me. I ducked and waited for about ten seconds. I stood up and I felt invulnerable. I felt superior, like possessed with the power to do anything. I started running downhill like a mad man. I looked to my left and, in the distance, I saw Sammy sprinting ahead of me. The sound of gunfire rang out again all over the place. Hundreds of bullets from automatic weapons were cascading all over the mountain. With few places to hide, we kept running as fast as we could. Suddenly an explosion knocked me to the ground. My ears were ringing. My body partially covered, by mud and branches. Everything was blurry.

"They are using hand grenades," I thought.

Despite my fear, despite an almost certain death, I was wide-awake and I knew I was ok. I reached for my silver revolver and I stayed on the ground face up, with my eyes closed, playing dead. All was quiet for a while, and then I heard the footsteps and the voices.

"We got one!" they said.

"Look! It's just a fucking kid!"

"I know! These brownies, son of the bitches, are the worst!"

"Let's finish him off!"

Lying on the ground, I opened my eyes. The first thing I saw was two alligator cowboy boots full of red mud almost on top of me. I looked up and raising my revolver, I aimed at the guy's waist, zeroing in on his balls and fired. He screamed and, dropping his gun, fell backwards, holding his bloody nuts with both hands. All of a sudden, out of nowhere, I heard a shot and I felt a sting in the left side of my neck. I turned around and saw the other deputy standing right in front of me, pointing his rifle directly at my face. He was shaking all over and he laughed. He laughed louder and louder. For the first time in a long time, I was conscious that I was facing death. It felt strange to be in a situation like that. I was extremely relaxed. I was calmer and more focused than ever before. The wound on my neck was bleeding profusely. Feeling the weight of my head multiply one hundred times, the blood pouring down all over my chest and shoulders, I wanted to react, but I couldn't move. So I smiled, a big smile, and looked up at the sky, searching for God, and kept on smiling. I could sense that the deputy was getting upset, ready to shoot and blow my head off. From the look in his eyes, I knew I was a goner.

"Keep smiling; asshole! You are dead!" he shouted. "Say *adios*, you fucking Mexican!"

Miguel, my guardian angel, standing at the end of the footpath with his M-16 aiming at the cop's head, was smiling back at me. The crack of the shot sounded like music to my ears. The head of the deputy exploded like a ripe watermelon, splashing blood and pieces of scalp and brain matter all over the rocks. Suddenly, out of the blue, like a fourth of July celebration, a hail of bullets poured from down below.

"Take cover, Juancho! Don't move! Stay put! Just wait for me!" Miguel yelled.

When the shooting stopped, Miguel crawled down the footpath, gave me some water, cleaned up my wound and put a handkerchief around my neck to stop the bleeding.

"You were very lucky, *pendejo*," he said. "It's just a scratch. That bullet missed you by less than an inch! A little more to the right and you'd be dead!"

We didn't know where Sammy was, if he was dead or alive. All was quiet again. Miguel searched the dead deputy's pockets and found two hand grenades. We looked down the hill, and didn't see anybody or any activity going on. There were no more than three hundred yards to go. We could see two patrol cars, with the lights still blinking, parked by the side of the road. The rain kept falling on our heads, big heavy drops. It poured harder and harder, it wouldn't stop.

"I want you to do just as I tell you," Miguel said, handing me a hand grenade. "Ok Juan, I guess there is one for you, and one for me."

Hesitantly, I took the grenade and put it in my side pocket.

"I go down first and then you follow me."

"And then?" I asked.

"Then, Juanchito, we run for it!"

Miguel spun around and raced downhill. I was close behind.

"I would indeed be lucky if I made it through a second time," I thought.

In no time, we sped across the wet footpath toward the side road and clambered down to the wet pavement. For an instant, I realized that nobody was shooting at us. Suddenly a beam of light coming from the patrol car lit the whole area. Standing behind the driver's door of the car, was this huge fat old dude, wearing a big white cowboy hat on his huge fathead, pointing a gun at Sammy's temple. We stopped. Motionless, looking at the fat cop, we felt defeated. On his shirt pocket, under the sheriff's badge, on a black plastic tag with white letters, we could read the fat pig's name: José Zapallo.

"Hello kids!" he chuckled. "I see that you like to play cops and robbers! As the saying goes, your money or your life!"

"He wants the money!" Sammy yelled. "That's all he wants!"

"Damn lucky for you if I don't kill you right now!" Zapallo said. He looked tired. "Just give me the two million dollars. I go my way and you go your's. No hard feelings, *muchachos*!"

I stared at Zapallo's puffy face, searching for some kind of a sign or facial expression in order to trust him. I saw none. He looked weird to me. Even at that distance, I could smell the whiskey on his breath and, when he talked, I could tell that he was drunk. As he talked, he kept caressing Sammy's temple with the barrel of his gun. Like all corrupted cops, he was a coward. Weak and with no character, he just acted tough.

"In case you're thinking of playing some kind of a trick on me, I thought you might like to know what happened to your friend Francisco a few weeks ago in the Mexican village of Iguala, where they also killed his son Faustino. My friend Zorro Porro set an example, so next time somebody thinks about helping a friend to cross the border, they will think twice."

"What happened to Francisco?" Miguel asked.

"He had his head blown off!"

"What about Anita, his wife?"

"They killed her too!"

I put my right hand in my pocket and stroked the grenade. I knew what could happen to Zapallo if I detonated the grenade in his fat ass. I could blow him to smithereens, his arms and legs everywhere, even his ears, his nose and his fathead blown to tiny pieces.

"Keep your hands where I can see them at all times, ok?" he demanded.

The two of us stood there facing Zapallo, not knowing what to do. I looked at Miguel and he looked back at me. As usual, at that moment more than ever, in order to kill the cop, it was necessary to have an absolute union of ideas and signs on our part. To kill or not be killed. Without saying a word, we knew how to proceed. At least I thought so.

"How do you want to do this, sheriff?" Miguel asked.

"You guys hand me the backpacks with the money and I let your friend go."

Both of us stepped forward holding the backpacks in our right hand.

"No!" He shouted. "One by one, first Miguel and then you, little prick!"

"Why do you have to call me a prick? You *pinche gordo!*" I yelled.

"Because that's what you are! Just a little Mexican prick!" he laughed.

Miguel walked forward and gave Zapallo his backpack with the money. I was furious. This fat son of a bitch, this *gordo hijo de la chingada*, was calling me a Mexican prick! Holding the backpack with my left hand, I walked toward him. When I got closer, acting quickly, in a flash, I changed the backpack from my left hand to my right and pulling the pin from the grenade, I put it in the side pocket of the backpack. From then on, I knew I only had ten seconds before the grenade exploded. "If I'm a little prick, then you are *El Grande Pricko,*" I said, just to catch him off guard.

I pressed the backpack against his chest pushing him back.

"Tackle him!" I yelled to Sammy.

Zapallo tried to hold Sammy by the neck and shoot him in the head, but he was too heavy, too fricking slow and too drunk to turn around on time. I heard the boom of Zapallo's gun close to my right ear. Sammy jumped from behind, elbowing him in the back of the neck. Zapallo fell forward and, being so tall, he fell real hard hitting the ground face first. We piled up on his back. His stomach was pressing the backpack against the wet soil. He sensed what our intention was and tried desperately to get up with all his might, to no avail. The explosion pierced Zapallo's body, cutting him almost in half, shattering our eardrums, knocking Sammy against the patrol car, and lifting Miguel and me almost twenty feet in the air. When we landed on our ass, all muddy and dazed, miraculously unscathed, there was bloody money scattered all over the place. All twisted like a big broken doll, Zapallo's body was half submerged in a crater full of bloody mud. His eyes were wide open. He had a certain expression; that astonished look we all have *cinco segundos antes de la muerte!* Those last five dramatic seconds, before we die!

"Spaghetti and ketchup!" Miguel shouted, pointing at Zapallo's open belly and the splattered bloody guts.

We started to laugh. *Juazzzz!* And laughed out loud. *Juazzzzz!* Jumping, and bouncing up and down. Our ears were still ringing from the explosion. Dancing like mad under the rain; yearning to wash away the blood, the dirt and all the bad memories from our body and soul. *Juazzzzz!* It was our own private celebration; celebrating life.

CHAPTER 13
To New York

At last, the waiting was over. We were in the car on our way to New York City. There was neither joy nor sorrow left in me, just a feeling of loneliness. I didn't feel like celebrating anymore. After what we had been through, I couldn't believe I was still alive and breathing.

"From now on, I need to replace fantasy with reality, and it's about time," I thought.

"Okay kids, here we go!" Sammy shouted. "Fasten your seatbelts! In forty-five hours, more or less, we'll be in New York City! The capital of the fricking world!"

"I have a friend that lives in New York," Miguel said.

"Where does he live in New York?"

"He lives in Washington Heights. On Broadway and 178th Street."

"That's the ghetto!"

"What's a ghetto?" I asked.

"The place where poor people live," Sammy said.

"That's offensive."

"Anyway, my buddy likes it there very much! His girlfriend is from *Santo Domingo.*"

"Everybody in that neighborhood is from The Dominican Republic. The people of the ghettos are mostly blacks or foreigners!" Sammy chuckled.

"How can that be?" I asked. "You just said that New York is the Capital of the World!"

"That's what excites me most about New York!" Sammy said, ignoring my comment. "It gives me a sense of life, when I'm among people from all over the world. In New York, the people shape the city, not the other way around."

"In Mexico, everything is different. Everywhere you go it's mysterious," Miguel said, reflecting a mixture of sadness and anger in his voice. "We don't have ghettos; we have poor barrios and poorer villages where people are living on a level of subsistence far below the people of your ghettos. Let me tell you, they are very poor and they really suffer. However, they suffer with dignity. For them to be poor is not so bad, on the other hand, to be a miserable being is just out of the question."

"I'm not surprised," Sammy said. "For those poor souls, Mexico is an inspiration, I guess!"

"And crossing the border; their motivation!" I said.

"Screw you, Juancho!" Miguel yelled. "It seems to me you've forgotten that you are a *Mexicano* too! *Pinche pendejo!*"

"*Nunca, primo,* never! Of course not! I'd never forget who I am!" I laughed. "I'm one hundred percent Mexican, and more clever than all of them put together!"

"You are very clever for a Mexican," Sammy said. "I've noticed that."

"Not just clever for a Mexican, *amigo.* I'm clever; period! *Comprende?*"

After saying that, I kept silent. I didn't feel like talking anymore. I closed my eyes. I was very tired. Sammy and Miguel in the front seat, kept rambling on about the New Yorkers, the ghettos and the Mexicans. Before falling asleep, I caught the weirdest fragments of their conversation. I was very much surprised because what both of them were saying was so unrelated to the nature of the *pinche* subject. I wanted to tell them that it takes somebody like Juan Sintierra to make a breach in the wall. A kid like me is primarily one who has faith in himself, who is not part of the herd, someone who doesn't respond to the normal stimulus like the common people. I'm not a drudge or a parasite. Like an artist, I live to express myself and in doing so I enrich the world. Besides, I'm absolutely single minded in my dedication to a task. From the beginning of my journey in Mexico, my top priority was to see Barack. He was my top priority. It meant that I believed in Barack's desire to help me without thoughts of return. I also believed that he will value me as a person. Even knowing that nobody else but Miguel and Blanca wanted to help me with my project, deep in my heart I knew that Barack would be willing to help me too, for the pure love of it.

I opened my eyes. We had slowed down and exited the highway. I looked out the car window to get a glimpse of the town. It looked bleak and uninviting to me.

"We are already in Santa Fe," Sammy said.

"Where is that?"

"In New Mexico."

"We are in Mexico?" I asked. I was shitless. "We are back in Mexico? Are you nuts?"

"New Mexico, Juanchito," Sammy chuckled. "New Mexico, USA!"

"Put it this way," Miguel said. "It's the same old *pinche* Mexico, but with a new owner."

"I don't understand what you're saying, *primo*."

"You don't have to, Juancho. When you meet Barack, just ask him. I'm sure he will be able to explain it to you."

We passed railroad trucks, factories and warehouses, and finally parked by *Taco-Toco-Tico*, a colorful fast food place. Everybody ordered tacos and sodas. Sugar King, a big pink soda, was included with lunch. Halfway through the meal, Sammy ordered coffee, left the car keys on the table, and got up to go to the bathroom.

"Are you ok?" Miguel asked.

"Yes," Sammy said. "I'm just tired."

Sammy walked away. As usual, when he had something important to tell me, Miguel slapped me on the head.

"I don't trust him," he whispered.

"You don't have to slap me on the *pinche* head just to tell me that! You *pinche puto!*"

When Sammy came back, we saw a police cruiser pulling into the parking lot. We finished our food and, in a hurry, we left the restaurant through a side door, walking separate ways.

"I'll meet you around the corner," Sammy said, and strolled to the car.

We walked around the corner, two blocks up the street into a small plaza. There was a bus stop and about ten people, brown just like us, waiting for the bus. We stood in line behind them, watching the upcoming traffic, waiting for Sammy. Miguel looked somber.

"Miguel, are you okay?" I asked.

"No," he said.

"Why?"

"All our money is in the trunk of the *pinche* car, *pendejo!*" he said angrily. "There is something about that *pinche* Sammy that doesn't add up!"

"Ah, I don't think so. You are just being too fricking paranoid!"

"I hope you are right, Juancho," he said, "but I'm still pretty good seeing through people!"

The people at the bus stop were speaking in Spanish. By their accent, I could tell that they were all Mexicans. Talking loudly, they were discussing among themselves going to a place called *Chimayó* Village, to some *Santuario* to pray. I overheard an old man arguing with the group. He was refusing to go with them, claiming that he was a Toltec. An old woman standing next to him, with her legs wide open, pulled up her skirt and started peeing at the old timer's feet. It was a disgusting sight. Her vagina looked like chopped liver. The stream of urine flowing out and splashing on the sidewalk formed fetid yellow foam. Holding her skirt up, like a toothless witch, she was smiling at us, comically gesturing with her index finger that the poor old man was crazy.

"There you have it, Juan. Our countrymen," Miguel said, looking at them with disdain. "We will never repeat this story. This moment belongs just to you and me!"

"There are different thoughts, for different folks! She just felt like peeing!" I giggled. "What's the big deal? What's wrong with that?"

We spotted Sammy's car coming down the avenue. As we stood on the sidewalk like two idiots, he slowed up, alongside the curb and, waving his hand out the window, shouted:

"Taxi, *amigos?*"

Out of the corner of my eye I saw the police cruiser coming the opposite way. All I prayed for was that the two cops inside wouldn't try to check us out. What I really wanted to do at that particular moment was to get out of New Mexico, even faster than when I escaped from my Old Mexico, *lindo y querido*. We climbed into the car. When Sammy drove off, like a good law abiding citizen, he was going at a leisurely pace, about thirty-five miles an hour.

"There's a strange thing about this town. I didn't see a single white person except for the two cops. Then it must be a ghetto!" I thought.

"Don't get panicky now boys," Sammy said, stepping on the gas. "Who's cool?"

"We are cool!" all of us shouted, giving high fives and laughing aloud. *Juazzzzz!*

When we got to Tulsa, Oklahoma, it was raining. We went directly to a local motel. The owners of The Hum Ping Inn Motel were a Vietnamese family that Sammy knew very well.

"I met the Ping Pong family when I went to Saigon with my father as a tourist years ago. My old man is a Vietnam vet in charge of some kind of a charity that builds cancer clinics for people that have been affected with Agent Orange during the war."

"Does your father work for The United Fruit Company?" I asked.

"United Fruit Company? What are you talking about Juan?"

"I don't know, my grandpa told me once about the United Fruit Company running some kind of monkey business with the bananas in Central America. I heard you just mentioned something about oranges in Vietnam. So I put two and two together," I said.

"Agent Orange is not a fruit, Juan! It's a very toxic chemical that was used by the armed forces to spray the jungle and kill the trees and people, when looking for the Vietcong."

"Just to give you an idea, Juanchito," Miguel said, cracking up. "If they would spray the bananas with Agent Orange, I'm sure they would grow straight!"

"Hey!" Sammy said. "Straight bananas! Not such a bad idea! A great marketing tool!"

Sammy and Miguel were laughing like crazy. I hated them! I knew I had said something stupid. All of a sudden, I felt better. Maybe I was immature and stupid, but at the same time, I was ready to face the most important moment of my life, meeting my friend Barack.

Miguel and I stayed inside the car while Sammy went to the front desk to get the room keys. We couldn't take any chances to be seen together yet. The killing of Zapallo and his deputies was all over the news. They appeared on the front page of The Tulsa Extra, accompanied by a photograph of Zapallo in full uniform.

"Authorities have evidence that a group of about fifty terrorists, heavily armed, all suspected to be members of Isis, Hamas and Taliban fighters, working together as a team in the area, were involved in the ambush that killed the five hero officers in Phoenix, Arizona."

I stopped reading. I couldn't believe my eyes and I was really mad. Mad like hell.

"Two Mexicans kids, Barack, and the Wall would be a much more interesting headline than all that nonsense!" I thought.

I ripped the newspaper in half and threw it in the garbage.

"What are the police doing?" I asked angrily, grabbing my laptop on my way to the bathroom.

"Hiding the real facts from the people," Miguel said.

"You can't blame them!" Sammy chuckled. "Zapallo and his deputies acted like The Keystone Kops!"

"Are you sure they have a good description of the three of us?"

"Yes! They know exactly who we are!" Sammy said.

"Then we have to change the car!" Miguel demanded. "As you well know, all car-rental transactions are computerized."

"How are they supposed to know it's the getaway car? Somebody else rented it for me."

"You never know, man. I don't feel secure riding in that car anymore!"

"I'll look into it tomorrow!" Sammy agreed.

I went into the bathroom and locked the door behind me. Suddenly I was horror struck, by the fetid stench of somebody's *caca* floating in the toilet bowl.

"That's all I needed today! What a pig! Looks like dark chocolate!" I thought, with my eyes fixed on the pile of crap. "I'm sure it's Sammy's. He's a big guy and he's full of it!"

Holding my nose, I flushed the toilet right away, still appalled by the treachery and deceit of criminals like Zorro Porro Neto and Zapallo, who for different reasons and with different tactics, acting with total impunity, were after brown kids like me. It's like we've been drawn into a war we never started and we don't want to fight. I remembered when I was only five years old, my grandpa telling me many stories about the coyotes, the border patrol and their innocent victims. In addition, all that goes on when ignorant and starving people try to cross the border. They believe the coyote's promise that, at any second, the reality to cross to the other side would be in their grasp, never noticing how the coyote was betraying them all the time.

"Crossing the line is a con game, Juan. A brutal plan, designed by a few sons of the bitches in power, just to make money," he used to tell me. "The biggest con game; in the whole damn globe!" Now I know, from my own experience, that he was right! With my senses still affected by the foul smell, I sat on the toilet, my moving oval office while on the road. I opened my laptop and I started to write.

CHAPTER 14

The Second Letter to Barack

Tulsa, Oklahoma, October 8, 2014 (1:00AM)

Dear Barack:

I have no idea if you received the e-mail I sent you on October first, because you haven't answered yet. Anyway, I wanted to tell you that at last I finally made it! I'm here in your fabulous country, about two thousand miles from Washington, closer than I've ever been to your beautiful White House. Let me tell you my friend, America is a Paradise and I hope I'm fit to live here. Since I crossed the border to visit you, I faced many problems along the way. Nothing major, I don't want you to worry about me. When I meet you in person, I'm going to make sure I give you a full report about certain American citizens, some of them in uniform that you should be aware of. I don't have to tell you again the admiring devotion that I feel for you, as a human being and as a leader of the free world. The other night, at the home of a friend, we had a discussion about the difference between the exiled and the immigrant. A discussion I'd love to have with you. Anyway, I was telling him my impressions of America and how my trip corroborated my positive intuitions about Gringo-Land. In fact, I feel at home everywhere I go in this wonderful land of yours. My friend told me that not knowing

America that well yet was probably the reason why I love America so much. To me it seems like a magical place, that's why I loved it instantly. It's the way I had dreamed it to be, even down to some ugly aspects, like the situation we faced in Arizona with an angry sheriff and his deputies. Nevertheless, the evil and corrupted people that I've met haven't bothered me. They are part of the picture that I had accepted in advance, before coming here. Since I was born, I felt the same way about Mexico. I loved the defects and the ugliness of it all, but as I was growing up, somehow everything started to repel me. On the contrary here, up to now, I don't know any part of Gringo-Land that I don't like. Here the people can voice their wishes in a direct fashion, without the intercession and the distortion of the politicians, like in a real democracy, where all values are not reduced to just *pinche escoria* or, like you would say in perfect English, reduced to slag.

Before leaving New Mexico which, according to my *primo* Miguel is still our same *pinche* old Mexico but with a new owner, I wanted to visit the place where the mysterious Manhattan Project was developed. This was an interesting subject my grandpa told me so much about, something worth seeing and analyzing. I still have many miles to cover in order to see you. Contrary to the lyrics of the famous Stones' song: "time is not on my side." Between you and me, believe it or not, I want you to know my grandpa loved The Rolling Stones and The Mariachi Vargas de Theloctlican, in that order.

Right now, we are here in Tulsa in a motel for the night, hiding from certain evil characters that I mentioned to you before. In a few hours, around five in the morning, we are planning to leave this nice motel. Don't worry, we are not trying to avoid paying the bill. We already paid cash in advance for two nights in order to keep the criminals chasing us off track. Also, to avoid been spotted by the local police who for sure right at this moment, are already looking for us. From here we are planning to go through Missouri, Indiana, Ohio, Pennsylvania and then *to New York City. We want to visit the office of Human Rights Watch regarding the disappearance of the forty-three students in Iguala. We are going to explain to them the real situation and what is really going on in that area. Even now, after all that happened, the government still hides the truth, and instructs the police and the army to kill civilians. Barack, in this instance, if people feel nothing for all those poor kids, there is no way they are going to do something for them. If, on the other hand, people are overcome by feelings of hate and revenge they can't control, then they will not be clever enough to make the right decision. That's why I still think that somebody cool like you, who cares a lot about what's going on in the world, is the only one that I firmly believe has the right solution for this tragic problem and can bring all these criminals to justice. I have to go to bed now.*

To be continued...

At the break of dawn we got up. Having spent a restless night on the hard motel mattress, I felt very tired. I put on my blue jeans and tucked my silver revolver into the right pocket. Sammy introduced us to Mr. Ping Pong. He looked a little primitive to me. In turn, he introduced us to his staff, a number of Vietnamese friends that he harbored and, at the same time, secured jobs for them. All these *chinos* were very grateful to him. That's why they swept his carpets, scraped the crumbs off the floor and kept everything absolutely immaculate. Mr. Pong was delighted to meet us, and he vehemently insisted that we stay for tea and have some sweet rice muffins his wife had baked for breakfast.

"You must come more often and teach me English, such a beautiful language, English. I want to speak it perfectly," Mr. Pong said to Sammy.

He took us to the back of the motel to a two-car garage. A young Vietnamese woman, who was sweeping the area around the garage, opened the garage door and showed us two cars, a white BMW and a silver Subaru station wagon. In the empty space next to the cars, there was a ping-pong table. Four beautiful oriental girls, giggling, jumping up and down and having a great time, were playing table tennis. When one of them bent over to pick up the ball, her perfect white ass and her black pubic hair was a pleasant sight so early in the morning. It was a sexy and exciting wakeup call! I could tell that none of them had panties on. It was a great *vista*.

"Maybe our good friend Mr. Pong is running some monkey business on the side," I thought.

Mr. Pong kept telling us to stay for breakfast. It felt funny to be in the company of all these *pinches chinos*, so early in the morning, in Tulsa, Oklahoma, of all places.

"Sammy, my friend, I know how much you appreciate European cars. You can take the BMW or the Subaru, whichever you prefer. Both are brand new."

"We'll take the Subaru," Miguel said to Mr. Pong, before Sammy had a chance to answer. "This way we keep a low profile and call less attention."

"Where are you bound for now?" Mr. Pong asked.

"Missouri. Is it very far away?" I asked.

"About four hundred miles," Mr. Pong answered. "Whatever you do, don't go near Ferguson! The police in that town are very nervous right now!"

"Why?"

"They killed a black kid. I think they shot him in the back! It's like a war zone over there!"

"And you call that a war?" Miguel asked. I could tell he was exasperated.

"Being a Vietnamese, Mr. Pong must know a lot about war," I said, trying to calm Miguel down and avoid an unnecessary confrontation.

"Before I forget," Mr. Pong said. "The Subaru is eighty thousand dollars cash, the paper work included."

"In the land of the fee," Miguel started singing. Sammy and I started laughing. *Juazzz!*

Mr. Ping Pong looked puzzled. A sweet oriental expression across his round yellow face, was smiling at us. "What you are singing is the University of Oklahoma's racist song that was posted all over the Internet?" he asked.

"No, Mr Pong, our song is just one of Miguel's weirdest ideas."

"Singing is good boys. It's good for the soul and the spirit. It'll keep you motivated all along your imaginary journey."

"It's not imaginary. It's *pinche* real!" I said.

I placed my computer bag on the back seat of the car while Sammy programmed the GPS. Mr. Pong and his whole clan were standing by the motel entrance, waving goodbye. Seeing the beautiful oriental girls, with the sunlight reflecting on their perfect figures, I wished I could stay and play ping-pong with them all day and all night long, non-stop. It took real effort and exercise of will power not to stay an extra night.

As we drove farther away from Tulsa, the buildings and the houses became more and more spaced out. Suddenly, we were in open country, in the middle of nowhere. After driving for almost three hours, Sammy looked through the rearview mirror with an expression of profound anxiety etched on his face.

"I don't want to alarm you but, all this time, far away down the road, I spotted a white vehicle tailing us."

"Is it a white BMW?" Miguel asked.

"I can't tell. Every time I slowed down to take a closer look, the driver wouldn't go for it."

I turned around to take a good look, when Sammy accelerated so suddenly, that my computer almost flew onto the floor. We were going so fast; that for one awful moment, I thought the car was about to flip over, killing everybody.

"Are you crazy? Slow down! All we need now is to be pulled over by the police!" I shouted.

I guess Sammy noticed the panicked expression on my face. He slowed down and skidded to a halt on the side of the road. I turned around to take a good look through the rear window, and I saw the beautiful blue Oklahoma sky and the wide empty highway. No white vehicle was following us. I opened the car window and spat to the ground.

Of course, to be in this situation isn't exactly fun for me. Nobody wants to be a fugitive. Nobody wants to be a loser. Nobody wants to lose hope. There is something wrenching and incongruous about murdering people. I opened my laptop and I started to write.

Joplin, Missouri, October 9, 2014 (3:00PM)

> *Barack, right now we are on I-44, on our way to Ferguson. To be honest with you, the more I travel your wonderful land, the whole atmosphere of your country and the people living in it are starting to confuse me a little. I'm noticing an atmosphere that's American and at the same time is not American in feeling and approach. I also noticed something wise and light in some people, and depressing and dark in others. Overall, I think that, the American people nowadays must recognize that they are near an awakening because, thanks to you and your leadership, they dream that they dream. You accomplished in a few years what other leaders couldn't accomplish in a lifetime. Where was the vision, the individuality, the courage and daring before you took over Gringo-Land? Every time I asked such a question, I always received the same response: "we're still a young country." Thanks to you, the country is maturing right now and going in the right direction. Do you know what? It's not easy to write while riding on the back seat of a moving car and, on top of that, worried about what's going to happen next...catch you later...*

CHAPTER 15
Missouri

When we got to downtown Missouri, the traffic was flowing fast and the moon was bright, almost global warming bright. There were Swat teams in armored vehicles and cops on foot all over the place. I noticed about forty patrol cars parked by this donut shop. Inside there were mostly overweight cops drinking coffee and eating donuts. There were no people walking the streets. It was extremely quiet.

"Donuts and coffee, a mean combination," Miguel said. "Too much caffeine and too much sugar give you bad energy!"

The three of us were not in a very good mood, grumbling about the lack of progress on our journey. We had to make a few stops, to make sure nobody was after us. We knew we were way behind schedule.

"Let's look for a place to spend the night," Sammy said.

The Shot in the Back Motel, with the colorful neon lights all over the façade, was a strange place. It stood across the street from a pawnshop, a bank, and a Kosher Restaurant. A red shingled, one-story house next to it called my attention. There was a big sign hanging up front - **THOMAS WILLIAMSON'S BULLET PROOF CAPES FOR SALE**. We drove around the block to check out the area and finally parked right in front. There were not too many cars in the parking lot. There were no signs of riots, or any kind of civil disobedience or altercation going on, between the police and the people in town.

"So far, so good," Sammy said.

We walked through the main door and signed the log. The black man at the front desk was standing still with his hands up, wearing a black cape. He looked very scared, wide-eyed and in shock. Two uniformed police officers flanked him.

"You can put your hands down now and take care of the clients," one cop ordered.

The black dude handed us the keys and rapidly raised his hands up in the air again.

"All we want is your damn cape, nigger!" and, after saying that, the cops took the cape off his shoulders and walked out.

"What's with the cape?" I asked.

"I bought it across the street," the black guy said. "These are bullet proof capes. All black people should wear one. They are reinforced and double shielded, especially in the back."

"I don't get it!"

"I can tell you are not from around here, boys!" he said. "In this town, black people get shot in the back all the time!"

"If I were you, I would get the hell out of town real fast!" Sammy said.

"I heard you man, but no matter where I go, I'm a black man and I'm scared. And nobody can change that!"

"That sucks!" Miguel said.

"I wish we could help you *amigo!*" I said, as we walked up to our rooms.

Ferguson, Missouri, October 9, 2014 (7:00PM)

Barack, we are here in Ferguson now; I don't know if you've been here before but let me tell you, when we came up, my first glimpse of the place was disappointing. I was saddened. The town looked bleak and uninviting to me. There were too many

*law enforcement personnel on the streets, reinforced by groups of
young rowdy police officers, drinking too much coffee and eating
too many donuts. I like tacos, so the spectacle nauseated me so
much that I wanted to go back to Mexico. I wish you were here.
You have a way of making peace and explaining things in a way
that I'm sure would lessen the pain of the black people here in
Ferguson. Now, as I sit here in this motel room, I don't even know
who I am anymore or why I'm here. After all, I'm just a Mexican
kid with a wish, and struggling to achieve a dream, wondering if
anything I'm doing or anything I have to say to you will have any
value at all. My thoughts of you and your example are the only
things that keep me going. I'm sorry if I seem confused but keep in
mind that English is not my first language, and it doesn't make it
any easier for me to integrate or try to make sense of your culture.
I know only what my grandfather told me about Gringo-Land,
and I think it's important for you to try and look at your country
from my point of view. You have to understand why I decided
to come here to see you and explain what my motivations were.
I think I have already told you about all the bad things going
on in Mexico while I was growing up. Moreover, let me tell you
man, here in Ferguson, it is worse than you probably imagine.*

Next day, when I got up, it was still dark outside. I realized
that it was five o'clock in the morning and that I just turned
fourteen *pinches* years old. I didn't want to say anything to nobody.
Anyway, I was used to it. Birthdays were never a big deal around
our house in Mexico. Sometimes I remember my mother singing
las mañanitas for me. Usually the whole fricking family forgot
my birthday altogether. I got dressed and put my silver revolver in
my right pocket. When I walked out, I saw a white BMW parked
next to our Subaru. I noticed that the door to Sammy's room was
wide open.

"Sammy?" I called. There was no answer, and I walked in.

Sammy was naked, and tied to the bed with ropes and tapes. His face was red and dripping with sweat. In his mouth, like a white dot, I could see a ping-pong ball used as a gag and secured with more tape. I called out to him again, but he couldn't talk, and didn't seem to hear me. Somebody touched my shoulder. When I turned around, I saw Mr. Ping Pong, in his underwear, standing in the middle of the room, with two of his oriental girlfriends completely nude at his side. They were smiling and pointing two big guns at me.

"I can't believe what a miracle it is to find you guys again," Mr. Ping Pong said.

"What are you doing here?" I mumbled, not knowing what to say.

"Henry from Mexicali told me about a backpack full of money! Do you know where it is?"

"Mikel, Mikel, where is Mikel?" One of the chicks shouted.

"I have no idea where Miguel is, bitch!" I shouted back.

Angrily she stepped forward and pushed me back towards the bed.

"Lay down!" she said and sat on top of me, smoothly going up and down on my crotch.

"Rape him! Rape him!" Ping yelled. "What are you waiting for? I love to watch!"

Now she was moving faster on top of me and, while pointing the gun at my face with her free little hand, she opened my zipper and started caressing my *pinga* and my nuts.

"Get it up! Get it up! You little faggot!" she screamed.

Ashamed, I was frozen! I couldn't get it up! "This is not rape, this is torture!" I thought.

All of a sudden and unexpectedly, I saw this guy wearing a black cape and dancing, doing the moonwalk and walking backwards into the room.

"Thank God for Michael Jackson and Batman!" I whispered.

Right away, the two chicks started shooting at him. All the shots hit the guy in the back, shaking him up a little. He didn't fall. He just kept dancing and moving backwards. I reached into my pocket and grabbed my revolver, firing a single shot in the neck of the girl on top of me. She grasped her throat and, looking stunned, collapsed to the floor. The dude with the cape turned around and shot Mr. Ping Pong twice in the chest. He wheezed and, falling backwards, exhaled his last breath. The other Chinese girl was terrified; pleading: "Don't kill me, mothafucka!" She dropped her gun, turned around and, holding her little tits with one hand and covering her hairy pussy with the other, ran out nude across the parking lot.

"Who's your daddy? Who's your savior? Miguel laughed. "How do you like my cape? Lucky for you *putos*, I went shopping last night! *Pinches cabrones!"*

With the gun in his right hand and pointing to the ceiling, going backwards in circles around the room, he just kept laughing and dancing like crazy. *Juazzzzzz!*

"Long live Miguel Jackson," I laughed. *Juazzzzzz*

Ferguson, Missouri, October 10, 2014 (7:00AM)

Barack, my friend, when I woke up this morning, I wished I hadn't. I know I'm going to disappoint you but I suppose bad luck is a constant in my life. Before leaving the motel, a band of criminals, ambushed us, they wanted to steal our money. Thanks to Mr. Thomas Williamson from Ferguson, Missouri, who invented "The Bullet Proof Cape", we were able to avoid being killed. As you can see, the American knowhow is still alive and well in your country, and Miguel and I, thank God for that. I don't want you to think for a moment that we are a pair of trigger-happy spics going around this wonderful land of yours killing people left and right. If you want to know the truth, the conviction that I'm going to meet you is the only thing that gives me the strength and really helps me to make it through the day. I hope you understand that the authorities and the criminals are both chasing me at the same time, and that in many instances, it's been very difficult for me to tell who's, who. Even so, I am trying very hard to adapt to your way of life. It is hard for me to reverse the old ways, so do not expect me to get better right away. Besides, until now, since you never answered my emails, I don't have any guidance or suggestions which I desperately need. As you can see, I write to you openly and just like you, I don't pretend to be somebody I'm not. I guess what I'm trying to say is that I'm sure I'll change little by little and that will show you that I'm worth a second chance. If you are reading this now, it means that I survived and we are on our way to Washington to see you.

CHAPTER 16
Indiana

When we left Missouri, Sammy was still mad, furious and driving very fast.

"The chinks raped me twice! Both of them!" he yelled.

"Cool it! It's okay," Miguel said. "If you worry about something enough, it's going to hurt you. So, just forget it!"

"They couldn't rape me!" I said proudly.

"They tied me up to the bed and the two chicks started to make love to each other next to me. Then Ping Pong jumped on top of them and joined the action. All that fucking and sucking got me aroused. I couldn't help it! I'm embarrassed. I don't know what I'm going to say to Nataya, my wife," Sammy said.

"You don't have to tell her anything!" Miguel laughed. "No big deal, at that particular moment you were not repressed and got yourself some stinky piece of Chinese ass! And whatever you call it, rape, sexual assault or simply fucking, I'm sure you enjoyed it!"

Miguel always said there was something about Sammy, something he was trying to conceal. He was a good person, perhaps a little too good to be genuine. Or maybe he was trying to hide his nervousness, ashamed of revealing his real emotions. Maybe this mask had become part of him. There was something in the way he acted, as if he was forced to do us a favor but, at the same time, he really didn't want to. I remember he was quite surprised when I told him the primary purpose in making the trip and the reasons why I wanted to meet with Barack. When he told us he wanted to go to New York to The Human Rights Watch office because he had friends there, he never named any friend in particular. In other words, Sammy never talked in detail about himself. Miguel and I instead blindly trusted him with our whole plan of action.

"There are four hundred miles to go to Indiana. This time let's make sure nobody is following us. I don't want any more surprises!" Sammy said.

"Are there a lot of Indians in Indiana?" I asked.

"No stupid!"

"Am I going to have the chance to meet this guy Indiana Jones?"

"You are really an a-hole!"

"No Indians and no Indiana Jones! So what's the big deal about Indiana?"

"The Indy 500, and NASCAR!"

"And what's that?"

"The most important car races in the world!"

"*MASCAR?* That means to chew in Spanish!" I said.

"No Juan, NASCAR, with an N, not with an M! *Pinche puto! Mascar* is what you do when you go to *Mc Mocos* and chew a Big Mc Moco, *cabrón!*" Miguel chuckled.

Well, at last, here we were in Indiana. A great lot of buildings, restaurants, parks, burger joints and war memorials, all designed to look like a huge outdoor mall, a familiar theme we'd seen before in other places here in Gringo-Land. Weirdly for me, one place looked just like the other, lot's of Main streets. However, Indiana, unlike the other places, had very little to offer. It was dull, soporific, cosmetic and distressingly boring. Unlucky for us, by coincidence we met a crazy nut that seemed different from the locals. Somehow, he broke the monotony of the moment. Even before shaking hands and introducing himself, he started offering us a deal, a big deal involving pure bottled mountain air.

"My name is Timmy Klansman. Bottled air is my own invention. I was also the person who invented the bottled water concept! My company is a life member of PFP INTERNATIONAL. Like bottled water, we are going to be a multibillion-dollar business. We are economically secure, and our profits are guaranteed forever and ever!"

"What's PFP INTERNATIONAL?"

"POLLUTING FOR PROFIT." You see, we have stock in other corporations around the world that, among other things like making war, are polluting the air and the water. In this particular case, as with bottled water, we came up with the solution, the way of the future! Pure bottled mountain air! Everybody makes money!"

"That's idiotic and *pinche* barbaric, *cabrón!*" Miguel said.

Timmy didn't pay any attention to him. "Can I tell you a secret?" he asked.

"Your formula?"

"Kiss my ass!" he said. "I'd never do that!"

"So, what's the secret?"

"Okay, then," he said in a loud voice.

After saying that, leaning closer to Sammy because he didn't want anybody but us to hear what he was going to say, he said,

"I'm a KKK member. I moved here with all my friends from Mississippi a long time ago."

"A KKK member? Nowadays? That's really stupid!" Sammy shouted, with purpose.

"You're right!" the guy said. "I ought to be smashed in the face and hung by the balls for what I've done to the blacks. However, now I'm a decent businessman and I deserve a second chance. I need your help!"

"What for?"

"I need capital badly, for manufacturing and distribution."

"What makes you think that we have money to invest?" Sammy asked.

"Well, don't get offended now boy. Anywhere I see a white dude flanked by two spics, I can tell that some kind of a drug deal is going on. Drugs and big money always go together."

I could tell that Sammy was in shock, and Miguel was furious.
"If you don't shut up right now, I'm going to kill you!" Miguel
said.

"Don't get mad Pancho," the guy joked. "It's all business!"

"Be cool, Miguel," I said. "He wants to get you mad!"

"You better quit saying that, Juan! You're getting me even
madder now!" Miguel yelled.

I looked across the street and suddenly I realized that we were
standing on the sidewalk across from the police station. I saw four
uniformed cops coming out through the main doorway. They were
coming towards us, and fast. As they got closer, I noticed Sammy
had gone pale. I was shitless. Miguel, as usual, was ready to kill.

"Hi Timmy, what's up?" one of the cops said amiably.

"Hello there, Sergeant Brybe. You look thirsty. Can I buy you
a beer?"

"No thanks, see you later Timmy. Who are these characters?"

"They're ok! They're my associates, Serge!"

"Listen, Timmy, don't forget to bring the envelope with the
cash for the captain tonight."

"No sweat, Serge! See you guys tonight!"

After the cops left, Timmy was humming a happy southern
song. I could tell he was feeling good, proud to be a KKK member
and in control of the situation.

"As you can see, I just saved your ass, boys! And that has a
price!"

After driving for more than one thousand miles, and almost
being killed in a couple of shootouts. After making pit stops on and
off the highway at gas stations and paying in cash. After staying
in lousy motels, and keeping to service roads. After respecting the
speed limit and avoiding tollbooths in order not to be spotted by
the police and the pack of criminals chasing us, in other words
doing whatever we had to do to steer clear of our pursuers, after
all of that, like three pinches *pendejos,* we ended up at the mercy of

this crazy nut, Timmy, a KKK affiliate living in Indiana and selling pure bottled mountain air.

"Do you mind stepping into my office, gentlemen?" he said, pointing to the bar at the corner.

It was after five in the afternoon when the four of us walked into the joint. Timmy was leading the way. There were only two or three customers, drinking and smoking at the bar. They looked retarded to me. A big no-smoking sign was hanging on the back wall. The acrid smell of cheap liquor and cigarette smoke was overwhelming.

"Let's take a booth," Timmy laughed. "It's more private, more romantic, and cozier."

As soon as we sat down, he spoke again.

"You know the deal boys, two hundred and fifty thousand dollars or I'll call the police!"

"You are out of your fucking mind! We don't have that kind of money!" Sammy said.

"I'll give it to you short and sweet, asshole," he smiled. "Henry, The Big K from Mexicali, sounds familiar?"

"Who?" Sammy was perplexed. "What are you talking about?"

"He is the king of the line. He is the ruler of the border! We are all internationally connected. We are one! Got it now, a-hole? Pay up, and shut up!"

I looked at Miguel. He just sat there. He was very quiet. He raised his eyes and looked at me only once, and that's when I smelled a different odor altogether, an odor that filled the whole place, an odor that I knew very well, since I had smelled that odor many times before. Miguel grabbed a knife from the table, stood up and, pulling Timmy's jacket over his head stabbed him once in the neck. Timmy didn't have a chance, Miguel was too fast and too lethal. The KKK member was dead before he knew what was coming to him. We threw him under the table like a sack of putrid potatoes and walked out of the bar the same way we came in. None of the retards inside the place noticed anything. We got into the car and drove off. The area around the bar was treeless, block after block, like an urban desert. The concrete and fiberglass buildings were all the same, a pathetic bland sameness and a cold uniformity. We drove slowly up Main Street directly onto the highway but, just before we reached the ramp, we saw a police cruiser with a cop behind the wheel parked by the entrance with his headlights on. We knew the face of the driver. It was Sergeant Brybe. Sammy's face flushed. Holding my silver revolver and looking at the cop, I could feel my heartbeat pounding in the center of my chest, tickling all the way to the tip of my index finger caressing the trigger. As we drove by, the cop looked up and, smiling pleasantly, waved goodbye.

"New York City, here we come!" Sammy yelled, happily pressing the gas pedal and hitting the wheel as hard as he could with the palms of his hands.

CHAPTER 17
New York City

While leaving Indiana, Sammy was sticking to the speed limit on the interstate. The road was clear. We made sure there were no police cars or any other vehicle following us.

"We are going to go through Ohio and Pennsylvania, and then to New York," Sammy said.

"Do you know how many more miles to New York City?" Miguel asked.

"We have about eight hundred miles to go. We'll make a few stops along the way for food and gas. We have to keep moving. We can't risk getting caught now."

I was exhausted. I sat back, opened my laptop and started to write

Indianapolis, Indiana, October 10 (4:30PM)

> *Barack, we made it out just in time! Now we are on our way to Ohio. I wish I could tell you what went wrong. It's a long story that I prefer to tell you when I see you in person. What I also discovered while traveling this wonderful land of yours is that a lot of people, especially the blacks, have a hard time trying to survive in Gringo-Land. Some of them don't even have money to pay the rent or put a decent plate of food on their table. Their kids go hungry. On top of all that they are harassed and killed mostly by*

racist police officers. It's hard for me to understand the mixture of racism and hatred I saw reflected in the eyes of some people here in Gringo Land. Who are they? Do they have a mother? A father? Are they custom made? Are they made in China? Korea? Taiwan? America? Cloned? Or just born out of a system? I wonder what produces these kind of murderers? I also noticed, in every city I went to, that you have many homeless people. Most of them are mentally ill and taking *siestas* on the streets. While I write this to you, I can still smell their bad breath and their strong body odor. I imagine that, if you have a chance to meet them personally, you will smell the same foul odor. That powerful and nauseating stench should be a reminder to you not to leave sick people to live and die like wild animals on the streets anymore. Those poor souls should be in a hospital. *Basta por favor, amigo mio!* It's strange how you can manage to feed the world, and not learn how to feed and take care of your own people. If you have all the power, I wonder why you don't change obvious things like that? Maybe because it's not profitable? Or, on the other hand, it is? In "the land of the fee", you never know! Are your character and habits not really what you preach? I ponder these questions as a humble Mexican kid watching firsthand what really is going on in your country. I wonder if you are alone and powerless to do anything humane for the people, especially black people. Maybe you are just a symbol, a façade reading a script in a Machiavellian play, written and designed by a mysterious director? If that's what it is, it doesn't surprise me. I always considered myself a mystery novel fanatic. Between you and me, I already read all the Harry Potter books. Please don't misunderstand me. I may not be a grown up yet, but I'm telling you all this as a friend. There are simple things that touched my heart here in Gringo-Land: watching the Arizona Mountains, standing in the middle of the desert in New Mexico, watching the blue Oklahoma sky, and looking at the Korean girls with no panties playing ping-pong at The Hum Ping Inn Motel in Tulsa!

We arrived in Cleveland late at night. We stopped at a gas station to get some snacks and go to the bathroom. There was nothing in the news about finding a dead KKK guy in a bar under a table in Indiana. In order to avoid the police and Zorro Porro's *pistoleros*, we kept a low profile and didn't get to see much of Cleveland. We just drove in and out. To me, it seemed a typical American city, thriving, prosperous, active, clean and spacious, including a few smelly and mentally ill people taking a *siesta* here and there all over the streets. The local people that we saw, including the dudes at the gas station, looked as though they were manufactured by some kind of a chain store. One looked just like the other, the same way as their cars, their houses, their cell phones, their homeless people and their computers. Somehow, it felt very good, leaving that pathetic town behind.

"We have five hundred more miles to go, children!" Sammy said cheerfully.

"I'm taking a nap guys, if you don't mind," I said. "I want to be rested and alert, to really enjoy New York, New York, the city that never sleeps!"

"New York; never sleeps? I wonder why?" Miguel asked skeptically. "It doesn't sleep at all? That's real fucked up, *cabrón!* No wonder they consume so much *pinche* flour!"

When I woke up, we were already crossing the Washington Bridge. It was a warm and sunny day, a beautiful global warming sunny day. There was a lot of noise and a lot of traffic on the bridge. We got off the ramp on 179th Street and Broadway. The people in the neighborhood were mostly black and Hispanic.

"Are you sure we are in New York?" I asked.

"I'm hungry, let's have something to eat," Sammy said, ignoring my comment.

"Where to?"

"Let's go to *El Malecón* and have some Spanish food. It's just three blocks away."

"What? *El Maricón?" Juazzzz!* Miguel laughed. "Let's do first things, first. Let's drive around the block and make sure we are not being followed."

We went around a huge old building that was across the street from the restaurant and parked at the back.

"Welcome to New York City," Sammy laughed. "Or better yet, welcome to Washington Heights, the Dominican Republic in upper Manhattan!"

"This is the ghetto where my friend Socrates lives!" Miguel said.

"This is The United Palace Theatre," Sammy said pointing to an old building. "Years ago, I worked for a big producer as coordinator for a couple of Spanish shows in this place!"

"That's great man! I wish I could do that!"

"No big deal!" Sammy said. "Just like any other business, it's all about money!"

"No matter what you do or where you go, *la lana* always rules! The *pinche* dollar is the boss *siempre, cabrón!*" Miguel barked.

After lunch we drove down Broadway to midtown. Along the way we stopped at Miguel's friend's building on 160th Street. Socrates was not living there anymore, and nobody in the dilapidated building knew where he'd gone or his whereabouts. Illegal aliens in the big city appear and disappear just like flying saucers in the sky.

"We are going to stay at The Empire Hotel, right across from Lincoln Center," Sammy said.

"What's the *pinche* Lincoln Center?"

"The Lincoln Center for the Performing Arts is the most important Cultural Center in New York City, where the Metropolitan Opera House is! The House of The Met! Where Nataya my wife is dancing tonight!"

"Your wife? Is she a real dancer?"

"Yes! She's a very famous ballerina!"

"Wow man! That's great! Congratulations!"

"And you little *cabrones* are invited to see her show tonight!"

"How did you meet her?"

"By chance. I used to park my car nearby Lincoln Center. She was a young émigré from Russia working as a valet parking attendant. It was love at first sight."

"I don't get it," Miguel said. "How come she's a famous ballerina now?"

"It's a long story," Sammy grinned. "We used to meet at this jazz bar called The Iridium next to the Empire Hotel for drinks. Her English was not too good at the time. Every time people asked her about her line of work she would answer. "Me work, do valet," and because she didn't know how to pronounce the "V" and the "B", people understood "ballet" and right away assumed that she was a ballerina, and treated her as such."

"*Juazzzzzzzz!* Really? You are pulling my leg, *cabrón!*" Miguel hollered.

"I'm not lying to you! She started believing and playing along that she was a real ballerina. She went to school to study Classical Ballet with the best in the business, and after that went back to Russia for one year to dance with the Bolshoi. The rest is history!"

"Wow!" I said. "That's magical! That's the pinche American dream, *cabrón!*"

"Screw that!" Miguel said. "That fricking broad has balls, that's all!"

"You bet man!" Sammy said proudly as he parked the car by the Empire Hotel entrance.

The hotel was a boutique type, small, with a nice bar in the lobby and the service was great. Compared with all the cheap motels we stayed in while on the road, this place looked like a palace to us. They even had organic fresh red apples at the front desk. For free! Not for a fee! Juazzzzz!

"A nice touch of class" I thought and started feeling good, like a Mexican big shot.

We met Nataya as soon as we arrived. She was waiting for us in the lobby. Looking like a typical ballerina, elegant and classy, skinny, tiny tits, fat lips and a wonderful smile.

"Nice meeting you kids! Sammy told me so much about you! Your personal story is amazing! It's out of this world!"

While saying that, she gave us two kisses each, pressing tenderly her wonderful fat lips on both our cheeks.

"Blow job! Blow job!" Miguel whispered in my ear. *Juazzzzz!* We cracked up.

"Ok boys, go to your rooms and get some rest. I'll meet you at seven at the Met by the stage door," Sammy said, laughing along with us, having no idea of our filthy intentions.

At a quarter to seven, we went across 9th Avenue to the Lincoln Center Plaza. It was a beautiful night. The fountain in the center of the plaza, with the water shooting up and the changing colors, was a great sight. Flanked by The Avery Fisher concert hall on one side and The Met lit up at the far end of the conglomerate, the whole place looked grand. Miguel smiled and raised his eyebrows slightly.

"I'm proud of you, Juan," he said. "This is what I call class!"

A huge banner, with Nataya's smiling face on it, was hanging between two giant poles right in front of the entrance to The Met, announcing the show.

Latin Culture Productions

Presents

For the first time at the MET

Directly from Moscow

A SWAN IN LAKE GEORGE WITH NATAYA DANZINGSOLOVA

(ONLY NEW YORK APPEARANCE)

We asked a funny looking security guard, trying hard not to laugh in his face, where the backstage door was. He was wearing a uniform too big for his small frame. He looked like a young Gandhi in uniform.

"Stage Deli?" he asked, his eyes wide open.

We could tell by the way he looked and by the way he talked, that he was what you commonly call cheap labor. He definitely was not a New Yorker, and that he really liked pastrami and corn beef sandwiches on rye, but he had no fricking idea what we were looking for. Therefore, we decided to leave the poor guard alone and just go around to the back of the building. Guess what, Sammy was waiting for us right by the backstage door.

"Here are the backstage passes. Put them around your neck and let's go in!"

As soon as we walked inside, the security guard checked our names on the guest list and let us in. I noticed a little old man holding a guitar, wearing blue jeans, a white t-shirt and a Yankees baseball cap, trying to go through security. He reminded me of Francisco.

"You can't go in," the guard grinned.

"What do you mean?" the little old man asked. "I'm Paul Simon, I have a rehearsal."

"Is this Paul Simon?" the guard giggled, looking at me, and pointing at the old man.

"Who's Paul Simon?" I asked.

"A very famous singer back in the sixties," the guard told me, letting him in.

"The American sense of humor is fricking weird," I thought.

We got into a cargo elevator with a bunch of fat dudes with big bellies, pushing big trunks on wheels. They didn't look very happy to me. Seeing all those huge bellies next to each other, I imagined all those bellies moving up and down and sideways dancing to Mariachi music.

"It would make a great beer commercial," I whispered.

"Who are they?"

"They are the stagehands, the guys who set up the stage."

"Why are there so many?" I counted about ten fat men.

"To work a show like this, you need a crew of at least thirty guys!"

"That's a lot of fat!" *Juazzzz!* I laughed.

"They are all union members and very expensive!"

"What do they do? What's the big deal?"

"Let me show you," he said, taking me onto the main stage.

When we walked onto the stage, it looked like a crazy house. All the fat guys were at work, sweating and gasping for air. There was a lot of hammering and banging, they were moving stuff all over the stage floor. Some younger guys in better shape than the fatsos, were on top of a ladder or a platform connecting cables and lights. Others were hanging huge decorations and setting up video projectors, while others were working in the orchestra pit, preparing the space for the musicians and plugging in the consoles for the instruments and the sound.

"That's a lot of work! But they don't seem to enjoy it much!" Miguel said.

"I know! Nevertheless, they make a lot of money! Give and take, we are talking about more than two hundred big ones! Only in stage labor fees! Remember kid, this is the land of the fee!"

"What good does it do, *cabrón*, to have money in your pocket if you are not happy?"

When Sammy heard that comment he put on a poker face, scratched his balls and smiled. "How do you know they are not happy?" "Are you a medium, or what?"

From center stage, we went to the dressing room area to greet Nataya before the show. She was fixing her hair and putting make up on her beautiful face. As usual, her fat red lips called my attention, and I felt a slight vibration and a warm feeling all over my little testicles. We wished her good luck and walked out, leaving Sammy alone with her in private, at least for the moment.

I'm pretty sure he appreciated that. Unexpectedly, I thought about Sammy's and Nataya's whole situation. If my sorry little testicles vibrated at the sight of Nataya's lips, I anticipated that Sammy's testicles would explode like an A-bomb after kissing her on the mouth. Once out in the hallway, my *pinche primo* Miguel got a little playful. He bumped me, pushed me and elbowed me, while hollering.

"Blow job! Blow job!"

"Good for Sammy, *pinche cabrón*! You are just jealous, *pendejo!*" I shouted.

When we got to our seats in the middle aisle, in the third row, the curtain was already up. The stage looked great. I could tell that the fat union crew had done a wonderful job. Looking around and watching the people sitting next to me, I felt completely out of place. I remembered being at the National Auditorium in Mexico once, but this place was an entire different story. The audience, the huge radiant chandeliers going up and down, and the whole theatre reflected real magnificence.

Gradually the lights went out and the music started. Nataya came out in the spotlight, and the place exploded with a round of applause and bravos, and a thunderous standing ovation. She bowed to the audience and started to dance. Swiftly, from one side of the stage, a *puñal*, a man looking like a gay Robin Hood and wearing pinkish pantyhose, jumped on center stage and, grabbing Nataya by the waist, lifted her up in the air, swinging her gently over his head. A big *jalapeno*, or some kind of a huge cauliflower, protruding between his legs called my attention. Two older women seated next to me, with their eyes fixed on the dude's crotch, screamed with pleasure. Meanwhile the guy with the *jalapeno*, compressed by the pinkish pantyhose, dancing like mad, was gently rotating in center stage, while caressing Nataya's body. She was spinning on her toes, flying like an angel all over the stage. It was a wonderful sight.

"If I were Sammy, I'd be very much concerned about my wife and the jalapeno guy!" Miguel cracked up.

"Whatever it is, *un jalapeno* o *un pinche coliflor*, it's fricking huge! I'd be worried too!"

Pandemonium, that's the only word that comes to my mind in order to describe what the reaction of the audience was at the end of the performance. People were yelling and applauding, and trying to climb up on the stage. Thank God Sammy came to our rescue.

Through a side door, he took us backstage again to the dressing room area. There were people all over the hallways, some of them from the press, others were friends and fans. Everybody was very excited and in a jolly mood. At the end of the hallway, there was a big dressing room for all the ballerinas. I noticed the door half open and, following the vibration of my little testicles, I walked up to the door and I took a quick peek inside. What I saw really shocked me. Lots of little tits, some of them looking like infected pimples, plenty of flat asses, and clean shaven pussy that looked like baked clams. Still in shock, feeling my *huevitos* vibration decreasing rapidly, very gently I closed the door.

"C'mon Juan! Stop snooping around and let's go out to dinner!" Sammy shouted.

"Hey guys! I'm going with you!" this tall skinny dude with glasses yelled to Sammy.

"Ok Brian! The New York Times is buying!"

Brian's answer came back quick.

"I forgot my wallet. I left my money at home, man!"

Twenty minutes later the four of us, and the reporter from the New York Times were sitting at a table in *Rosa Mexicano*, a restaurant across the street from the theatre. Everybody ordered guacamole. Miguel ordered *carnitas con frijoles*, a side order of tacos, a beer for him and a glass of orange juice for me. Brian Badreview ordered everything and more. It was amazing how much the *pinche cabrón* could eat. Nataya didn't order much. She was on a diet. Out of solidarity for her, Sammy was on a diet too. "The review of the show is going to come out in Arts & Leisure next Sunday." Brian said.

"What we could have used was a preview. It helps to sell tickets, you know?" Sammy said, scornfully.

I could tell that Sammy was mad at first but then he smiled, grabbed a glass of wine, stood up and said:

"Let's drink to the producers! Let's have a toast for more previews!" Sammy said.

"I hope you forgive me! I hereby return your stolen goods," Brian said, giving Sammy a white envelope full of money.

We all just sat there in silence as Brian got up, grabbed the guacamole dish and, without saying a word, left the table and hurried out of the restaurant. Sammy asked for the check.

"Ok boys, let's call it a night! Tomorrow we leave for DC at three in the afternoon!"

I'm not much of an expert, I'm too young for that, but what I saw going on that night at that table was completely wrong. I want you to know that I'm not talking about the guacamole. While all this was happening around her, Nataya was motionless in a dream state and in a completely different galaxy, still savoring her after performance blues, the standing ovation, the audience's love and the applause. She didn't notice what went on between Sammy and Brian Badreview.

At nine o'clock next morning, we met Sammy at the hotel lobby to go to the offices of Human Rights Watch.

"They have an office at walking distance on West 58th Street."

We walked on Broadway up to Columbus Circle and turned left on 58th Street towards 7th Avenue. The building was right at the corner. A dreadful old man, his face full of wrinkles, opened the front door for us.

"My name is Ramiro Doorman. Can I help you?"

"We are looking for Dr. Bert Brown, Human Rights Watch office."

"Tenth floor," Ramiro said.

"I've never been in a building where the doorman introduces himself to the visitors." Sammy said.

"In this building, everything is different and anything is possible," Ramiro grinned.

We took an old elevator to the tenth floor.

Sammy rang the bell. A long time passed, about five minutes. Finally, a young black woman opened the door, fixing her hair, putting lipstick on, buttoning her blouse and pulling down her skirt, doing all that, almost at the same time. She moved very quickly.

"Practice makes perfect!" I thought.

"Dr. Brown?" Sammy asked.

"Do I look at all like Doctor Brown?" she laughed. "C'mon in boys! He's waiting for you!"

When we walked into the office we could hear Dr. Brown breathing heavily, standing by his desk. He waved to us to sit down. He looked old and tired, half of his shirt was outside his pants, he had his fly open and he needed a shower.

"How was your trip?"

"A little too complicated."

"Did you fly in?"

"We came by car."

"Wow! Literally, that's a real pain in the ass!" he laughed.

After saying that, he just stood there, waiting for Sammy to say something.

"Miguel and Juan here are the only two students that escaped alive from Iguala, and they want to report what is really going on over there!" I knew that Sammy was lying.

"I know. That's a tragedy!" Brown said, handing a bunch of papers to Sammy. "Here, you have to fill out these forms, in English and Spanish. Sign them, I'll notarize them, and send them to the proper authorities for filing and processing."

"That's it?"

"For now, it's all I can do! I'll keep you posted!"

"Same fricking story everywhere, nobody cares about those forty-three kids!" Miguel said, angrily.

"We do care, my child," Brown said sadly. "There are thousands of children being kidnapped and murdered every day, not only in Mexico, but all over the world. For some people, trafficking and murdering kids is a good business. They even sell their organs. There is just so much our organization can do. Keep in mind that we must work within the system, in many instances a complicit system. This makes everything more time consuming, more complicated and extremely difficult."

Brown's speech was over. How long it lasted, I couldn't say. When he finally stopped talking, I realized that we were sitting practically in the dark. Apparently, Brown and his secretary liked the darkness. The sound of high-heeled shoes moving across the floor finally broke the silence.

"It's time to go now, boys," the black girl said. "I'll walk you out."

Without saying goodbye, we left the office. Brown, with his eyes half closed, was making a telephone call. It seemed like he had somehow fallen asleep and had just woken up to find a telephone in his hand.

"I can't believe what I just saw! Such an important organization is run by a crockpot!" Sammy said as we got into the elevator.

"You didn't know?" Miguel barked at him.

"I had no idea."

"You are lying."

Sammy said nothing. When we got down to the lobby, there was a different doorman standing by the main door. He was a younger guy with a big belly and wearing huge Ray Ban sunglasses. All dressed up in his doorman uniform, and with big sunglasses hanging from his red nose, he looked like a typical Latin American dictator.

"My name is Luis Doorman. Thank you for coming to our building," he said and proceeded to shake our hands. "Have a nice day!"

"These guys are weird!" Sammy whispered.

"Same last name. They must be brothers!"

We went outside and walked towards Central Park West and 7th Avenue. It is difficult for me to pinpoint exactly why we went to Brown's office or what we expected from him. Probably, at that exact moment, they were blowing away another forty-three kids in Iguala and nobody in power was willing to confront the killers to stop the massacre, or take drastic action against those murderers and get rid of them once and for all. Standing on that corner at ten in the morning, knowing that I was so close to the final leg of my journey to see my friend Barack, I tried hard to get rid of those thoughts. I had no reason to worry anymore. Everything that had happened to me was a great learning experience, more exciting and more fascinating than I could ever imagine it would be.

"I have to pick up Nataya and take her to the airport," Sammy said.

"She's not coming with us?"

"Her flight to DC is at noon! She's dancing at the Kennedy Center tonight and needs to rest!"

Okay! We'll see you at the hotel."

"Don't forget, we are leaving at two. Try to be on time."

We went across the street into Central Park. It was a sunny day and the park looked beautiful. There were many people walking and talking to their dogs. Watching the dogs and their owners, I was under the impression that it was the other way around.

"I want to see Strawberry Fields," Miguel said and started to walk faster.

On the corner of 72nd Street and Central Park West, there was this guy on crutches, singing in Italian and yelling "*pagliaci, pagliaci,*" while holding a paper cup in one hand and asking for money. He was wearing a white button-down shirt. It was wrinkled and too big for him, the sleeves way too long, and it was baggy at the waist of his black pants. He had no shoes on. Miguel laughed at the guy.

"You look like an unemployed opera singer," and stuck fifty bucks in the paper cup.

The bum laughed back, put both crutches on the park bench, jumped up and down celebrating the fifty bucks, and ran over to kiss Miguel's hand.

"Thank you, kid! You made my day! Now I can have lunch!"

We didn't have to walk too far. Strawberry Fields was crowded, mainly with young kids wearing jeans, some of them in matching t-shirts with Lennon's face on, the words "imagine" or "give peace a chance" written across their chest. Older women, dressed just like the boys and sitting on the floor forming a circle, were singing Beatles' songs. Miguel and I stood at the side of the circle, watching the women sing. A young and pretty one, with curly black hair, wearing tight jeans, her voice real sweet, caught my attention.

"Blow job! Blow job!" Miguel whispered to me.

"You are a real ass, *primo!*"

After I said that, I noticed two twin dudes, wearing the same jeans and the same t-shirt, standing next to the girl. There was something odd about them, as if they were trying very hard to blend in with the crowd but somehow they couldn't. Both of them were cross-eyed and sweating profusely. Suddenly, before I had a chance to tell Miguel about the two characters, our friend the unemployed tenor, moving fast to the music, was coming our way holding three brown paper bags against his chest. He gave us one each. When I looked back up, the cross-eyed twins were gone.

"Cold beer to celebrate our friendship, kids!" he said, smiling and clinking his paper bag against Miguel's and mine. The foam started to flow over the top of the brown bag and we had to drink it fast. It was ice cold, the best tasting beer I ever had in my whole life.

"They are *Negra Modelo.* I hope you like the taste!" he said happily.

After that first toast, we couldn't get rid of him. He went across the street to the Deli at the corner and brought three more beers. He seemed to be very happy.

"How come you are not walking your dog this beautiful morning?" he asked.

"I am," Miguel laughed, pointing at me.

"That's real funny," he said casually, not paying too much attention to Miguel's lousy joke.

"Honest, in America, a dog is more than a mascot, he's family. Whenever, on the streets, beaches or in the parks of America, you see an owner and his dog walking together, you never know who the owner is or who's walking whom. We love dogs, in some cases even more than our kids. We the dog owners are a huge market. We spend billions of dollars a year and it keeps growing. In America, God, flag, country and dog is a cultural thing. I wonder how come we don't have an image of a dog on our flag yet."

"And where is your dog?" I asked.

"It's a sad story. I can't sleep ever since," he said, and started to cry. "My dog, Skeleton *Flaco,* was a greyhound. He was the fastest ever. He was Florida's State champion *for* many years, won all races, was unbeatable, I made millions," now he was sobbing uncontrollably.

"So, what happened?"

He stared at me. He was very sad.

"It was the summer of 2010. I'll never forget that day. We had the most important race in Las Vegas. The purse was over four hundred and eighty million dollars and Skeleton *Flaco* was in top shape. I bet everything I had, my cash, my mansions, my ten yachts, my entire fortune."

He was crying hysterically, he could hardly keep on talking.

"So, what happened?" Miguel patiently insisted.

"Skeleton *Flaco* lost!" he shouted. "He lost the race! He came in last," and started crying again.

For about five minutes, we all remained quiet. We didn't know what to do or say. Suddenly he started laughing; he was crying and laughing at the same time.

"So, what happened?" Miguel asked again.

"I put him to sleep! I had to!"

"What do you mean, you put him to sleep?"

"Blame the fricking French!"

"What? Why blame the French?"

"Skeleton *Flaco* wanted an authentic French croissant for breakfast, instead I gave him a regular one from the coffee shop at the hotel. He got so mad and lost the race!" he said angrily.

"Wait a minute! Miguel asked. "And how do you know all that?"

"My dog told me!"

After saying that, he got on his crutches, hopped back to the corner and, holding the paper cup, started singing "his *pagliaci*" again.

We left this particular stranger on the same corner where we found him in the first place, and this particular stranger kept singing this beautiful song. I just couldn't imagine that in a desperate situation, he had the strength to kill his own dog, and all because of money.

"See what happens to people when they live too long in the city that never sleeps?"

"I know, they never kill their dogs; they just put them to sleep!" Miguel laughed.

That set us off. We laughed like old times, *Juazzzzz!* Like when we were back in Sinaloa. We laughed aloud and both at the same time. We kept laughing while walking all the way down to Broadway. It was the most awesome moment we had experienced in a long, long time. Suddenly I realized that, from the moment we are born, Mexicans are displaced and victimized. That's why, even when it comes to suffering and death, we know how to laugh and have fun because deep in our soul we know, that when it comes to death; laughter and tears are pretty much the same.

When we reached 72nd Street and Broadway, while waiting for the light, I saw the cross-eyed twins again, standing at the next corner.

"I saw those *pinches cabrones* in the park," I said, glancing in their direction.

"Me too *pendejo!* Do you think I'm blind?"

That's what I loved about Miguel. He was always alert. He would never let his guard down. I know him better than anyone else and his influence on me was more than obvious. At least, that was at the beginning. As I grew older, some things changed. I was not entirely comfortable in his presence. It was a mixture of envy and the suspicion that he was somehow better than I was. There was more innate goodness in him than in others, and that goodness I believe was keeping him alive. He was more truly himself than I could ever hope to be.

"Move,*pendejo!* Follow me!" Miguel shouted.

He started running down Broadway ahead of me. He was going too fast. It was almost impossible to avoid bumping into people while running next to him. Lucky for me it was a short dash. Three minutes later, breathing heavily, we were standing in Central Park West in front of this modern high-rise building. A huge copper sign, with the words *TRAMPA* TOWERS engraved on it, was shining like the sun right above the glass doors by the main entrance. Two large men standing right at the top of the sparkling clean marble stairs, were looking down at a group of about two hundred brown people carrying signs.

I'M PROUD TO BE A MEXICAN! - TRAMPA GO BACK TO FLORIDA! – I'M NOT A RAPIST I'M A STYLIST! - TRAMPA KING OF THE *HAMPA*! - YOU ARE FIRED! - NO MORE HAIR SPRAY FOR YOU! - *TRAMPA CABRON!-TRAMPA PUTOOOO!*

They were jumping up and down, holding the signs, and shouting insults in English and Spanish.

"*Trampa, hijo de la chingada!*"

"We want to cut your ridiculous hair!"

"*Trampa, pinche racista!*"

"Come out if you are a *macho* man! *Bocón!* Big mouth!"

Across the street on the other side, I noticed about twenty people holding red, white and blue signs that read: GREEKS FOR DONALD TRAMPA! LET'S MAKE AMERICA GREEK AGAIN! I couldn't believe my eyes!

"*Esta gente esta muy confundida.* These people are very confused," I thought.

Miguel and I were standing way up on the marble steps, looking at the screaming crowd. Suddenly this tall, middle aged man, well dressed and with his blond hair combed like a yellow bird's nest, walked into the crowd and yelled:

"Down with Donald *Trampa!*"

Everybody applauded! He walked through the crowd with one hand out in the open, waving to the people, while picking everybody's pockets with the other free hand. Suddenly he stopped and, standing tall in the middle of the crowd, looking down at them with the look of a man who has just been released from the nut house, he started asking questions.

"What are you doing here?"

"Rallying against *señor Trampa!*"

"You must be nuts!"

"This is a free country!"

"For me it is!" he said pounding his chest. "Besides, you don't belong here!"

"Yes! We do!"

"Have you any money?"

"Nope! We have no money!"

"How about if I get you some beer?"

"Yes! *Si!*" they shouted.

"Won't you get drunk?"

"Sure! We'll get very drunk!"

"And then what?"

"We go home!"

Abruptly, the tall guy with the yellow bird's nest on his head, with both hands in his pockets, turned around and looked at us.

"Hey!" he yelled. "You two kids, come over here!"

Miguel looked him right in the eye. I knew that look. I sucked in a deep breath and I went ahead, trying very hard to keep Miguel away from him. I shook the guy's hand. As I got closer, I noticed that the skin on his face was orange. He shook my hand and smiled.

"Maybe he's the famous Agent Orange from Vietnam!" I thought, and smiled back.

"Are you part of this crowd?"

"No" Miguel said. "We are just passing by."

"Can you guys do me a favor?" he asked lowering his voice.

"Sure!"

"Here is my card," he said, handing me a gold plated business card.

"Go inside and tell the bartender to get ten waiters to bring cold beer for these people! And that's an order!" he said while waving to the big brutes by the door to let us in.

Miguel kept looking at him straight in the eye, and again, I knew that look very well. I grabbed him by the arm, walking hurriedly through two double glass doors into the lobby. To the left we saw the bar and the bartender. He was a stocky guy, about fifty years old with a ponytail. He was standing behind an enormous glass bar and its many mirrors, looking like a modern version of the Wizard of Oz. I handed him the business card. He looked at it and smiled.

"What is the old fart doing out there hanging out with those folks?" he asked.

"He wants you to serve free beer to the people outside!" Miguel told him.

"He must be going crazy!" He started shouting orders, calling the waiters to come. As a group of about ten Spanish guys in uniform gathered around the bar, I noticed that they were very young and each one of them looked just like the demonstrators outside.

"For a moment I thought we were in Mexico again." Miguel said.

"What do you mean, *primo?*"

"All these *pinches pendejos* look Mexican to me!" *Juazzzz!* He laughed.

As we turned around to leave the building, the old dude with the yellow bird's nest on his head was walking into the building.

"Thank you kids!" he said.

"*Cabrón hijo de tu chingada madre!*" Miguel yelled.

All of a sudden all hell broke loose. Miguel charged forward and, grabbing the tall guy by the arm, pulled his hair. To my surprise the yellow bird's nest was not his hair, it was a wig! The guy's orange face went pale! One of his bodyguards handed him a red baseball cap, with the "Let's Make America Great Again" slogan written in big white letters, to cover his baldhead. The whole scene seemed ridiculous to me, like right out of a Marvel comic. As I ran after Miguel, I started to laugh. Meanwhile, Miguel was standing outside on top of the marble stairs, holding the yellow hairpiece high up in the air with his right hand. A white label attached inside caught my eye, it read: Made in China! Miguel swung it around and threw it into the crowd.

"Here, *pendejos!*" he shouted. "I have more than enough with peaceful demonstrations! It's about time you wake up and kick some ass! *Pinches cagones!*"

Señor Trampa wearing his red baseball cap anxiously followed us outside.

"C'mon kids! Don't do that! You know how much I love Mexicans!" he pleaded.

As he was saying that, I saw in the background down the avenue, the two cross-eyed twins coming our way.

"Hurry up! Let's take the subway!" Miguel shouted.

We ran towards Columbus Circle. I looked up and saw the statue of Christopher Columbus, standing tall on his pedestal among the traffic noise and the toxic fumes in the middle of the circle, watching me approvingly. I waved him goodbye as we rushed downstairs and jumped over the turnstiles. The guy in the token booth yelled something but we were not listening. We made it to the platform just as a train was pulling out of the station. Hiding behind a column, we saw the two twins wandering through the station looking for us. When they got too close, we had no choice but to jump onto the rails and climb to the other side of the platform. As we emerged from the subway, we ran like rabbits all the way to Seventh Avenue and 57th Street and went down again into the subway station. We took the R train downtown and got off at Times Square. We emerged to the bright lights, to the "melting pot" smell, to the crowds of people and the noise. I tried to stay five or ten steps behind Miguel to make sure we weren't being followed. All this time I kept thinking of my friend Barack. I vowed for the hundredth time that, once I met him, I would change my ways and become a different person. Miguel stopped, turned around and looked down the street for a long minute.

"Do you see those two twins, *hijos de la chingada?*"

"I think we lost them," I said.

"Let's go back to the hotel and make sure they're not following us."

We walked up 42nd Street all the way to Bryant Park, watching our backs and making sure nobody was after us. We sat on a park bench to rest a while and have a soda and a hot dog. I opened my laptop and set it on a little metal table. Just as I was about to write, I decided that I was getting fed up. Barack never answered my e-mails anyway. I closed the laptop; I got up and followed Miguel out of the park.

"Where are we going?" I asked. "Are we going back to the hotel or what?"

"Of course, *pendejo!* I just wanted to make sure those putos twins are not on our ass!"

We walked one block to Grand Central. The station was crowded. There were passengers getting on and off the trains. Out of nowhere, people were surging around us, people of all ages, shapes, colors and odors.

"By the way they look and how they smell, these people must be part of the famous melting pot," I thought.

Miguel, immobile among the moving crowd, stood there and just watched. As usual, he never let his guard down. After about half of the passengers were gone, somebody tapped me on the arm. When I turned around, I saw this white thin man smelling of liquor with a paper cup in one hand and a cardboard sign in the other, which read, **Homeless with aids**. I reached into my pocket and gave him a fifty-dollar bill. He nodded in gratitude and moved on to the next person. At that moment, I glanced to my right, surveying the rest of the crowd. What happened next defied all expectations. Directly behind the "aids" bum, just inches from his shoulder, one of the cross-eyed goons that I saw in Central Park took an automatic out of his pocket and, with an effort, tried to point it at my chest. A bit thrown off balance by the crowd, he was uncertain whether to keep pointing the gun at me or let the others pass by him. The people around us came and went by too quickly to pay any attention to what was going on. Suddenly, the "aids" guy threw the paper cup into the face of the gunman, and that gave me a chance to grab Miguel by the arm and run away. By now we knew what we had to do. I went right and Miguel went left. I headed straight for the subway staircase, squeezed under the turnstile and calmly walked onto the platform for the Times Square Shuttle.

I took a deep breath and, as I was starting to relax, I froze. Slowly making their way down the final staircase, I could see the two gorillas looking all around the platform. They were wearing the same Lennon t-shirts that somehow made them look totally out of place and ridiculous. Standing beside the platform, next to each other, they didn't see me. Now I was standing right in back of them, hiding behind a column. When I saw the train approaching the station, I didn't hesitate. I jumped forward and I pushed them down onto the tracks. I heard a soft boom, like a big balloon suddenly losing air. People at the station, not knowing for sure what really happened, started to scream, trying to get help. Without stopping or turning around, I began walking up the stairs slowly. When I surfaced on the corner of 42nd Street and Broadway, I caught my breath, looked at my phone for directions and began walking up Broadway along the west side of the avenue towards 57th Street. Two young cops, sitting in a patrol car and drinking coffee with donuts, chewing happily, not even looked at me.

"Not bad at all, Juan! Not bad!" I thought.

I was feeling like a hero and a sick laugh rose up from my stomach. I looked straight ahead and kept walking. At a streetlight, I glanced up. The New York sky was calypso blue, decorated with huge white clouds looking like giant cotton balls. The city that never sleeps was vibrant with activity nobody seemed to have the time to look up at the sky. I felt a sudden homesickness and guilt. I thought of Miguel. I couldn't call him. Those were his strict orders, no telephone calls, no twits and no texting. On the way to the hotel, I stopped at a coffee shop to have a sandwich and a soda, and make sure nobody else was following me. While having lunch I opened my laptop and I decided to start writing again.

Manhattan, New York City, October 12, 2014 (1:30PM)

Barack, in my last e-mail I told you about the beauty of the Oklahoma blue sky. Today, after seeing the New York calypso blue sky over Manhattan decorated with huge white clouds, I felt that inexplicable feeling that I was witnessing the best version of nature's work of art. It felt almost like when in Sinaloa the strong wind blowing from the north, carrying the sand and the debris to the foothill slopes, exploded like a Mariachi fiesta enveloping the whole valley. Anyway, the important thing is that I am here in New York and on my way to Washington to see you. After all, that's my ultimate goal. I must confess that during my journey here on this side of the fence in your Gringo-Land, with all the difficult situations I have had to face, and not getting any answers from you, I sometimes thought of packing my few belongings and go back to Mexico for good. What kept me going forward was the fact that I was finally going to have the chance to meet you and, somehow, you and I together would work out a rational solution to all the problems affecting my country and yours. As I write this note, I also sense that you must be a very busy person with a lot of work to do, here and all over the world. I can imagine "globalization at its best" and all the hard work that it takes to impose that "innovative system" upon humanity. By the way, I just saw you on TV last night, and I couldn't help noticing that you looked very tense. You also have a few more wrinkles and a lot of new gray hair. It seems to me that you've aged very fast. Even your body language is changing alarmingly. I worry about you, my friend, and I hope you are doing ok. Hope to see you soon. Juan

After having lunch, I packed my computer and continued walking on Broadway towards the hotel. When I got to the corner of 65th Street, I saw Miguel standing across the street watching the hotel's entrance. I waved to him to cross the street and join me.

"I saw what you did in Times Square, *pendejo!*" he said angrily.

"No other end would have been possible for those criminals who keep following us."

"It doesn't matter, *cabrón!* Every time you kill somebody, you are also the victim."

"Look who's talking!"

"A real Mexican builds his world in his own image, *carnal,*" he smiled.

His smile had the ruthless calmness of conviction. We walked silently into the hotel lobby. We saw Sammy waiting for us.

"You are a half hour late!" he said impatiently.

"We got lost," Miguel said.

"So, how was your tour of Manhattan anyway?" Sammy asked, as the three of us walked out to the car.

"It was great!" I said.

"New York is a beautiful city! Don't you love it?"

"To love a thing is to know and love its nature," Miguel laughed, "and I don't know New York that well, since we've only been here for one *pinche* day, *cabrón!*"

CHAPTER 18
Washington DC

We arrived in Washington around six in the afternoon. We went directly to the hotel where Nataya was staying. After checking in, we went straight to our room.

"Go to your room, take a shower and change. The show is at eight, we don't have much time," Sammy said.

When we came down, Sammy was already in the lobby.

"Nataya is in the limo outside, ready to go to the theatre" he said hurriedly. "You, Miguel, take the Subaru, and I'll go with Juan in another car."

"And how am I supposed to get to the *pinche* theatre, *cabrón!*" Miguel shouted.

"Use the GPS, you little peasant!" Sammy laughed.

We went outside to see Miguel getting into the Subaru and driving off.

"Drive carefully!" Sammy yelled. "We don't need any more problems right now!"

Sammy climbed into the back seat of the limo and kissed Nataya passionately on her fat red lips. It was a long and hot kiss, so hot it almost lit up the whole vehicle.

"I'll see you after the show. You are the best! Go break a leg! I love you!"

He stepped swiftly back down onto the sidewalk. We looked about the area around the hotel, making sure the coast was clear, and carefully covering each other's back, we strolled to our car. When I opened the car door, I noticed that the back seat was full of flowers. There were purple orchids everywhere, with some potted plants placed on the floor. The smell was pleasantly overwhelming. "Are we going to somebody's funeral?" I asked.

"Thank God I got the purple orchids," Sammy laughed. "Nataya loves them!"

We drove down New Hampshire Avenue to F North West Street and parked two blocks away from the Kennedy Center, next to the silver Subaru station wagon.

"Miguel is here already," I said.

"We'll meet him inside. I have three backstage passes."

"What about the orchids?" I asked.

"Before the show is over, we'll bring the car around to the stage door, give the flowers to the stagehands and they'll take them to her dressing room. She'll be delighted!"

"Can I keep one?"

"What do you need it for?" Sammy thought I was joking.

"For my *amigo* Barack!" I said. "I think it would be a good gesture on my part!"

"Boys don't give flowers to boys, Juan! Especially orchids!" he laughed.

"*Por que no?*" I asked. "Actually it's not funny, our friendship is very special."

When I walked into the theater lobby carrying the purple orchid and with Sammy at my side, everybody was looking at me. I felt a surge of adrenaline, similar I used to feel in Sinaloa when going around making deliveries. This time it was different. It was a good feeling, the kind that made me feel fearless and able to do good things. I had never been among this kind of a crowd before. All the people around me were so different. They didn't look Mexican at all and, as usual, blending in was not my strong point. I saw everything in sharp detail, happy faces, and beautiful women wearing long dresses, white-haired men, some of them looking like bankers with gold-rimmed glasses. I also noticed Miguel dressed in black, standing next to the bust of JFK opposite the main entrance of the opera house. To the left, there was a marquee with a big color poster of Nataya on her toes, in a dance stance, with wide-open arms and smiling. In big bold letters you could read:

Latin Culture Productions

Presents

A Swan in Lake Tahoe with Nataya Danzingsolova

And the National Ballet Company

Only Washington DC appearance

Exhilarated, I waved to Miguel and, walking at a moderate pace, holding on to the purple orchid, I crossed the lobby to greet him, suddenly realizing that in about two hours, Barack and me would meet for the first time, face to face, in that same spot.

"I'm going inside to see the show, guys," Sammy said, handing us the backstage passes.

I was too excited to go in, sit still for more than an hour, and watch the whole show. Not tonight, I mean, I loved Nataya and, in different circumstances, for sure I would happily watch the entire show like I did at The Met in New York City. However, in this instance, I wasn't in the mood to see that show again. No way!

"Let's go outside and take a walk," Miguel said.

As we walked out, we could hear the roar of the audience applauding. It was eight o'clock on the dot. I imagined Nataya coming out on stage, bowing down and greeting her fans.

"I like that! It must be a standing ovation!" I said.

"Me too! It must be nice to have so many people admiring you all at once!"

We sat on a bench facing the Potomac River. A river older than the United States, this river was flowing even before George Washington was President. There are all sorts of myths and legends surrounding rivers. I mean, we are Mexicans and we like to make up stories about rivers and that night, looking at the river, we felt we were not afraid anymore. Everything we did in the past was probably stupid. Okay, it was stupid. It's not that we were trying to be heroes or anything. We were terrified at failing and, no matter how old I get, I think I'm always going to be scared of failing. Miguel, sitting next to me, was meditating.

"Let's go back inside," I said.

"You go first," Miguel said.

I walked back inside the lobby and, when I looked up, the lights hit me right in the eyes. The ceiling got excessively tall, and I got dizzy. I walked up to the JFK bust standing in the center of the lobby and I leaned on it to regain my strength. I saw a young black man wearing a tuxedo with gold buttons, a white hat, white shoes and black gloves, stepping away from the bust. He called my attention. I couldn't ignore him. He turned suddenly and stared at me. I looked hard at him. He grinned at me with enjoyment and got closer to Miguel as he was walking in, tapping him once with his index finger on the back of the neck. Scratching the back of his neck, Miguel kept walking towards me. The black dude turned his head and winked. There was the distant sound of people coming out of the hall. At last I was going to meet Barack. I saw Sammy, next to the president, surrounded by at least twenty secret service agents, hurriedly walking towards me. My mouth got dry and I was shaking all over. Finally, I was going to shake hands and embrace my friend Barack. I saw the black dude approaching me. His black gloves caught my attention. Suddenly my cell phone rang.

"Juan!" It was Blanca. "You have to get out of there, fast!"

"What?"

"It's a trap! Zorro Porro sent somebody to kill you! Run, Juan! Run!"

I looked up and, out of the corner of my eye; I saw a black glove with a needle on the index finger, aiming at my neck. I grabbed the guy by the arm and, jumping forward, I smashed his nose with my forehead. With all my strength, I pushed him backwards against the JFK bust. I heard a soft sound, like a huge egg breaking up in little pieces, and I saw the black guy falling to the floor face first. There was a lot of blood flowing from a huge hole in the back of his head. I looked up and I noticed that the bust was also bleeding from the nose. Still holding the purple orchid with my left hand, I said,

"Thank you Mr. President! You saved my life!", giving the bust a military salute before twenty overweight secret service agents, screaming like mad dogs and smelling of cheap perfume, piled up on top of me and my purple orchid. I passed out. I don't remember anything else that happened that night.

Next day I woke up in the hospital. When I opened my eyes, Nataya and Sammy were in the room. A purple orchid was on the night table next to my bed. Nataya was holding my hand and crying. There were two young guys in uniform standing by my bed, one on each side.

"Juan, I'm so glad you are ok!" she said.

"You are a hero, kid!" Sammy shouted happily. "Take a look at this!"

On the front page of the Washington Post under the headline: **"TWO YOUNG MEXICAN HEROES SAVE THE PRESIDENT'S LIFE"**, there was my picture and Miguel's.

"You guys are in every newspaper and every news outlet all over the country, and all over the world!" Sammy said.

"What have we done?" I asked.

"Can't you read? You saved the president's life!"

"We did what?"

"Read, Juan! Read!" he said, handing me the newspaper.

And there it was, in bold letters, and in black and white.

At least nine people were wounded inside the lobby of the Kennedy Center for the Performing Arts when a lone assassin tried to kill the President. The quick intervention of two Mexican kids, subduing the assailant, saved the President's life. Together with Prime Minister Putin of Russia, the President was walking out of the hall into the lobby after attending the premier of A SWAN IN LAKE TAHOE, performed by the Bolshoi's famous ballerina, Nataya Danzingsolova. The assassin, ready to strike, was waiting for the President by the exit door, but was confronted and thrown to the ground by Juan Sintierra and Miguel Meromero, two young Mexican nationals that happened to be in the area at that moment. The local authorities, for security reasons, have not released the name of the assailant, or the trademark of all the gardening tools found at the site. The President commended both young men for the Medal of Honor, and is expected to meet with the two young heroes at the Rose Garden, Monday of next week. According to a statement released by the White House, when the President was asked what he was going to talk about with the two young heroes, he said: "Among other things, we are going to talk about gardening at our borders, and about the American people's and the Mexican people's similarities..."

I stopped reading. I couldn't believe my eyes, Miguel and me, two national heroes.

"Hey!" I asked. "Where is Miguel?"

"He's in intensive care."

"Can I see him?"

"Not just yet, Juan."

"Why?"

"Because he is very sick and you two are in the care of the United States government!"

"So?"

"There are rules and regulations, Juan. A huge investigation is going on."

"You mean we are prisoners?"

"I wouldn't say that. The proper authorities are investigating the two of you. That's all."

"Then we're screwed! Miguel and me, we are not proper at all!"

"I don't think so, kid. In your particular case, there are too many political implications."

"I don't know what you are talking about!"

"You don't need to know, Juan. Everything will be ok, you'll see."

The two young white guys in uniform standing by my bed, staring straight ahead, were smiling. Both looked the same to me. They were not moving at all. Standing still, they looked like two perfect statues, like two toy soldiers in a window display.

"Who are they?" I asked. "*Federales?*"

"No, Juan! They are US Marines!"

"You mean these are the same guys as in that picture, holding the flag on the mountain top?"

"Yes and no, Juan," Sammy laughed. "Those were marines too. It's an old picture and it was taken a long time ago."

"*Orale, cabrón!* As long as these two guards are not *federales*, we are cool!"

For the next three days, two FBI agents, one old and one young, were in my room asking me the same questions, constantly. They even took samples of my blood and my saliva to the FBI lab. Somehow, checking my e-mails, they had linked me to a man called Barack Orwelson from Chicago. My answer was always the same.

"I came from Mexico to Gringo-Land to see my friend Barack, your *presidente*. I have no idea who that other Barack from Chicago is or what you are talking about."

"You are no genius, kid, but you are highly intelligent. You are cleared, we have nothing on you or your friend," one of them said. "This is off the record of course!"

After saying that, they got up ready to leave. Looking at them, I didn't think they were giving me a compliment, more like they were realizing how much shit was about to hit the fan if I really opened up my mouth and told the truth to the whole world.

"You can go and see your friend Miguel now!" the older agent said, before walking out.

When I opened the door, I saw Miguel lying on the bed with his eyes closed and all these tubes connected to his body. He was breathing normally. A young nurse and two marines were standing by the bed.

"He's in a coma," the nurse said.

"For how long has he been like this?" I asked nervously.

"Four days already."

"Will he be ok?"

"I don't know. Right now, from the head down, he is temporarily unable to move. The poison is all over his body!"

"But he'll live, right?"

"Where there is life, there is hope, Juan. Miguel is very strong. But you have to be prepared for the worst."

I couldn't cry and I felt my body invaded by an immense sense of peace. I was sure Miguel would live. That was all that mattered to me.

"I would like to be left alone with him for a moment," I said.

"Of course," the nurse grinned and she walked out.

The two marines didn't move an inch. It felt like two deluxe prison wardens were watching me.

"Are you all right, *primo?*" I said, holding his hand.

He smiled and squeezed my hand. I shifted uncomfortably in my seat.

"He's not in coma," I thought.

"I'm going to die, Juan," he mumbled, suddenly. "I can feel it!"

"No you won't, *pinche cabrón!* Not if you put your mind to it!"

"*Silencio, pendejo!*" he said angrily. "Let me talk, I don't have much time left!"

Miguel's brown eyes were half-open, looking into mine, his right hand now weakly clasped around my arm, was very cold. The clock on the wall showed twenty minutes past ten in the morning, which meant that Miguel had decided to die exactly five years to the day we first met.

"Juan," he whispered. "Blanca's child is my son. Promise you will take care of him."

"I can't believe what you are saying! You must be going mad!"

All of a sudden the door opened and the nurse, together with the two FBI agents, burst into the room pushing me aside and, standing by the bed almost on top of Miguel, furiously started interrogating him. Suddenly, Miguel's eyes closed. I knew he was dead.

"Get Juan out of here!" somebody yelled.

The two marines escorted me out to the elevator and took me directly to my room. Sammy was waiting for me.

"I'm sorry, Juan."

"Is all this show of power necessary, all this fricking madness, all this *pinche* brutality? We are just two little people!"

"Little people talking little harsh words can be very dangerous and you could be booked on suspicion of terrorism by the legal system."

"I thought that only in Mexico you could go to jail, because a cop or a judge didn't get an answer to some questions or didn't like your ideas!"

"That's the way the cookie crumbles, kid! The good news is that you are free to go now and tomorrow morning, at ten, you are meeting the President at the White House."

"What about Miguel's body?"

"First they have to perform an autopsy on him. After that he'll be sent in a sealed coffin back to Mexico for a State Funeral."

"A State Funeral, in Mexico?"

"But of course, Juan!" Sammy shouted. "Remember, you must be present at the burial. You are two national heroes!"

That same afternoon, Sammy took care of everything. He took me to a barbershop to get my hair trimmed, and he bought me a dark gray suit, a white shirt, a red tie and black shoes.

"I sure look like I'm going to a funeral," I said.

"The protocol requires for you to be dressed conveying confidence, like the President."

Next morning, four secret service agents in a black Cadillac SUV picked us up at our hotel at nine thirty sharp. The person in charge ordered one of them to use some kind of scanner to check if we were carrying any weapons.

"Isn't the kid holding the purple orchid one of the suspects?" The agent in charge asked Sammy.

"For your information, Juan is a national hero," Sammy said.

"All I know is that he is a person of interest in my investigation."

As I was climbing into the car, all dressed up and feeling confident, like the President, I looked myself in the rearview mirror.

"Why the hell am I feeling so nervous? I am not going to jail! I'm finally going to meet Barack!" I thought.

My heart raced as we approached the White House. Surrounded by the secret agents, we got into the compound by a side gate and went through three more security checks before reaching the Rose Garden. At the first gate, we had to pay a fee of twenty dollars each in order to get in, at the second one, forty dollars, and, at the third one, fifty dollars. At all the checkpoints there were huge signs with big red letters stating: "Payments in cash only, no credit cards, checks or money orders allowed."

"You're on your own now," Sammy said, pushing me forward. "It's the show you've been waiting for!"

A very elegant, middle-aged woman with a beautiful smile came to my rescue and, taking me by the hand, escorted me to a chair next to a lectern, flanked by the American and Mexican flags.

"Nice meeting you, Juan. My name is Hillary Flipton. I'll be assisting you throughout the ceremony," she said.

When I sat down, still holding the purple orchid on my lap, I saw about three hundred very happy people sitting all over the lawn, facing me, some of them setting up TV cameras on tripods, while others, smiling and pointing at me, were typing away on their laptops. I heard like a symphony of cell phones ringing in the background. Everything seemed like fun, as if they were all caught up in a big *fiesta*. I felt like a celebrity, like I was Luis Miguel giving a press conference before a show at the *Auditorio Nacional*. My *primo* was dead and I was feeling very sad about that, but all this attention was flattering and it was hard not to enjoy the moment. "Relax kid, don't be nervous, it will be over in ten minutes. But first, read this," Hillary said, handing me an eight by eleven white paper sheet, with the presidential shield printed on it. I started reading.

10.00 AM, The President's speech opens the Medal of Honor Ceremony.

10.02 AM, The President greets Medal of Honor recipient.

10.03 AM, The President invites honoree to the podium.

10.04 AM, Honoree stands next to the President, posing for pictures.

10.05 AM, Honoree thanks the President, praising democracy and the American way of life.

10.06 AM, The President and the honoree exchange red roses and purple orchids.

10.07 AM, The President presents the honoree with the medal.

10.08 AM, They shake hands and embrace each other for the official picture.

10.09 AM, Holding up their hands, they both smile and wave to the press.

10.10 AM, They embrace once more and get down from the podium.

Important note: Honoree must keep smiling at all times for the cameras. There will be no interviews of any kind, without a pre-approved script. After the ceremony is over, the honoree must leave the area. No dialogue between the President and the honoree permitted, at any time.

Warning: For security reasons, honoree would be shot dead on the spot, if he does not follow the above-mentioned instructions to the letter.

"These gringos don't play games! They are real *locos*, the pinches *cabrones!!*" I thought.

I folded the note and put it in my pocket. I looked at my watch. It was exactly one minute to ten. At ten o'clock sharp, Barack climbed onto the podium, waving and smiling. The crowd went wild. Approaching the microphone under the sunny Washington sky, waiting for the audience to quiet down, he looked presidential.

"My fellow Americans, we are gathered here today to honor Juan Sintierra for saving my life. As you well know, when you are the President of the most powerful country in the world, you attract a lot of attention and there are certain acute disadvantages in attracting attention. Evil people start hating you because you have the power to discipline them when they don't respect the rights of others on the world stage, or when you say things about them that they don't appreciate. And let me tell you, I know that what I've been saying lately has gotten me into a lot of trouble with the bad guys. But luckily for me, and for the American people, there are also good and valiant young men, like Juan and Miguel, willing to give their lives if necessary, to defend and protect our freedom. Today I want to cut my speech short. At this moment, words cannot express how I feel about this young Mexican hero for saving my life. I want all of you to meet Juan Sintierra!"

Hillary grabbed my arm and helped me to get to the podium. Standing next to the President, holding the purple orchid and feeling like an idiot, I got closer. He smelled of perfume, his eyebrows were graceful and he smiled nonstop.

"Come closer, kid! I want to shake your hand!" Barack said.

I noticed the camera guys started filming and everybody else was taking pictures. When we shook hands, some people started yelling and applauding. I tried to make eye contact with him but he looked the other way.

"I want to talk to you alone," I whispered, when we embraced each other for the first time. Gesturing to the microphone, he completely ignored me. Feeling rejected, I was starting to get upset. Hillary, as usual smiling in a motherly way, pushed me closer to the microphone.

"*Dear amigos,*" I said. "I'm glad to be here in the capital of the planet next to my friend Barack. I'm not an Alien not even a Martian, I'm just a humble Mexican kid and I want all of you to know that I did what I had to do, just with my two little hands. There was nothing to it! I want to thank you and your president for this honor! I love Gringo-Land and I love you all. *Gracias!*"

While delivering my speech, I was holding the purple orchid with my right hand. However, with my left hand behind my back, I kept my fingers crossed.

I got a standing ovation. Barack gave me a bunch of red roses and put the Medal of Honor around my neck. I gave him my purple orchid. We shook hands again and embraced for more pictures.

"I want to meet in private with you," I whispered in his big ear.

"No way, that's not possible," was his abrupt answer.

Once again, the people started applauding and cheering. Standing next to each other, we waved goodbye to the crowd. When we embraced for the last time, I insisted, asking him once more for a private meeting.

"Listen, kid, there's nothing to talk about!" he answered angrily and got off the podium real fast.

"Come this way, Juan; good job! You did real well," Hillary said, escorting me out of the area.

Walking at a slow pace, I followed her, holding the bunch of red roses in my hand. My first feeling of attraction and admiration for my friend Barack had faded. It suddenly started to rain. Hillary took me inside the White House through a metal door down a corridor to a private office. I knew my face was radiating anger and pain.

"Read this," she said, handing me a note while putting her arm around me as we waited.

OFFICIAL NOTICE

Dear Mr. Juan Sintierra,

You have 72 hours to leave the country voluntarily. After that period, you will be breaking the law and considered an illegal alien. According to the law of the land, you would be incarcerated and deported to your country of origin.

Best,

Mr. Ike D. Portyou Jr.

Operation Wetback Team

IMMIGRATION AND NATURALIZATION SERVICE

When I left the White House that day, I felt disappointed and relieved at the same time. I left on cordial terms with Hillary. She turned out to be one of the nicest people I met during the ceremony. She was kind, cultured, unassuming and obsessed with work. She confided to me how bored she was with her actual job. Boredom was a small price to pay for peace of mind. She wanted to return to her former life in the country and become a quiet private citizen. When I told her that she could become the greatest spiritual leader of our time, she got very emotional and started to cry.

"Your destiny is to become the first woman *presidente* of Gringo-Land," I said.

"Thank you, Juan!" she said. "I have to leave Washington to fly back to New York in the morning but you know how to reach me. You will let me know if anything happens to you. Promise me that you are going to be back in Mexico within seventy two hours."

"Of course I will *madre!*" I answered and, after saying that, I left.

Back in my hotel, I went directly up to my room. When I opened the door, I saw my passport, my laptop, my cell phone and my silver revolver on top of the bed. The FBI old timer was lying in bed next to my stuff, watching TV.

"What are you watching?" I asked.

"Watching basketball!"

What's the score?"

"95 to 78"

"Who's winning?"

"95, stupid!" he barked and started to laugh like crazy. I laughed too.

"*Juazzzzz*! That *pinche* joke is older than you, *cabrón!*" I said.

"But I got you just the same, kid!"

Suddenly he stopped laughing.

"I thought you might like to know that your friend's autopsy confirmed that he died of poisoning. Right now he is in a nice coffin and ready to travel with you to Mexico. As a matter of fact, we made all the arrangements for you guys to travel together on the same plane, you in first class and Miguel in the cargo compartment."

"What about Miguel's killer?"

"We cremated him and his ashes were sent back to Chicago, to his father's house," he said. "Anything more you'd like to know?"

"No," I said. "Just leave me alone now. I need to be by myself."

Standing by the door and holding a huge Macy's shopping bag, he stared at me in silence.

"*Amigo*, whatever you do with your fricking life, good luck *kid*!" He opened the door, shook my hand, waved goodbye and left. Being a Mexican, no matter where I am, I don't trust the so-called authorities that much. Therefore, I checked the whole room for hidden microphones, cameras or any other recording devices. When I checked the bathroom, the soap, the toothpaste, the toothbrush, the dental floss, the shampoo, the toilet paper, the box of tissues and all the towels were missing.

"I guess the FBI field agents don't make such a good salary anymore," I thought.

CHAPTER 19
The White House

It was early evening when I arrived at The Ghetto Inn Motel. A young black girl in white slacks sat at the front desk. She didn't even say hello. She just gave me the rate.

"Its fifty dollars a night, for a single room, cash in advance only."

"How do I get to the South Side?" I asked.

"You are on the South Side now. Everything is in walking distance."

"Do you know George Orwelson?"

"Of course I do!" she smiled faintly. "He's my friend Barack's father. They live at the White House, at number 1984, just six blocks up the street!"

"1984? Orwelson? The White House?" I asked startled.

"Yes! He lives in a house that his father painted white! Is there something wrong with that?" I could tell she was a little upset.

"Of course not! I was just asking."

"I hope you like it up here. It's very quiet," she said, ignoring my answer and handing me the room key.

The motel seemed empty. The corridors were very dark. The only activity going on was the cleaning woman, making a hamming noise with her vacuum cleaner. I unlocked my door and walked in. The windowless room looked barer, than the little room in my trailer at the Elota River. A single bed, one night table, a small dresser, and an ugly and stained gray carpet, gave the place the look of an old sanatorium. I sat on the bed and opened my laptop to check my mail.

Welcome to the South Side, Juan. I hope you are well. I'll be waiting for you at my White House. Remember, no phone calls or txt msgs. The "crazies" are watching us at all times. Best, George

I answered right away.

I'll be at your place in twenty minutes. Juan

I went downstairs. The girl at the reception, with her hands flat on the desk, was looking at me. She leaned forward and pointed in the air with her forefinger.

"As you exit, go left, young man, go left," she laughed.

I went out and down the steps leading to the street, and there I was in the middle of the ghetto on the South Side of Chicago. I squinted my eyes and I tried to imagine that I was back in Sinaloa. No Elota River here but perhaps I could run into one of *Lobo's* ex-bodyguards. I opened my eyes wide and I saw rows of dilapidated buildings, flanked by vacant lots. As I walked by, I saw a black woman hanging out of a fifth floor window in what looked like a deserted building. She was showing her big black tits and yelling:

"Come up! Light up my world! God is Love! The Lord belongs to everyone!"

I didn't pay any attention to her. She looked positively insane. The street was deserted; except for some rats running by the curb and into the sewer looking for food. I was carrying two million dollars in cash in my backpack, but somehow I felt secure. Maybe it was my imagination, but there was something special about the ghetto, everything was serene and peaceful. Suddenly, right in the middle of the block, painted in white and surrounded by vacant lots, standing alone like a white fly standing on a brown turd; was Barack's White House. What a difference that house made on that particular block between the slums, sparkling white, decorated with colorful Christmas lights and a huge garden full of flowers. A big fat white man in sunglasses, wearing a suit and tie, sweating and puffing, was shoveling dirt in the garden. On the front porch, the number 1984 painted in gold, shone in the morning sun. A post card like that in the middle of the ghetto seemed astoundingly strange and unreal to me.

"*Señor* Orwelson?"

"Juan?"

He gave me a funny stare, started to say something, then shook his head, put the shovel against the fence and shook my hand.

"Welcome to the White House kid!"

"*Gracias!* I'm so glad to meet you, George! What a beautiful house!"

"C'mon inside kid!"

We went into the house. He opened the door with that striking leisure only fat men ever achieve. He was large and wide, not too old or too handsome. However, somehow he looked distinguished and very strong. The neck of his blue shirt was unbuttoned, it had to be because his neck, like everything else on him, was so fat. His big fathead still had a decent amount of blond hair. His motions were quick and determined. There was nothing slow about the way he moved. He was smiling all the time. When we sat down next to each other on a black leather sofa, he continued smiling.

"It's nice of you to come and see me," he said. "I needed closure."

"Everything happened so fast that night. Barack tried to kill me and I reacted. I was protecting myself."

"I know kid. I'm not blaming you anymore."

"You doubted me over the phone, so I had to come and convince you."

"You don't have to give me two million dollars to convince me kid!"

"Like I told you over the telephone, I want you to open **THE MIGUEL MEROMERO YOUTH CENTER** here in the South Side." I said, handing him the backpack full of cash.

He listened without moving a muscle on his face. When I finished talking, he made a vague gesture towards a big color picture of Barack hanging on the living room wall. "No matter what Juan, my son Barack is dead," he said sadly. "If it's important to you, I know who's responsible for his death and he's coming here tonight."

"Who is he?"

"Here, read this" he said handing me a laptop. "I'll be in the backyard. I'm barbequing for you and my pets tonight."

He got up slowly and went outside. I noticed he was wearing alligator shoes one size too big. I opened the computer and started to read. Outside on the street, the sound of gunshots reminded me of Sinaloa. I felt a bond with the South Side of Chicago as if it was my own neighborhood.

Hi, my name is Barack Orwelson, I'm twenty years old and I'm not the typical American you see everywhere. I'm black, with a bland expression reflected on my face, pseudo serious and definitely shrewd. I live with my white father. He's my blood and he looks like no other father in the world. He owns the only family house still standing on our block, a house that my father painted himself, all white. Nowadays, it's surrounded by a cluster of dilapidated buildings that according to my father, were once brand new and architecturally in good taste, before the white people moved out and we the blacks took over. "Barack you are my son and you deserve to live in a white house, no more no less," he told me one afternoon after he finished painting our home. My father always dresses in a cheap ready-made suit, his shiny handmade alligator shoes one size too big. Like a pseudo-intellectual, he's always carrying an old newspaper under his arm and, of course, he wears sunglasses, the same model that Ray Charles used to wear. He is a man who eats and drinks too much, smokes too much, sits too much, talks too much and is always relaxing too much. "What's the point of having money in your pocket if you can't enjoy yourself?" is his mantra. He's the type who departs from the norm, but he is my father and I love him just the way he is. Let me tell you, I love him very much.

I live in the ghetto of the most typical American city. There are acres and acres of vacant lots. It looks like a bombarded citadel. You can see piles of smashed, almost pulverized bricks and plaster all over the place. Hundreds of charred buildings standing up looking like some kind of big black Godzilla monsters battling against the Chicago gray sky. Nothing is too dilapidated to discourage us, the locals. We love our neighborhood and, no matter what, we keep moving forward. Here in my town we are jovial, disputative, crazy and independent. We disagree with everything, because we know its all hypocrisy and lies we hear, day in and day out, anyway. That's the reason why we can accomplish everything we want to. There is a spirit here that even years of misery and deceit has not smashed just yet. Now and then, I get out of the house to stretch my legs and take care of business. I go by the only hotel left in the whole neighborhood, The Ghetto Inn Motel. All kinds of people stay in this dingy place and that's where I find my best customers, the hungry buyers. They pay top dollars for a joint or any other heavy shit. All they want is to get high and blow their minds out. Today, I'm here to meet a guy from Mexico who sent me an e-mail a week ago offering me a job.

I'll be in Chicago next week and I would like to meet with you to discuss some important business. I'll be staying at The Ghetto Inn Motel. I believe it's in your neighborhood. Please feel free to answer via e-mail. Gracias! Zorro Porro

I answered him right away.

Mr. Porro, thank you for your e-mail. I'm definitely looking for a job. They keep telling me that I'm overqualified. I have a lot of free time right now, and I need a job badly. They disconnected my cell last week. I'll look for you at the motel. Barack Orwelson

When I finally met this obscure Mexican guy, he was quite a figure, walking across the shady motel lobby dressed in a very expensive suit. He told me that he was a man without a country and all because of some vicious kids that ruined his life.

"I would give an arm and a leg to be able to find them," he told me.

"Did they steal from you?"

"I don't think that's any of your business," he said angrily.

"What can I do for you, bro?" I asked, nicely.

"I want to kill the mother-fuckers!"

"I can see you are upset," I said. "How much are you paying?"

"Fifty thousand dollars!"

"For each one?"

"Yes!"

"For one hundred big ones, consider it done!" I said happily.

Here I was in the middle of the ghetto, making a deal with this older Mexican dude about killing two kids I didn't even know, for one hundred thousand dollars.

"Come back tomorrow morning, around ten, and I'll give you all the instructions," he said.

"I guess that's all," I said, before walking away.

When I came out into the street, I saw a beautiful black chick hanging out in front of the motel. It was Monday night and, just like me, she seemed to have nothing to do.

"How about going to my white house and do nothing together girl," I said grabbing her by the waist.

She stared talking, but I wasn't paying attention to anything she was saying. All the time I was thinking about her nude body lying next to mine. I turned my eyes upward to thank God and I had no doubt, that from up there he was talking to me. I knew it was the Lord himself.

"You're very lucky Barack. With all this money, you are going to be able to get out of the ghetto, go to school and grow up to be President!"

Next day, at ten in the morning, I waited in the shabby motel lobby for the Mexican guy. He came downstairs at ten past one. He was wearing a long black coat, a red shirt, blue jeans and a black cowboy hat. He looked like shit. When he walked out with his face all contorted, not even looking at me, I followed him close behind. He was walking real fast and I tried to catch up with him.

"Stay back!" he barked. "Just follow me!"

We walked for about five blocks until he turned left into a corridor of burned down buildings, the locks dismantled, the doors unhinged and the balconies full of garbage. There was a small park covered by discarded old furniture, and burnt up books and newspapers. Except for the sound of the skate-boards in the distance, the place was practically deserted. An older black man and a young oriental woman sat on a charred sofa, smoking weed. They stood up and looked at us without expression. They just stood there like two animals lost in a field. Suddenly the Mexican slowed down and spoke to me.

"I have a black maid working at my hacienda in Mexico. She has a pretty good life, as a matter of fact, a much better life than you people have in this lousy place!"

"I feel sorry for you! With all your wealth and everything, you don't seem that happy to me!"

"How do you know?"

"You want to kill two people, don't you?" I laughed. "You have a very peculiar way to show your happiness!"

"It's nothing personal. It's just business!"

He looked puzzled. He turned around and retraced his steps. His voice grew stronger.

"Listen kid, here is the deal. These two kids I'm talking about are inside the country right now on their way to Washington to meet with the President. Juan, the younger one, sent two e-mails to an e-mail address he believed belonged to Barack. We intercepted the messages. We know all their plans. Your job is very simple. This coming Sunday they are going to be at the Kennedy Center to see Swan Lake and meet the President in the lobby of the theater after the show. I'll give you a pair of gloves, specially designed with needles in the index fingers containing a very powerful poison. You just have to get close enough to prick the little fuckers and then walk away. They'll never know what hit them."

"That's all?" I asked.

"Yes boy! They'll be dead in less than an hour."

"What about the secret service?"

"No problemo! You'll be done before the President even meets with them!"

"How do I get paid?"

"Cash! Fifty per cent now and the rest after you finish the job!"

"Consider it done!"

"Listen, Barack, one more thing."

"What?"

"If you talk to anybody about this, I will have no choice but to kill you too!"

"No sweat man! I'll keep my trap shut! I love life too much!"

After I finished reading, I closed the computer and I put it down, very slowly on the sofa, and stood up. The Venetian blinds were down across the back window, giving the place a sleepy look. The back door was not quite shut. I gave it a little push and it moved outwards with a little click. The backyard was big and well kept. There was a swimming pool enclosed by a wooden fence with pines and bushes around it. The smell of barbecued meat was overwhelming. I went farther into the yard, and I stood peering around and listening, hearing nothing except those strange sounds coming from the pool and having nothing to do with human activity. At the far corner, by the side of the pool, I saw George standing by a huge barbecue grill, surrounded by a cloud of smoke.

"Come closer, Juan!" Do you want a beer?"

"Okay," I said. "That's a lot of meat!"

"I told you! It's for you, me and my pets!"

"What pets?"

"Dick and GW! Do you want to meet them?"

"Of course, I do!"

He gestured to me. I followed him along the side of the pool.

"There they are!" he shouted. "Dick, GW, this is Juan!"

I couldn't believe my eyes. In the center of the pool there were two giant crocodiles, with some kind of a black belt strapped around their bodies, swimming softly our way, obeying their master's command. I jumped back. I was scared shitless.

"Don't be afraid Juan, they are two lovely animals. I raised them myself. At night I let them loose in the backyard and they are better than a guard dog."

"You really do that?"

"In this neighborhood, people use to jump over the fence to try to rob me. Not anymore!"

"Why?"

"After Dick and GW devoured a few of them, I guess the others got scared and got the message. Word of mouth, you know?"

"How do you know they eat people?"

"The morning after, I usually find a bloody sneaker or a shoe. Dick and GW don't eat junk. They love human flesh. They're picky eaters!"

"What's that black strap around their belly?"

"That's a set of wheels I designed myself, custom-made just for them!"

"What for?"

"This way, when they are out of the water, they can move much faster!"

While talking to me he was slapping the water with both hands and tenderly calling them. When they got closer to the edge of the pool, he laughed, bent over and patted both animals on the head. I was ready to scream. Then he blew them a kiss. Both reptiles splashed the water with their tales, as a sign of affection I guess. I was in shock. I couldn't help it. I pictured my body going through those jaws and heard the grinding of their teeth cutting through muscle and bone. It gave me the shakes.

"Tonight both of them are having a good dinner and a good dessert. They deserve it."

"I get it!" I said. "The dessert is coming to dinner!" We both had a good laugh.

When Zorro Porro arrived on the South Side of Chicago, it was almost midnight and it was very hot. Everybody was outside, drinking, smoking weed, listening to music and dancing. It was one great big party. On the way to Barack's White House, his custom- made suit called the attention of the people loitering in the streets of the ghetto. They seemed to be glad to see a classy dude like him walking in their neighborhood. The black boys and the black girls were all smiling at him. He took a handful of fifty-dollar bills out of his pocket and handed them to the kids.

"Nice to see you, boss!" they yelled amiably, while taking the money.

"This place seems poorer and louder than before," he thought. "I don't want to stick around here for too long. I have to find that Barack kid and whack him, before he opens his big mouth!"

He looked up the street and, well, there it was, Barack's White House! A beautiful little English Tudor house painted white, shining like the sun, standing in the middle of a vacant lot amongst the slums. The house glowed, decorated with Christmas lights. Zorro Porro, standing by the front lawn, made sure his right hand fitted the grip of his forty-five gold-plated pistol, and walked quite naturally up to the front door. He knocked twice. When the smiling big fat white guy opened the door, the smell of grilled meat exploded in Zorro Porro's face.

"Welcome to my house! How are you?" The fat guy said good-naturedly.

"Mr. George Owerlson?"

"Yes! That's me! I was expecting you earlier."

"I've come to see Barack, your son."

"C'mon in! I'm about to have dinner."

"Thank you, but I'm here for only one reason and I recall having expressed that reason."

"May I ask you again, what that is?"

"Don't you remember? To pay your son the money I owe him for a job well done!"

"He just went out. We can wait for him while chewing a good steak!"

They walked into the backyard. On the deck outside there was a big table with three bottles of red wine and three tall wine glasses on it. Two big benches that looked like two rectangular wooden boxes bordered the table. Zorro Porro scrutinized the whole place. He even walked up to check out the barbecue grill and the swimming pool. He noticed huge pieces of meat cooking on the grill, and the big empty pool.

"I just emptied the pool this morning. I have to fix it and paint it new!"

"Nice place you have here!" Zorro Porro said, sitting down on one of the benches.

"Relax," George said. "Have some wine. Barack will be here soon."

All this time, I was hiding inside the house and to be honest with you, I had to force myself not to go out and shoot the *pinche* Zorro Porro in the head. As I stood waiting for George's signal for me to come out, I wanted all this to be over, no more killings. Just to go back to my *lindo y querido Mexico*, where I belong.

"Let's drink a toast," George said, raising his glass. "To Barack, and Miguel!"

"What are you saying, *gordo cabrón*"? Zorro Porro mumbled.

That was the signal! I pulled open the door and I ran out onto the deck. When Zorro Porro saw me, he tried to get up while pulling out his golden forty-five.

"Juan!" he screamed, his voice trembling with anger. "You *pinche hijo de la chingada!*"

"Dick! GW! Dessert is ready! Go for it!" George shouted.

Suddenly all hell broke loose. I saw the two wooden benches rising up and breaking into little pieces. There was broken wood flying all over the place. Zorro Porro landed ass first on the floor and dropped his gun. He looked at me, terrified. He had no idea what hit him next. Moving at top speed on their set of wheels, in no time the two crocodiles were on top of him, shredding his body to pieces. In less than three minutes everything was over. All that was left on the floor was a pool of blood, Zorro's golden-plated forty-five gun, a Rolex watch, a wedding ring, a gold chain, a wallet, a huge black vibrator, and a pair of cowboy's boots.

"See, Juan?" George said smiling. "I told you, they are picky eaters! They don't eat junk!"

He turned around, grabbed the hose and started to wash the blood away. Meanwhile the two beasts were on the floor motionless, waiting. With one eye they were checking me out and with the other eye they were looking at George. I was starting to get nervous.

"Dick! GW! Go back in the pool! Go now!" George commanded.

To my relief, the two animals turned around and slid down the deck, gliding real fast on their set of wheels all the way back to the swimming pool.

"At last, we can have dinner and celebrate kid!" George said happily. "Go and get some chairs!"

I didn't go back to The Ghetto Inn Motel that night. I stayed with George in his backyard all night long underneath the stars, drinking wine and talking, in that order. We talked about his son and Miguel, and about Ronald his dead crocodile.

"He died of an overdose."

"Died of an OD, a crocodile? What happened?"

"Some time ago, there was this gang called The Brainless, roaming the neighborhood. One night they got high, and came up with the stupid idea of invading my house and robbing me. Dick, GW and Ronald gulped down the ten of them. The bad news is that they were carrying a backpack full of pure heroine, and Ronald was not a picky eater," he said sadly.

"Wow!" I said. "What a story! That's movie material!"

"I loved Ronald so much that, as a tribute to him, I saved his skin in my garage and every couple of years I make myself a new pair of shoes."

When he said that, he was actually crying. By the third bottle of wine, George started thanking the Lord for being alive and well, and asking God to take care of Barack's and Miguel's souls and forgive them for their sins.

"God, you must forgive these two kids. They grew up like animals in no man's land and the people spat on them. Particularly my son, who grew up on the South Side of Chicago, a vast lunatic asylum where nothing can flourish and there is no way out. He was like a prisoner, a scary rat in a dark cellar. Miguel, on the other hand, was born brown, poor and in Mexico, a big graveyard in the making, in a home that was a mix between some grim catholic institution and a Bronx sanatorium. Both of these kid's lives were an inevitable disaster. Both of them were on a collision course and when these two kids, who had more love for the others than the others had for them, finally crashed that tragic night at the Kennedy Center in Washington DC, their whole past came toppling down and engulfed them..."

The sun was already up. I didn't want to listen to this middle-aged man, with a set of false teeth and an old newspaper under his arm, anymore. A completely new life was waiting for me back in Mexico. I have many years ahead of me. Moreover, as I had promised to Hillary in Washington, I had less than forty-eight hours to leave Gringo-Land for good. George just kept talking and drinking wine. I kissed old fat George on the forehead and I got up and left.

It was a sunny day in the ghetto. No one was outside. There was a strained silence. I looked at the house again. It looked grand. Maybe it was an illusion or a ghost from the past. I imagined a huge red, white and green banner, the Mexican flag color's up front: **MIGUEL MEROMERO YOUTH CENTER.**

"It would be a terrible thing for Chicago if this house ever disappeared," I thought.

I went back to The Ghetto Inn. The same young black girl, wearing a white silk blouse with a blue scarf around her neck, sat at the front desk. She held an e-cigarette in her tiny fingers. The fingers holding it were full of rings. When I asked her for a car service to the airport, she looked sharply at my empty hands.

"No luggage?" She asked.

"Nope, just me," I said. "What about getting me a taxi to the airport?"

She pressed her lips and, still holding the e-cigarette, pushed her index finger around the middle of the lower one and then she smiled. The smile flashed like a beam of light and changed her whole face. She looked like a little girl and suddenly I wanted to stay.

"I'm afraid I can't tell you exactly how much. Nothing is precise in this neighborhood, but I believe a town car to the airport would cost you about forty-five dollars plus the tip," she said.

"What about an UBER?" I asked.

"UBER cars coming into this area, I don't think so! At what time is your flight?" she asked and gave me a comic stare.

"Leaves at nine."

CHAPTER 20
Mexico Lindo Y Querido

After boarding the plane, I slumped into the seat and closed my eyes. I tried to relax, keeping my back straight, flexing my thighs and knees, imagining that I was lying on my back on the floor, a position in which my little brain functions best.

I was on a plane on my way back to Washington DC. My heart felt heavy and my mouth felt dry. Painfully, I began to go through everything that had happened after we crossed the border and everything that was waiting for me in Mexico. Miguel's smiling face swam towards me out of the darkness. I stared at the face, trying to hold it in my mind, but it was fading rapidly. There was no smiling face waiting for me in DC. It was only Miguel in the cargo compartment, dead and forever young, inside a brown wooden coffin.

When I arrived in Washington, the airport security kept me in an enclosed terminal. My next flight to Mexico City was leaving in two hours. Nataya and Sammy, were allowed to come into the holding area and see me.

"A complete statement to the press will be made within twenty four hours," Sammy said abruptly.

"I need a drink of water," I said.

"Here," Nataya said, handing me a bottle of Gatorade.

Looking at her sexy red hot lips, I couldn't help but remember the first time we met her at The Empire Hotel in New York and Miguel whispered in my ear: "Blow job! Blow job!"

"Do you think I'm going to have a chance to see Barack before I leave?" I asked.

"No, Juan, he doesn't even know who you are!"

"I don't get it! How did they find out about us?"

"Henry, The Big K from Mexicali, remember him? He keeps them informed about everything that goes on at the border. You are a good kid, you deserve the world, but in this instance you were just used as a poster boy. The politicians in Washington needed a picture with a young face like yours next to the president. And Henry got it for them."

"What's that picture for?"

"The election year is coming up, and everything about Mexico and the illegal aliens is big news in this country, and there are millions of Hispanic voters across the nation!"

"But then, why make me a hero?"

"It was an accident!"

"What do you mean an accident?" I couldn't believe what Sammy was trying to imply.

"You see, at the beginning the idea was to stage a different story, more romantic. Two Mexican kids crossing the border just to meet the president was a lovely story. But when this Barack Owerlson from the South Side of Chicago entered the picture, trying to kill you guys, he changed the script and the story got much more interesting, and more dramatic. Just imagine, two Mexican kids, saving the president's life! That was big news! Get it now?"

"So, everything was a lie!"

"It didn't hurt anybody!"

"It did hurt Miguel and me!"

"It's hurting you because Miguel was the only good thing in your life. He was the guy who told you never to give up. All the people around you are giving up. They are all defeated. Not you Juan. You can't give up. You won't give up. You must keep going!"

"I have to board my plane now," I said.

He grabbed me by the shoulders.

"Just remember kid, as far as we're concerned, we never had this conversation. If you happen to need anything, don't you ever think of contacting me again! Understood?"

"Okay," I said laughing.

Sammy was not laughing at all. He was not even smiling. He took Nataya's hand, turned around and walked away without saying goodbye. Now, at last, I was starting to understand how the big game is played, a game that sometime in life, everyone must play, but not everyone knows the perpetually changing rules or how it is played.

Washington DC, October 20, 2014 (11:00PM)

Barack, lucky for me, I'm very good at writing letters, so I know for a fact that writing to you via e-mail and letting you know how I feel is the best way to make myself very clear. Today, while I'm typing this email, I'm on a plane on my way back to my Mexico lindo y querido with my dead primo in the cargo compartment. I don't think I'm ever coming back. I wish I could tell you that my visit to your country was better than I imagined it would be, but in all honesty, I can't, I'm disappointed. Not only disappointed, but actually saddened. Gringo-Land soul wise, how should I say this, it's short of just about everything. Boredom reaches its peak. People are too obsessed with personal security, money and material things. People are lonely, even in a crowd. It's a "me-first-me" society. Is the ability to make money and the ability to survive one and the same? Is this the meaning of true wealth? What is it that people fear? What is it they don't understand about humanity? Your so-called civilized citizen is not that different from a savage in this respect. Every time I met somebody on this side of the fence, I was looked upon as a worthless crackpot. They made me feel different, like I was carrying with me a sense of violation and profanity. In my humble opinion, for your society in general, what's dead is sacred, what's new, what's different, is evil, dangerous or subversive. A new world is made with a new spirit, new values. Probably, that was the main reason why you refused to talk to me when we met at the Rose Garden. From the beginning, I was interested in being your friend because of your stated positions, which I thought were as progressive and evolutionary as mine. However, that was until I realized that the corrupt nature of the system, the same *pinche* system that gave you the power to govern Gringo-Land plus the stronghold the corporations have on government, limited your authority and in a way tied up your hands. So with what's available to you, almost like in Mexico, you have to preside over near non-Democracy. I apologize for my skepticism, or maybe I'm just getting restless, but I'm still sure that, because of you and your legacy, a great change is coming over America. There is no doubt about that. We are witnessing the prelude of something unimaginable. Maybe Hillary, that sweet old lady who was so nice to me during the ceremony at the Rose Garden, will become the first woman president in Gringo-Land, and that's only the beginning. I can feel it. I have to admit that your Rose Garden is peaceful and really beautiful, but somehow I didn't like the look of your White House. There is something cold and austere about the structural design. Between you and me, I liked George Owerlson's White House on the South Side of Chicago much better. It was also a pleasant surprise to meet Barack Owerlson's father, a real working class hero. As an American, he's a different breed, a man with the most stimulating mind, liberty loving, free of prejudices and hatred. You need more men like him on your side, men that are noble and morally fit, just like you. As you well know, the cowards and the ignorant can't work together. That's why, now more than ever, you need a united front to face your enemies and your detractors. Men like Mr. Orwelson should be part of that united front.

I want you to know that, even if you won't talk to me, I'll keep trying to communicate with you because I still care about you and I want to help you. I know you have accomplished a lot of things in your life, but I'm not entirely convinced that you'd be able to manage all this by yourself in the near future. I can imagine you seated on a comfortable chair in the oval office as the Commander in Chief, surrounded by all your staff, and yet paralyzed with fear and anxiety. Considering all that, and just because I'm your friend, I'm going to send you my grandfather's teachings, that not long ago came in very handy for me and saved my life. I'll try to be brief, I promise!

THE WORLD ACCORDING TO MY GRAMPS, FROM ONE TO TEN

1) *In a society of free people, there is no room for prejudice and hatred.*

2) *In the land of opportunity, there is no room for senseless sweat and struggle.*

3) *People that recklessly plunder from the earth, under the maniacal delusion that this activity represents progress, are just insane.*

4) *War is also a form of insanity. War is confusion. War teaches us nothing, not even how to conquer our fears.*

5) *To fight is to admit that one is confused. It's an act of desperation, not of strength.*

6) *The only war worth fighting for is man's bloodless war against his despotic nature. This is a real war, because it can go on forever, and it's called evolution, and the battlefield is in the heart.*

7) We inhabit a mental world, still finding no solutions because we are still asking the wrong questions. We find only what we look for, and even today, we're still looking in the wrong places.

8) The most terrible thing about our society and the world in general, is that there's no escape from the nightmarish treadmill we have created.

9) We are trying to defend what's old, useless, dead, indefensible, not realizing that every defense is a provocation to assault. That's why we are not happy, not contented nor radiant, and not fearless.

10) We have land, water, sky and all that goes with it. All together, we could create a beautiful and shining world. We could radiate peace, joy, power, benevolence, and have a better way of life. However, greed has made us blind.

As you can see, my grandpa has a different view about the world than the so-called "leaders" and very different ideological principles. According to him, the world is changing very fast and, if we don't destroy it, maybe, just maybe, a man of genius may step up to the plate and stop the indiscriminate killings that are going on all over the place. People are confused and terrified. We must stop plotting revenge. Too bad you and I couldn't get together even for a little while. I'm still convinced that you and I can do a lot to change things. However it was your decision not to pay any attention to me and, because of that, nothing much is going to change. As of now, I'm still a stranger in a strange land and you treated me pretty much the same. I know what you're thinking, "Okay Mr. Brown Mexican boy, how many ways are you going to tell me how rejected you feel?" Okay, maybe I'm overstating my case, maybe exaggerating, but let me tell you just a couple of more things that I discovered here in your pinche

Gringo-Land. First of all, I learned that I'm smarter than most people around here. In some places we went by, the littleness of spirit and the ignorance were monumental. You know what's really weird? Most of those people were white! They didn't like brown Mexicans and blacks that much! Of course, I also met some people that were a little smarter, smarter than 99.9 per cent of the others. I also discovered that too many people here in your country feel like failures, or maybe they don't know what they want or what they are feeling. Some of them can't even get an education, much less a part-time job, and they feel trapped. I believe that, if you don't treat each citizen seriously and with respect, then you are not serious about governing. Anyway, most of the people here are ignorant but nice, just like in Mexico. I know it seems funny, but Mexicans and Americans could be best friends. That's why I wanted to talk to you about the mexicanos' and gringos' similarities. Before I finish this letter, I should thank God that you guys didn't kill me. Not that you didn't try! Juazzzzzz! At least for once, God was on my side! Coming to Gringo-Land was a good experience in life and helped me to grow up real fast! I laughed like crazy and wailed like a mad man! I also killed a few no-good bastards and made very good friends. Even though you closed the door on me, I want you to know that it was me who really wanted to walk away. I had enough! Now, hoy, looking back, I can picture you standing by the window of your oval office, holding my letters, thinking of me walking free on the other side of the wall. A wall that you guys out of an attack of paranoia built, not me. I can sense the envy and the sadness in your heart, and I just know you must miss me, too. Un abrazo,

Juan Sintierra

My arrival in Mexico was out of this world. A multitude was waiting for me at the airport, waving Mexican flags and calling my name. There were Mariachi Bands playing music all over the place. It looked like our national soccer team, our beloved Tri, had finally become world champions. Looking at the people jumping up and down and smiling happily, for once in my life I couldn't help feeling so proud to be a Mexican and a hero!

"Here is where you belong, Juan," I thought.

I had always known that I was a different kind of Mexican, daring and ambitious. My family, especially my grandfather, expected me to do the greatest things possible. For grandpa, seeing his *nieto* leaving for Gringo-Land was truly a strange idea and a waste of time. Instead, my mother quickly agreed with my plan. She wanted a better life for me. What she didn't know was that I was running away to find something and my excuse was Barack.

From the office of the *presidente* they sent a Mercedes Benz limo, escorted by an army of police cars, to pick me up and take me to *Los Pinos* for the big reception. On my way to the presidential residence, there were thousands of people on the streets and out on their terraces, waving flags and cheering my name. They even hung huge banners on every pass along the way to Los Pinos, with my picture on it:

JUAN SINTIERRA *NUESTRO HEROE MEXICANO!*

There were two big gorillas in the limo, the driver and a bodyguard.

"You are very famous, *pendejo!*" the driver said, handing me a note. "Read this."

7.00 PM, El Sr. Presidente speaks.

7.02 PM, El Sr. Presidente greets Juan.

7.03 PM, El Sr. Presidente invites Juan to the podium.

7.04 PM, Juan stands next to el Sr. Presidente posing for pictures.

7.05 PM, Juan thanks al Sr. Presidente, praising democracy and the Mexican way of life.

7.06 PM, El Sr. Presidente presents Juan with the Mexican Medal of Honor.

7.08 PM, They shake hands and embrace each other for the official picture.

7.09 PM, Holding up their hands, they both smile and wave to the press.

7.10 PM, They embrace once more and get down from the podium.

Important note: Juan must keep smiling at all times for the cameras. No interviews with the press allowed. After the ceremony is over, Juan will be escorted out of the area. No dialogue between El Sr. Presidente and Juan will be allowed at any time. Warning: If Juan doesn't follow the above mentioned instructions to the letter, for national security reasons, he could be shot to death on the spot.

"I already know the *pinche* script, *cabron!* Everywhere it's the same *mierda!*" I said, tearing up the note and tossing the little pieces out the window. "If you were not under the international witness protection program, I'd shoot you in the pinche head, *puto*," the gorilla said, putting his big hand over my face and pushing me back all the way against the seat. After that, there was no more dialogue between us. Of course, I was not going to argue with the *pinche* beast! I wasn't even there.

They dropped me off by the main gate of *Los Pinos*. A very beautiful girl with a gorgeous smile put her arm around my waist and escorted me to a chair next to a podium, flanked by the American and the Mexican flags. To the left of the podium, wrapped in the Mexican flag, Miguel's coffin was placed on a steel platform. In the background I could see a beautiful pine forest. I started counting the pines, one by one.

"Nice meeting you, Juan, my name is Lupita, I'll be assisting you throughout the ceremony," she said, squeezing my arm and leading me to the chair. She had the sweetest smile.

"I counted five hundred pines! This is no *pinche* Rose Garden!" I thought.

I sat down and I saw about four hundred people standing all over the lawn, drinking and laughing. Some of them were carrying hand held TV cameras on their shoulders. Nobody was paying any attention to me. They were yelling and pointing at this tall guy wearing a white cowboy hat. He was not facing me. I could only see his back.

"*Señores y señoras, con ustedes, el Sr. Presidente de Mexico!*" shouted the announcer.

When the guy in the white hat turned around to face the microphone, I almost fainted. There he was, Zorro Porro himself. I couldn't believe my eyes. It can't be! I almost got up and ran away. I was shaking all over. It felt like I was having a bad dream. I didn't know what to do. I closed my eyes and tried to reach my Zen mode.

Everything went precisely as planned and I performed my part on the podium according to the script. It was my greatest performance, the performance of my life - my speech, my smile, my posing for the pictures, the hand shaking and, at the end, the embrace, holding each other and waving goodbye to the people! It was picture perfect!

"Lupita will bring you into my office, we have to talk," Zorro whispered in my ear.

In less than five minutes, everybody had left the compound and, strangely, nobody paid any attention to me. I sat on a chair looking like an idiot, by myself, waiting for Lupita to pick me up. Suddenly, I don't know why, I had a hard on. It was a good one, it felt so good that it made me feel powerful and proud. When she finally showed up, she grabbed me by the hand and helped me get on my feet.

"You were great, Juan!" She told me kissing me tenderly on the lips.

Lupita escorted me out of the compound. She was silent now and, staring at me with wet eyes, she started sobbing.

"What's wrong?" I asked her.

"You are free! I want to go with you!" she screamed.

"Let's go!" my hard on and me answered at once, in that order.

"I can't, Juan, we are all prisoners here!"

When we walked into Zorro's office, he was drinking and smoking facing a long and dark oak table, in complete silence. Behind him was a large window from where you could see the garden and the five hundred pines. He seemed to be upset and was breathing heavily.

"*Gracias, Lupita,*" he said, slapping her nice little round ass. "You can go now."

I sat down across from him on a large sofa. It smelled brand new. He took the cigarette out of his mouth. Then he looked at me. His eyes went over me, slowly, examining my face.

"Maybe I'm wrong, but to me you don't look at all like a hero. You look more like a *pinche pendejo,*" he laughed, putting the cigarette back in his mouth. He turned around and went to the bar at the back of the room, poured himself a drink and turned on the lights. The glare from the lights blinded me for a moment.

"You listen to me and listen to me good, *cabrón!* I'm going to be very brief," he said. "As of now you are a free man in this country. I have an agreement with my boss in *El Norte* and these were his strict orders. You can go back to your old neighborhood and do whatever you please. You can go back to your old business at your own risk if you wish, or you can collect a monthly pension of five thousand dollars from the government. This deal is top secret. If by any chance you disclose this information to anybody, I have rigorous orders from my boss in the north, and Henry, The Big K from Mexicali, to terminate you. If you want to live a long life and die of old age, you'll know what to do."

"Can I ask you a question?"

"What *pendejo*?"

"Who are you?"

"I'm your worst nightmare! Your *pinche Presidente, cabrón!*" he laughed.

"But then, who was that guy in the White House, that house in the South Side of Chicago?"

"You can't figure out anything, can you, little shit?" he grinned.

He stopped talking and drew his breath. He got up and leaned forward with both hands on his hips.

"Don't tell me that he was playing your double!" I said, looking at him straight in the eyes. "The guys from the cartels do it all the time! They even try plastic surgery!"

"I'm a leader!" he shouted. "I can't afford to die, *cabrón!* I must live forever!

"Wonderful casting," I said. "That guy on the South Side eaten by the crocodiles looked just like you!"

"Or maybe he was me and I'm him. You'll never know who's who, you *puto!*" he laughed. "Now get the hell out of here! Get lost for good! *Pinche pendejo!*"

Once I was out of *Los Pinos*, my breathing and my heartbeat returned to normal. I was relieved that, in my meeting with Zorro Porro, no guns had gone off. At last, I had a pretty good idea about my situation regarding my past and present problems with the law here in Mexico. But that didn't mean that my personal safety was secure or guaranteed. I also knew that my relation with Zorro Porro and his cronies wouldn't get better for some time, if ever. I saw a taxi turning the corner towards the avenue and stop at a red light. I retraced my steps and got into the cab. My bus to Sinaloa was leaving at ten.

"To the bus terminal, *por favor!*"

I opened the front door of my trailer and Blanca came running from the small living room throwing her arms around me. We embraced and kissed, and fell to the floor crying and laughing like when we were two wild little kids.

"Miguelito, come and meet *tio* Juan," she yelled while lying next to me on the floor.

To my amusement, a very energetic and good looking little child, screaming and laughing, jumped on top of us.

"He looks like Miguel's double," I thought.

"I'm junior," he giggled. "I mean, I'm Miguelito."

I was ashamed. Maybe I have impressed the little kid now, but on that tragic night in Washington DC, I couldn't save Miguel's life. Because of me, Miguelito had no father now. I hated myself for that. Again and again, I have tried to let go of the past to enjoy my present. Nevertheless, I can't.

"C'mon Juancho. Like the good old times, let's take a walk by the river. There's a full moon out tonight and grandpa is waiting for us!" Blanca said.

We walked slowly in silence that evening, submerged in our own thoughts. Miguelito was running ahead of us playing, picking up small branches and pebbles. The full moon was shining on him. It had rained the night before and the only sound was the murmur of the river's muddy waters flowing rapidly downstream.

"I love you, Juan," Blanca whispered. "But this is the last time they will let me see you. I'm the new governor's wife! I'm part of the system now!"

Suddenly, before I had a chance to answer, grandpa jumped out from behind a tree, waving a big tree branch like a sword.

"I'm Conan the Barbarian! Just back off now, I'm keeping this child hostage!" he yelled, holding Miguelito by the waist. Surprised, Miguelito stared at grandpa for a moment before bursting into laughter, and, giving him a warm hug, kissed the old man on both cheeks.

"Welcome back, Juancho," grandpa said, shaking my hand. "Here is where you belong, *muchacho!*"

Staring at the face of the moon reflecting on the river; suddenly, deep in my soul something shifted. Gradually, I had a vivid recollection of my state of mind before leaving Mexico. It framed itself inside my head next to the memories of my travels to Gringo-Land. Listening to the river flow, I closed my eyes and I sensed Gramps, Blanca and Miguelito's souls deep inside me.

"North America is no place for a brown Mexican," I thought, before opening my eyes.

At that moment, I felt the need to make up once more with my native land. I wanted to embrace it. At long last, all the wounds were finally healed.

"What happened to our river grandpa? What happened to Mexico, to all of us?" I asked.

"Juan, not too long ago there were thousands of dream places in Mexico. You could sit on a bench by the sea or by the riverbank, stand on a mountaintop overlooking a lake, or just sit on your front porch or in your backyard, and appreciate the awesome beauty of it all. The air was soft, fragrant, the atmosphere charged with magical names that created a great symphony of human and humane activity. It is all over now kid. A brand new Mexico is being born. Everything that was beauty, courage, principles, honor and compromise has been smashed and hidden under a mudslide of false progress and violence. Now we live in a country commanded by a band of criminals. Our Mexico *lindo y querido*, is buried under a pile of trash, a big graveyard. But there is hope Juan, there is hope, as long as the ashes are still warm."

ABOUT THE AUTHOR

Néstor Lacorén was born in Buenos Aires, Argentina. The former reporter is now a music producer and promoter who travels the world. Néstor currently resides with his wife, Helene, in New York City. Two Mexican Kids, Barack, and the Wall is his debut novel.

Printed in the United States
By Bookmasters